FORGOTTEN

ALEX SIGMORE

Dark Woods Press

First edition ebook ISBN 978-1-957536-04-0

Paperback ISBN 978-1-957536-05-7

To those that love, unconditionally.

Chapter One

WINTER

AT ALMOST FIVE O'CLOCK THE DOORBELL RINGS.

I'm not expecting anyone, though I'd left my work clothes on as I'd been patiently waiting for the mail to arrive so I could finally retrieve it, change into something more comfortable, and finally relax. I was in for the night, and the day had been more than exhausting enough. After all the shit that had gone down with the Williamson project, I'd left work early on the excuse of a headache and come home wanting nothing more than to grab my favorite pajamas and scrounge up some good wine.

But when the clang comes out of nowhere, I'm ashamed to admit I jump. Felton installed one of those doorbells that rings through the house like the Hunchback is working overtime and it gets me every time. After chastising myself for being so jumpy, I roll my eyes, wondering who could be darkening my doorstep on a Friday afternoon when all I want is a moment of peace to myself. Felton hadn't installed the surveillance cameras since they "clashed with the architecture", so it was either ignore whoever was on the other side of the door and hope they went away, or gather up what energy I have left for interacting with people and do the decent thing. I almost let it go, but I need to make a good impression on the neighbors, especially if I'll be living here full time now. At least I can use it as an excuse to go retrieve the mail.

I slip on Felton's old sneakers he'd left haphazardly by the door, unable to keep a smile from forming across my face. These are my *fiancée's* sneakers, no longer my boyfriend's. I wouldn't call myself a sentimental person, but I am a bit of a romantic, so I notice the little things. And soon enough I'll be putting on my *husband's* shoes at the last minute when I need to meet someone unexpected at the door. It's been a long road, baby, but we've made it.

I take a deep breath to reset myself, plaster a fake smile across my lips and open the door, praying this interaction doesn't take long. But instead of someone standing on our doorstep, there's nothing but a small brown package leaning up against the timber. Left by the mailman no doubt. I drop the smile, relieved I don't have to interact with anyone else today, even if it had only been one of the neighbors needing to borrow something. People still did that, right?

I can't help but notice he left it leaning on to the more "traditional" side of the house. I'm not an architect, I'm an engineer, so my concern lies in the practical. Felton…he's the artist out of the two of us. And he calls this house an architectural "dream". His words. If I recall correctly, it's classic English Tudor merged with post-modern impressionism. You'd think the result would be an ugly mish-mash of glass and wood, metal and shingles, but somehow Felton fused them perfectly and made it beautiful. The door itself is set into a small alcove with cross timber over wattle on one side and glass on the other, the entrance sitting between them at the end of a short path winding down from the driveway. He told me when he first found this house there had been nothing here but an old Tudor-style home built sometime in the middle of the nineteenth century. It didn't even have an indoor bathroom and had fallen into neglect and disrepair. But slowly, over the course of two years, he managed to transform it into the magnificent swan it is today, the pride of the local community and the recipient of the AIA Connecticut Design Award for best single-family residence in the state. The award had made him something of a minor celebrity in our little town and, oddly enough, was what first brought him to my attention. So you could say, in a way, this house was what brought us together. It's appropriate this is where we'll be starting our lives together.

Ignoring the package, I walk down to the driveway and then finally to the mailbox itself, where I retrieve a small stack of flyers, advertisements, and what I suspect are at least two bills. We've only been living together a short time and I haven't had a chance to learn about all his financial habits yet. The freezing air whips across my exposed face and I shiver as I make my way back up the long drive, the wind blowing in short, but powerful gusts. A cold front moved in last night in the middle of what had been a very pleasant start to spring, bringing with it the chance of snow on all the newly opened flower and tree buds.

Even though I know it's silly, it still makes me sad to think about the trees that had worked so hard to begin blooming, only to have the cold snap strike, threatening to kill everything all over again. Trees are hearty beings, they'll get over it, but I can't help but wonder if trees and flowers could think, would they get as exasperated about the weather like we do? Would they lament the cold, always hoping for the warmer days, or would they take each day as it came, knowing it was all part of a necessary cycle?

God, I must be more tired than I thought. Here I am about to freeze my ass off worrying about the trees and plants. I eye them carefully as I make my way back up the driveway.

If they had their way, I'd be nothing more than food for them, their roots feeding on my rotting corpse.

Winter! Stop it! You need to get ahold of yourself. I take a deep breath, bend down and grab the small brown package leaning up against the entryway, and make my way back inside. The security system beeps twice as I open and close the door again. I kick Felton's sneakers off and immediately trash the junk mail, setting the two bills aside to leave in Felton's—wait, no —*our* home office later. I'm about to leave the package as well since it's addressed to him, but I can't help but notice the stylish calligraphy on the front. Perhaps calligraphy is too generous a word, but the writing is almost certainly that of a woman and, it seems to me, contains a bit of a personal touch to it. Maybe it's in the way the end of the "F" in Felton's name almost forms a heart.

I'm being ridiculous. I toss the package on top of the rest of the mail, cursing myself for being so goddamn paranoid. I don't do that, not anymore. Cammie would have called me on it if she'd been here. I can't forget all the progress I've made and the glowing endorsement Dr. Hobart gave me on our last session. He said I'd come a long way and that as long as I made intentional decisions, I could live whatever kind of life I wished. One free from what caused me so much trouble in the past.

Still, it's hard to deny some woman sent my fiancée a package. I know most of his friends and family, who would do such a thing and leave no return address? A prank, possibly? The postmark was from the Brighton post office, not more than five miles away.

I pick up the package and shake it, feeling its heft. It's dense, like a book. But not like one of those coffee table books he's always going on about, this is shaped like a regular-sized book. He doesn't even read books, not paper ones anyway. Most of Felton's books are electronic. Plus, if it had come from a store, there would be an indication of that on the cover.

Winter. Stop it. You're better than this. It's Felton's package, he'll deal with it when he gets home and then you don't have to worry about it anymore. You're being possessive and paranoid.

I put the package down, resigned not to think about it anymore until he comes home. But as I walk away, I can feel it *watching* me, tempting me to unwrap its secrets. The packaging isn't held together by more than a couple of pieces of scotch tape. I could…

I rush back over and before I can stop myself, peel the top edge open, allowing me to see into the package itself. It is indeed a book. My heart does a little flutter at the confirmation, and I manage to slip the paperback out of the brown wrapping without ripping the packaging.

"What the…?"

I stare at the cover a minute, trying to understand what it is I'm seeing. If this really is a book it's got the most god-awful cover I've ever seen. I'm no art snob, but even I know this reeks of someone's poor photoshop skills and a home printer. "*Simple Desires* by Miranda Maryweather?"

The title reminds me of one of those trashy novels my grandmother used to keep on her bedroom shelf, but the image is nothing more than purple mountains set against a darkening sky. Is this a prank? The book itself is thick enough to be a novel, but it doesn't smell like a new book should. It has the musk of age to it. The back of the cover isn't much better. There's no image of Miranda Maryweather herself, just a brief description of what the book is about. No barcode either, which means this is someone's pet project. But the image that wraps around cuts off in a black strip, not extending all the way to the edge. The strange part about it is if this is someone's craft project, the spine is actually glued like a real book. It's the only thing that seems to have any quality to it.

I check the wrapping again to make sure I haven't missed a note or explanation as to why this has showed up on my doorstep, but there's nothing inside. I flip through the first few pages, half expecting them all to be blank only to find its laid out like any other book would be. Title page, table of contents and…a dedication page.

As my eyes scan the dedication my heart picks up again and I realize opening this package might have been the smartest decision I've made all day.

To my best supporter, F. I love you.

F.

F for Felton? It has to be; why else address the book to him?

I have to take a few deep breaths. Think. Who could have sent this? A fan? Someone who saw Felton's name in relation to the award? Maybe some crazed person out there looking for attention? But there's something about the dedication that doesn't sit well with me. *My best supporter.* Who is he supporting?

Oh, Dr. Hobart would not like this. This is exactly what I'm *not* supposed to be doing, but look what I've found! If I hadn't gone snooping, I might have never known about this secret admirer.

Winter, remember you're not to make any assumptions. You have to communicate with those you love, not assume.

Right, right, I know. He's right of course. But the damage is done now. I might as well keep going. It isn't like this could get much worse. I turn a few pages to the first chapter, intrigued about what kind of support my fiancée has given

Ms. Maryweather and I have to stop myself from laughing out loud as I read the opening line.

"It was a dark and stromy night,"

"Nope!" I slam the book closed, laughing and shaking my head in disappointment. Stromy? Not even a spell-check, *Miranda*? Maybe I don't need to read this thing after all. Whoever Miranda Maryweather is, she's obviously an amateur. Even I know better than to start off by copying one of the most famous openings in history. And if I were to do it, at least I'd have the decency to spell check myself! This is obviously some nutjob and I've already spent way too much time on something that isn't even an issue. I carefully slip the book back into the book-sized package and gingerly fold the ends up. Felton won't even be able to tell. I place the package back on top of the other bills that came in the mail. I'm about to leave it all for future Winter to deal with, but then remember.

In the corner of the large room lined by windows on the north side sits a crate full of shipping tubes for Felton's designs. It takes me a second to dig through everything, but after a moment I retrieve the small roll of packing tape wedged into a corner of one cabinet. At least I can tape it back up better than Miranda had, so someone who isn't supposed to look can't go snooping.

After carefully taping the end back up and replacing the tape, I take one last look at the package and then put it out of my mind, focusing instead on my warm pajamas and that glass of pinot noir.

Chapter Two

No MATTER how hard I try, I can't seem to get those words out of my head.

To my best supporter.
I love you.

I love you. There's one thing I'm damn sure of: "F" had better not be for Felton. Otherwise there are gonna be lots of other "F's" thrown around. Who would dedicate a book to him? I grab my phone and google Miranda Maryweather in the greater Connecticut area, but nothing comes up. Pen name. Has to be. He hadn't had a girlfriend for at least five years before we got together, that much I know. After everything I've been through, it always comes out on the first date. Sometimes that's not a good thing, but then again, it really weeded out those who couldn't handle it. It's just one area where I'm not flexible.

I huff in frustration and take my wine glass to the kitchen, pouring the remainder into the sink. I've lost any taste for it. The kitchen is located in the modern part of the house, which means it's mostly glass and steel and looks out on the woods in the backyard and at the long, winding driveway out the front. I can barely make out the streetlights at the end of the drive, but the path lighting along the driveway is visible enough. The neighbors are just a little too far to see from here, but only a five-minute walk. It's one of the things I like best about this place, secluded but not cut off from everything. It has all the appearances of an isolated home in the middle of nowhere but is quite close to modern society; all part of the illusion of extra luxury.

It's the same illusion I strive for in my own designs. Civil engineering isn't quite as revered as architecture, but it still has its own artistry. Simple lines, functional supports, aesthetically pleasing to the viewer's eye without them knowing exactly why. And since I can't get that damn book off my mind, I might as well work on something. There will be no relaxing until Felton returns home from work and explains himself.

Just as I turn away from the view of the driveway, movement catches my eye. It's brief, but I could swear there is something out there. Some*one*. Dusk has settled and darkness has seeped into the air, making it difficult to see. But one of the lights illuminating the driveway cut out for a moment as someone or some*thing* crossed in front of it. I turn back and peer out, trying to make out what I saw. The night is perfectly still. I scan, hard, not wanting to move for fear that my movements in the house might somehow obscure my vision. Then I see it, a dark figure, standing just at the end of the drive, beyond one of the large stone pillars that flanks the entrance.

"There you are," I whisper.

My first instinct is that it's a man, in a long coat that almost brushes the ground. But I can't tell if he's facing the house or away from me. Something inside tells me it's the former. That he's watching this place, that he's watching *me*. I snatch my cell phone from my back pocket.

"Hey Janet?" I ask before the voice on the other end can say hello.

"Win? Is that you?" the elderly voice answers on the other end.

"Hey, yeah, it's me," I reply, trying not to be impatient with her. She is almost sixty, after all.

"How are you, dear?"

"Good, good. Are you at home?" I ask, not blinking for fear of losing sight of the figure.

"I just got home. Is everything okay?"

"Can you do me a favor and look out towards our place? Do you see someone standing at the end of our driveway?"

"Someone at the end—what's going on?" Janet asks, her voice cracking a bit. Janet is pretty tough, but still. She's in her sixties. It's not like I expect her to just head on out and ask this person what they're doing at the end of our drive. *This* was why she'd been trying so hard to meet all the neighbors. It was important to have a community for situations just like this. Well, maybe not exactly. It wasn't as if I'd ever expected to see a creeper standing at the end of my driveway, but situations where we can watch out for each other. I don't want to be one of those people who lives twenty yards from four other families and don't know any of their names. People are already too cut off as it is, and I refuse to be a part of it. Janet, for all her flaws, is the neighbor I trust the most. I haven't garnered all the details yet, but I know the woman is single, recently divorced from her husband of almost thirty years, and sharp as a whip. If someone is being a peeping tom or something similar, I'm pretty damn sure Janet would go out there and beat them with her own shoes if she had to.

"I don't know, but I'm staring at what looks like someone standing out here and I'm just trying to figure out what they're doing. But I'm too far away to see them clearly."

"Hang on." I hear rustling in the background. "I had to get my binoculars," Janet says, her voice slightly muffled. I assume she's holding the phone between her shoulder and ear while looking through the binoculars. "Where was he again?"

I squint out the window, but small halos are forming in my vision from looking at the bright driveway lights, and I realize I've lost the figure. "He was right there, at the end of our drive, by one of the pillars. I can't make him out anymore. I don't even know if it was a him."

"It was definitely a him," Janet replies, disdain in her voice.

"You see him?"

"I don't see anyone, but no woman would be standing out there looking at you in that glass box you live in. Probably some pervert."

"But you don't see anyone?"

"Not yet, hon, but I'll keep looking."

"That's okay. You're probably right, just some nut. Or maybe someone admiring the house. We've had a few of those since the articles came out," I lie, trying to make myself feel better. No one has come out to see the house, despite all the press about it. But it didn't mean someone couldn't, though it was late in the day for a viewing.

"I'll keep checking anyway. What else do I have to do?" she asked.

"Thanks Jan, I'll talk to you later."

"I'll call back if I spot the bastard!"

I hang up, slip the phone into the pocket of my pajama pants, and cross my arms. A cold shiver runs down my back. Could it have been my imagination? It has been a long day.

I stand in the same spot, watching, waiting to see if I see them again; maybe they'll reappear, or I can at least figure out if I'm seeing things or not. If I can see them clearly, I'll be able to give the police an ID if necessary. Realizing that I'm standing here like a scared little victim, I shake the shivers out of my body and stomp over to the closet, grab my overcoat, and pull it on over my pajamas. Two strange occurrences in the same day means something weird is going on. First the book and now this person. And I'm not just going to stand here and take it.

I walk out into the cold, the wind blowing my coat up against my silhouette and I hitch my breath. It's dropped more than a couple of degrees since I was last out here and that wasn't more than an hour ago. Regardless, I trudge on down the driveway again, sliding my eyes from side to side, keeping an eye out for any movement in the darkness beyond the driveway. I don't know exactly what I'm going to *do*, but I'm not just going to wait for whoever is out here to come to me. Though part of me can see the headline now: *Civil Engineer dies in brutal murder because she was stupid and left her house.* Part of me grins at that.

When I finally reach the end, I pull my cell phone out and turn on the flashlight, scanning the area with the weak beam. Janet's house is visible from here and I can see the older woman in her bedroom window, the binoculars still glued to her face. I smile and wave, and Janet waves right back but doesn't take her eyes off the area. She's keeping an eye out for me, which I appreciate more than she probably knows.

I scan the road again, looking for any trace of the person who could have been out here, finding nothing. No dark figures lurking in the shadows, no footprints, nothing the person may have dropped or disturbed in any way. Part of me is disappointed. But another part of me is relieved. It must have just been in my imagination after all.

The wind is blistering, and I'm already chilled down to the bone. That's what happens when you come outside with nothing more than an overcoat and some pajamas. Taking one last look around, I finally head back to the house for the second time this evening. I'm about halfway up the drive when bright lights illuminate my shadow on the house. Behind me, Felton's car rumbles up the driveway, the loose gravel crunching under the tires. I move to the side to let him pass but he slows and rolls down his window.

"Winter? What are you doing out here? Aren't you cold?"

My first instinct is to ask him about the book. Maybe there was someone out here watching me, but I can't help but think about that damn package, sitting in his office. I want to throw a thousand questions at him, get my explanation and find out just who the hell is sending love books to my future husband.

But instead, I just bend down and kiss him through the window.

"Hi sweetie, welcome home."

Chapter Three

"So, why were you outside in your pajamas?" Felton asks, shrugging off his satchel and hooking it over the end of the kitchen counter stool. I'd headed back through the front door while he'd pulled into the garage. I couldn't help but sneak a cursory look into the office as I passed just to make sure the package was still there.

"I can go out in my pajamas if I want to," I say, smirking, trying to remain playful. I know how I can get sometimes and I don't want to start this off accusatory.

"Yes, but why would you want to? It can't be more than thirty out there by now." He makes his way around the counter to wash his hands; a peculiar little habit he'd always had ever since I've known him. Whenever he gets back home from somewhere he always takes a few minutes to wash his hands, as if he's scrubbing off the dirt of the world. As if dirt wasn't allowed in this place.

Almost like the house is responding to his commands, the heat kicks on automatically, and a low hum reverberates throughout the house. I've still got my coat on, trying to warm the chill from outside. But I don't want him to know that.

While he's got his back to the sink, I pull the coat off and rub my arms before returning it to the closet.

"I wanted to get the mail. You got a package," I say. He's given me the perfect opening. Maybe now he can just open the book, he can explain and all of this can be over before we sit down for dinner. Nothing but a nice, relaxing evening ahead. I'm not going to tell him about the figure out at the end of the drive, not until I'm sure it was real and not a figment of my imagination. He could blow things out of proportion—something we have in common—and I'm not about to ruin his night by telling him there might be a prowler around. If someone did try anything, our security system will scare them off. If that doesn't work, I'm a decent shot, and the gun is right in the back bedroom.

"I could have grabbed it," he replies, drying his hands. He comes over and gives me a deeper kiss than the one we shared outside. Now that he's back home and situated, he's much more comfortable. He pulls away. "Thank you, though."

I'm struck by his earnestness. The mention of a package doesn't faze him; which means he wasn't expecting it. He's not trying to hide it. That makes me feel a bit better, but also a little worse because now it's a totally unknown element. *Some*one sent that thing to him and I'm *going* to find out who it was. At least if he'd been expecting a prank—maybe he'd played one on a coworker—and some sort of recognition had formed in his eyes I could have explained it away. But if it was a prank, it's a damn poor one. Who mails a book as a joke?

"It's kind of heavy," I say, trying to steer the conversation in the right way without overshowing my hand. But he's not moving. Just standing there staring right into my eyes.

"Hmm? Oh, the package." He snaps his gaze away. "Maybe someone sent us an early wedding present."

"Maybe," I say, keeping my voice light. We haven't even registered yet, he knows that. I mean, not even that many people know; he only proposed two weeks ago. He obviously doesn't expect it to be anything nefarious, yet I did. What does that say about me? "I left it in the office."

He turns back and gathers me into his arms, pulling us together. "How about we skip dinner?" he buries his face into my neck, sending a different kind of tingle through my body.

But I tense up a second later. I can't relax until I know more about that book.

Just let him explain it, then you can both have a nice night together.

"I'm really hungry," I say, pulling my palms up and placing them on his chest. My brand new, three-carat engagement ring catches my eye as I say it. "Playtime after."

Felton laughs. "Want to fuel up, huh? I gotcha." He gives me that near-irresistible smirk and pulls away.

"Why don't I get started?" I ask, hoping he'll find his way into the office.

"Then I," he says, loosening his tie, "will go find something more comfortable myself."

I turn towards the refrigerator and grind my teeth together. At this rate he won't look at it until the morning. "I think I saw something else in the mail too, something from AIA maybe? I'm not sure," I lie. That should do it. He won't be able to resist the possibility of another award nomination. God, I'm such a shit sometimes.

"Oh?" He perks up and turns from his path towards the bedrooms, swinging around the large partition wall and descending the two stairs into the office.

"Finally," I whisper to myself. This will all be over in a few minutes. I pull out the pinot noir I'd opened earlier and pour myself a fresh glass. Maybe I can actually enjoy this one. For a brief second I consider pouring one for Felton before thinking better of it. If someone kept lighting a cigarette for me and I had to refuse each time, it would do nothing but put me even further off them. No, better to let him see how much I enjoy the wine and make the first move. Attract, don't push, right? He'll come around eventually;

going your entire life without wine is worse than going without sex.

To busy myself, I begin retrieving ingredients from different places around the kitchen. Tonight will be a good night for taco bowls, sans tacos. No need to add all those extra carbs into their diet when the bowls have plenty of nutrients in them.

A sound catches my ear: the rustling of paper being torn away. He's opening the package. I can already breathe easier knowing that, one way or another, this package business is about to be concluded.

He doesn't return immediately, and no other sounds reach me from the office while I prepare the meals. Maybe he's just processing it, trying to figure it out himself. Or maybe he's trying to decide what to tell me. I return to chopping peppers, trying to put it out of my mind.

I wait nearly ten minutes. Enough time for me to completely finish fixing everything. The bowls sit on the counter, a small bit of steam rising from each. My glass of wine remains rooted in its spot, untouched.

This is ridiculous. What is taking him so long? I take a deep breath and head to the office, poking my head around the partition without actually descending the stairs. "Hey," I say, keeping my voice soft.

He's hunched over his computer, but from this angle I can't see the screen. I *can* see the tension in his shoulders. He jumps at my words and stares at me a minute, like he's coming out of a trance. But then his eyes relax. "Hey."

"Dinner's ready," I say, my heart picking up speed. This is not the reaction I was hoping for, and as I scan the office, there is no trace of the book anywhere.

"Oh. Great, I'll be in there in a second."

"What are you doing in here?"

"Hm?" he asks, looking up again. "Oh, just some work stuff. I just wanted to get it done real quick."

My heart is hammering now. "So," I say, trying to keep the myriad of images and possibilities from running wild through my mind, "do we have a new knife set or something?"

He looks at me as if my head is screwed on backwards. "The package?"

"Oh," he says, pausing. His eyes flicker away, then back again. "No, it was just junk mail, one of those promotional packages."

Even if I hadn't already opened it, I would have recognized the lie. "Promotional package from whom?" I try to keep my voice from shaking. He was unapologetically lying right to my face.

He shrugs. "Just one of those small, no name societies, probably wanting me to join just to give them some prestige. Junk mail." He returns his attention to the screen, all his former warmth gone.

This is not happening. Not now, not after I put this ring on my finger. I have to push. There's no other way, not if we're going to build a life together. I won't do that again, I won't live in a relationship built on secrets. "It looked like something personal. It didn't have an official label or anything."

Felton stops typing for a split second, then resumes. "They must have interns doing some grunt work, probably think it will make things more personal."

Oh my god. He's not going to stop. I struggle to keep breathing. Not only is he lying, but he's doing it without hesitation. Should I call him out right now? If I do, there is a one hundred percent chance we'll have a fight about it. He was supposed to come home and explain this thing, not cover it up! This isn't the man I agreed to marry. For the entire three years we've been together he's been nothing but honest and upfront about everything…right? Maybe I've missed something. He can obviously lie without compunction, what else hasn't he been telling me? I recognize the spiral beginning and pull it back. Focus on the problem, not the emotion, like Dr.

Hobart says. We can deal with the rest later. I'm going to have a hell of a session coming up.

"Felton?" I ask, that familiar sensation of wetness building in my eyes.

He glances up again.

"Where's the book?"

Chapter Four

HIS EYES FLASH and recognition dawns on him. I see it all over his face before he has time to wipe it away. If I hadn't surprised him he might have been able to hide it. And now it was all out in the open.

Why couldn't he have just told me? Was it really so bad he had to lie about it? I hold his gaze while using considerable strength to resist looking down at my ring finger, as if to say, *You promised you'd never lie, you made a promise, and here's the physical proof.*

"You opened it," he says, his eyes falling.

"I did." No sense in denying it. I'm not the liar here.

He sits at the computer a moment longer, then taps the power button and stands, crossing the room to one of the suspended cabinets on the far wall. He removes the package with its torn wrapping.

Part of me is confused. If he'd been trying to hide it, there are far better places than inside the cabinets we both use on a regular basis.

"Here," he says, tossing it to me with no warning, hurt in his eyes. "Happy?"

It isn't a hard toss, just an awkward one. I fumble the

catch, but manage to grab it before it hits the floor, though my grasp only reaches the outer wrapping. As I pull at it the wrapping tears even further, producing an audible *rip* that echoes through the room.

"Why did you lie about it?" I ask, staring at the horrible thing, the tear having revealed the amateurish cover plastered with her name.

"Why did *you* open it?"

He's accusing me? "I'm not the one keeping secrets! I'm not the one lying to my spouse. I gave you the chance to come clean about it and you hid it from me. How is that supposed to make me feel? Knowing that my fiancée has a secret admirer out there is bad enough, but to lie about it on top of that?" I take a breath. "I thought you understood." Yep, one hundred percent chance of a fight.

"Secret admirer?" He frowns, but his brow is creased in confusion.

I huff and tear the wrapping away from the book and toss the brown paper with the feminine writing on the ground. He's playing dumb and I've almost reached my limit. I angrily flip to the dedication page and shove the book back at him.

He scans the page, and for a split-second I see something in his eyes: sadness maybe? Regret? It's so quick that it's gone by the time I realize I'd seen anything at all.

"F," I say, not wanting to let go of my anger. "That's you, right?"

"Yeah, maybe," he answers, still looking at the page. I'm being more than patient, daring him to lie to me again, but he remains silent. He's not going to give anything up without me ripping it out of him.

"Okay, so who is Miranda Maryweather? And how does she know you?"

"I knew her in school," he says softly. I'm almost surprised by the admission. Part of me thought he'd just keep denying it. He turns to the first page and scans the words on the page.

As he begins reading, I catch the faint upturn of one corner of his lips.

"In college? You never said—"

"No, younger. Back in high school, a long time ago. That's who I was looking for on the computer. I haven't talked to Miranda in probably twenty years."

"Why would she dedicate a book to you?"

He shrugs again and closes the book, seemingly unconcerned. "She used to have a thing for me way back when. That's the only reason I can think of. I swear I haven't talked to her in a long time." It's like he's run out of energy, like something zapped the fight out of him, and I can't help but pity the bastard, cursing myself as I do so. He shouldn't be getting off this easy. He'd still lied, and for what? Should I take this high-school-sweetheart idea at face value? I don't want to make this any harder either, but he needs to give me more.

"Why didn't you just tell me that from the beginning?"

He glances up and purses his lips. "I *was* going to tell you, but I wanted to find out about Miranda first, so I could give you the whole story all at once. I didn't think you'd come in here and start browbeating me. Had you given me time to research I probably could have found out tonight."

"But instead you lied to me."

"Yes. I did." Still defiant. I have a hard time accepting it. "Because you caught me off guard! I know what you've been through, and I wanted to give you all the information at once. I thought you'd drop it but you're just so damn persistent...I should have known better."

I stare at him, not sure what to say.

"Oh, and by the way, there's no AIA letter in here. Obviously." He glares at me, his eyes accusatory.

"That's different," I say. I wasn't trying to hide anything; my lie was to expose the truth. They're two different things.

"Be honest. If I'd come back into the kitchen and told you I'd received a strange book from someone I used to know back in high school, what would you have done?" Before I can answer, he continues. "You would have started asking me questions. Who is she? Why is she sending me a book? Why now? Where does she live? When was the last time you saw her?" He stands and closes the distance between us. I want to back up but remain resolute. "I know how things get some-times, and I wanted to be able to tell you everything at once. I know you hate not knowing what's going on and you want all your questions answered immediately. That's all I was trying to do. Why didn't you just tell me you'd opened it when I got home? We could have avoided this whole song and dance."

Dammit. Now I'm not as upset with him as I am with myself. He's right, I should have confronted him immediately. Normally, I would have. But this just...felt *different*. Like I needed to hide it for some reason, or at least make him come to me with it instead of the other way around. I'd wanted him to prove himself to me, which he shouldn't have to do and now I feel like shit. That's not how I want this relationship to start. This is the man I love, not one of those others. He isn't like Thomas or Sal or Scott, because he actually loves me back, and here I am grilling him over a stupid package that neither of us knows anything about. Love means he shouldn't have to prove anything to me.

But...that nagging voice in the back of my head won't shut up. What if I hadn't opened it? Would he have even mentioned it to me? Or would he have just tossed it and never told me about it? I don't like the implications of that thought. This is my chance to do what I should have done from the beginning.

"Maybe it wasn't right," I say, "but I saw the writing on the front and I couldn't help myself. Tell me, would you have told me the truth about it if I hadn't known? Or would you have kept it secret?"

He stares directly into my eyes. "I would have told you. I don't want to screw up something so perfect." He smiles. "I would have gathered all the information I could find and then presented it to you. Maybe even set up a whole PowerPoint presentation."

Okay. Now he's just rubbing it in. "Smartass." I stifle my own smile. "You would tell me, right? If there was something going on. You know I can't—"

"Winter," he says, in that way that always means he knows this is important and he wouldn't hurt me. "I promise on my grandmother's grave I am not having an affair or seeing anyone else. There is no one but you, okay? I swear to it."

His voice doesn't waver, and his eyes don't shift. He is dead serious. Even if I don't completely buy the high school thing, it doesn't matter, because this is real.

"Did you find her yet?" I ask, attempting to shift the attention away from me now that I've made a complete butt out of myself.

He shakes his head.

"When you do, you should tell her to hire an editor, and someone to take care of that atrocious cover."

His mouth breaks into a smile and he pulls me into a hug. "I will definitely relay that message."

After basking in the warmth of his comfort for a second I pull back. "And would you please tell her to stop sending my future husband books telling him she loves him?"

He chuckles, clearly relieved that the danger is over. "Yeah, I don't know *what* that's about. I assume the 'F' is for me, but it could very well be a Freddie or a Franklin or a Ferdinand."

"Did you have any of those in your class back then?"

"Probably. But I'm not sure she's working with a full deck, if you know what I mean."

I place my hand on his chest. "What *are* you going to say when you find her?"

"To not send me anything else and suggest she never

contact me again. If she does have some kind of infatuation I think it's best not to encourage it."

I smile. The perfect answer. "I'm sorry I opened your package."

"I'm sorry I didn't tell you." He pauses. "Or maybe I'm just sorry you're too damn impatient for your own good."

I move to smack him again, but before I can his lips are on mine. For the first time since it arrived, I don't give a damn about that book anymore.

Chapter Five

FELTON

FELTON STARED AT THE CEILING, LISTENING TO HIS FIANCÉE'S long breaths. He wasn't sure he'd ever be able to sleep again.

He glanced at the clock: 2:22. Ominous. Beside him Winter was fast asleep, having exhausted herself first with worry, then with some very intense sex. Felton had struggled to focus on their lovemaking, the book pushing itself—no, shoving itself—to the front of his mind. Long after he'd climaxed he let her continue to ride him; one of them might as well enjoy it. He had to pretend he finished at the same time, all a carefully crafted performance so she wouldn't suspect. Afterward they'd eaten some cold dinner and then come back to bed, where he'd been lying awake ever since.

This cannot be happening.

He'd nearly had a heart attack when he opened the package and seen the author's name. A name that had plagued him for years: Miranda Maryweather. There was no way it could be her. It just couldn't. All that had been taken care of long ago. But some part of him had always expected this day to come. Those first years, he'd had night terrors and his days were wracked with panic. It all grew a little easier as time went on, lulling him into a false sense of security. And then he met Winter and slowly stopped thinking about *Miranda Maryweather* so damn much. He'd almost been able to convince himself it hadn't happened. That somehow he'd invented the story and built it as a real memory in his mind.

But then. Then there was the other part that told him this would never be done and would haunt him for as long as he walked this Earth. That it had been inevitable.

He turned and checked his future wife again; she was out like a light. This couldn't wait until morning. Whoever sent that book was out there, and they knew exactly how to find them. And as much as he didn't want to get anyone else involved again, there was little choice. This went beyond just him, now.

He grabbed his phone off the nightstand and silently slipped out of bed.

They usually only left one light on in the house at night, a small one in the office, and he was able to make his way back there easily without tripping or making any noise. The lamp illuminated the far corner of the room, bathing it in a soft, warm light. The far side of the office was nothing but giant glass panes that looked out on the forest behind the house. Felton had intentionally designed it to be open and exposed. During the day it almost felt like he was outside as he worked at the computer or used the drafting table, which sat facing the windows. He likened it to an artist's easel facing a beautiful landscape, ready for a masterpiece. They'd both be using that drafting table now; that was, if this *fucking book* didn't screw everything up.

He walked over and grabbed the horrid thing, studying the poor quality of the print on the cover. Pixels stood out everywhere. He flipped through the pages again, just as he'd done as soon as he opened it, looking for a hidden message of some sort. Why did Winter have to open it? Couldn't she have left well enough alone? She was always so damn curious. Given what she'd been through he couldn't really blame her. But now that it was here, he couldn't just ignore it. Someone had sent him this message. That meant someone else knew about *her*. About *them*.

The thought unnerved him. He wiped a thin line of sweat from his forehead and pulled his phone out, his fingers shaking as he typed out a text message.

Are you up?

He waited a few minutes for the response, turning the book over in his hands. It felt so strange like this, in semi-official paperback form. The last time he'd seen it, it had been nothing but a loose collection of typewritten pages, held together with clips and staples. He turned to the dedication page and read it again. It was still exactly the same. Then the first page, the mistake still there in the first line. Almost like a signature. Whoever had reproduced this had gone to great lengths to make it exactly the same.

Unless.

Unless there was some possibility it *was* her.

His phone vibrated on the desk and he snatched it up before it could wake Winter.

What do you need at this ungodly hour?

Felton snapped a picture of the front of the book and sent it over.

Is this a joke?

I wish. It showed up in the mail today.

He watched the screen, waiting for a response. And when the phone vibrated again he nearly jumped. Only this wasn't another text.

"Awake now, huh?" Felton asked, answering the phone with a hushed voice.

"If I were you, I don't think I'd be so chipper," his brother replied on the other end. "Tell me what happened."

Felton relayed the story as best he could, leaving out nothing. He thought about not including his conversation with Winter, but Brian needed to know everything. He kept his voice low; the house was big, but not that big. Winter might miss his presence in bed and come in here at any minute and he wasn't exactly sure how he was going to explain himself if that happened. He turned to the computer and switched the monitor back on. He'd have to say a dream had inspired him on his latest project.

"Do you still have the wrapping?" his brother asked.

"I'm not an idiot."

"You said it was hand-addressed. Does the hand-writing match...*hers*?"

He grabbed the brown paper from where Winter had discarded it. It looked feminine, but not necessarily familiar. "I don't think so. But it's been so long I'm not sure. I'd have to find something with her handwriting on it and I don't think any of that exists anymore."

Brian paused. "Let's assume for a minute it isn't from her, because I'm pretty sure that's impossible. Who else knew about you two?"

Felton furrowed his brow. "It wasn't exactly a secret. We were together for a long time. Everyone in the family, for one—"

"You don't have to worry about us," his brother replied.

"Yes, I know. But family friends, anyone who was at the wedding. I dunno, probably thousands of people in the end."

"Yes, but who else *knew*?" He said it with such intensity that Felton experienced the same nausea he had all those years ago. No one was supposed to know. That was the point.

"I don't know. I sure as hell didn't tell anyone."

"I may have to talk to Dad. We'll need his resources."

Felton's ears burned. "You can't do that," he whisper-yelled into the phone. "I don't need his help. There has to be a way to figure this out without his involvement."

"And how are you supposed to do that without any leads? And don't forget, it isn't just your ass on the line. We all have something to lose."

Felton ran his hand through his hair. "I know. And I'll find something. Maybe I can go down to the post office, see if anyone remembers anything."

"For God's sake don't do anything stupid." His brother's voice was harsh. "You start asking questions and people get suspicious. Small towns like this talk. Listen, you don't need to do anything. Just sit on your ass in your big, fancy house and let us take care of this. Does Winter know?"

Felton cheeks burned. How dare he tell him to stay out of this. He was the one with the most to lose. "She opened it but I think I was able to convince her it was nothing."

Silence on the other end.

"Brian?"

"This would have been so much simpler if she hadn't found out."

Felton wiped his brow again. The sweat wouldn't abate. "You know how she is. If I'd been here she never would have found it."

"Woulda coulda. Go back to bed. I'll call you tomorrow, at work. Do something with that book. Get it out of the house."

Felton took a deep breath. "Yeah. Okay, right."

Brian disconnected on the other end. Felton grabbed the ripped brown paper and folded it carefully, placing it and the book back in the cabinet. The same one he'd gone to when Winter asked him where the book was. Had she seen the panic on his face? He'd gotten pretty good at hiding his true feelings when he needed to; it was especially useful for stubborn clients, the ones who thought they knew better, who wouldn't take yes or no for an answer. Maybe that's why he'd been so successful; he was just so damn agreeable.

But when Winter had asked about the book he'd panicked. What else was he supposed to do? Tell her the truth?

Tell her that yes, he did know Miranda Maryweather better than he'd known almost anyone in his life? She wouldn't have handled that well.

Especially after he told her he'd never been married before they got together.

Felton sighed. But that was what he was supposed to do. Pretend like none of it ever happened and move on.

Felton moved over to the large floor-to-ceiling windows and stared into the darkness. There could be someone out there right now, watching him. Plotting against him for what he'd done. He wanted to scream into those woods. To tell whomever was out there to come and get him already, because the guilt and anticipation were taking much too long for his liking. Maybe this was exactly what he deserved. And maybe Winter could do better.

A ghostly form appeared in the glass, startling him. He jumped back, unsure what he was seeing until he realized it was a reflection. He turned to find Winter standing at the doorway, her eyes searching him. His heart dropped. How long had she been there? How much had she heard?

"What are you doing in here?" she finally asked.

He glanced to his monitor, then back to her. "I had some late-night work I wanted to get done. You didn't give me a lot of extra time this evening." Flirting always threw her off her game.

She reached out a hand. "Poor thing. That workout should have knocked you out cold. Maybe I should have tried harder. Give me a second chance."

He smiled, but if he could have punched himself without looking suspicious, he would have. Though maybe his brother would give him a good kick tomorrow for good measure.

"How about we just hold each other?" He wasn't sure he could pretend through a second session.

She tilted her head and grinned. "How uncharacteristically romantic."

He had to enjoy this while he could; because very soon it could all come crashing down around him.

Chapter Six

WINTER

I AWAKE WITH AN UNEASY FEELING IN MY STOMACH. WHICH doesn't make sense. Everything has been resolved, Felton told me everything and we'd had some great makeup sex. So why do I have this pit at the bottom of my stomach? Am I just being paranoid about finding him in the office last night?

I woke up to a cold spot beside me, which isn't the norm. Sometimes Felton uses the bathroom in the middle of the night, but he's never gone so long that his side of the bed grows cold. After the strange night I couldn't get back to sleep without him there, and finding him hadn't taken long. Despite the fact he was trying to be quiet, in a house as cavernous as this, sound travels, though I hadn't been able to tell what he'd been saying. I tell myself he'd just been muttering to himself over his latest project, as he sometimes did when he got excited.

I also tell myself the fact that his cell phone wasn't on the nightstand either doesn't mean anything.

I've already made more than a few wrong assumptions in the last twelve hours. I don't want to continue down that path.

But then he'd been staring out into the dark woods beyond the house. Had he seen someone out there too? The computer was on, but the chair was still under the desk and something about the whole scene didn't feel right to me. Did I ignore my instincts and ask him back to bed instead of pressing the issue? Yes on both counts. I decided not to tell him about the person at the driveway even then as I still don't know if they were real or not.

I get up and shower, leaving him in the bed. By the time I'm dressed and ready for work he's already in the kitchen, coffee in hand. But he has dark bags under his eyes and he hadn't bothered to shave yet. I would have commented that he looked homeless, but he didn't take jokes about his appearance very well, so I let it drop.

"Did you get any sleep last night?" I ask while I pull a bottled water from the fridge.

It doesn't escape my notice that his hand tightens around his coffee cup. "Yeah." He pauses. "Yeah, I think I'm just frazzled by this project."

"What is it?"

He glances up like he didn't hear me. "Hmm?"

"Your project. What is it?"

"Oh," he replies, taking a sip from his coffee. "Angel's firm wants four new designs for one of those subdivisions down south. But he wants them to be modular so he can get six or eight variations out of them. You know the type. Sprawl."

He says it with such disdain. Why does he keep accepting these jobs for subdivision work if he hates it so much?

"Sounds about like my day. I have to meet with the city planners for two new bridge overhauls. At least you have a budget to work with." I smile, taking a few sips from my bottled water.

"Yeah. Don't let them screw you over."

"I never do." Obviously he's not in a talking mood this morning, which doesn't make me feel any better. I grab my coat and pull it on over my suit jacket. With as cold as it was yesterday I'll need the extra warmth. Especially if we're going out on site today. I never tell anyone but site visits are my favorite part about being a civil engineer. I love seeing the structures up close, or the areas that will soon be transformed by my designs. It's like seeing into the future, watching the landscape change before my eyes to accommodate her gleaming structures. If today's bridges were as bad as the initial reports had indicated, there was a good chance they'd need to be completely torn down and rebuilt, which is the best situation, really. Starting from scratch gives me more confidence than when we have to do an overhaul. I haven't won any design awards yet like my soon-to-be husband, but I suspect I'm close. The rumors mill is going strong.

"Well, have a good day," I say, leaning in to kiss him on the forehead.

"No breakfast?" he asks.

"I'll grab something on the way. I may be home late."

"Good luck out there. Love you."

"Love you too." I wave to him, that feeling only growing. As I pass the office on my way out I can't help but notice neither the book nor the wrapping are anywhere in sight.

ALMOST FIVE HOURS AND AN UNSATISFYING CROISSANT LATER, I finally find the time to hop in the car and go look for my lunch. I spent all morning on both sites and the odds we'll get one of them to start from scratch look promising. Maybe both if we're lucky. For some reason I always forget I do better under pressure, even when there's plenty that could be distracting me. On the way to work I'd been worried I'd be thinking about either the book or the shadow person all morning, but as soon as I walked into the office all thoughts of home life fell to the back of my mind and I got to work. I'd prefer to keep it that way. The deal with the book was over and done with. Now if I could just manage to keep my mind from running wild I'd be in good shape.

For these jobs our firm wasn't hired directly by the city, instead we were hired by a general contractor bidding for the job. I originally formed a loose partnership with a couple of other engineers right out of college, and over the past ten years we've built our firm to substantial reputation. GWH is my pride and joy, and I love the work of not only designing, but implementing those designs so they become reality. It's not unusual for me to be on site for the final surveys; it gives us the edge over the competitors. And if we land this contract, there's a good chance we'll be hiring a few extra people to help with the workload. But Henry and Sidhara can wait until I get back to their office before delivering the news. I want to see their faces in person.

But as soon as I start thinking about faces, Felton's gaunt visage from this morning pops into my head and won't leave. What *was* he doing last night?

I need to talk to someone, get another perspective. Maybe I'm too close to the situation to be objective anymore.

I pull over into the parking lot of a small cafe and dig my phone out of my purse. There's only one person I can trust with this, who will keep it quiet if I ask her to.

"Hello?"

"Hey, Cammie?" I say. I love hearing her voice. She's always so chipper.

"Winter! Hey!"

"Are you free this afternoon?"

"Why, what's wrong?"

"Nothing. I just thought we could catch up."

There was a snicker on the other end of the line. "You do

realize this is me you're talking to, right? You typically don't call unless something big is going on."

No, that isn't true, is it? "I call."

"Yeah, when you need something." Cammie's voice is still light and playful, but it makes me feel really bad. Do I only call when I need something? I hang my head, while keeping the phone pressed to my ear. Why is that? Why don't I ever call for fun?

"You're right. I'm sorry, I shouldn't do that. Not to you."

"You're fine," Cammie says, drawing out the word *fine*. "It doesn't bother me. I know you're super busy and you like your privacy. So what's up?"

"Something might have happened. Something at home."

"You're pregnant," Cammie replies, the excitement building in her voice.

I almost drop the phone. "No! *No*. Nothing—it's about Felton. Something is going on. Can we meet somewhere?"

There's a pause. "Oh, I'm sorry, Winter. I thought things were going good between you two."

"They were, I mean…they are. I just need another set of ears."

"I don't have an appointment between four and five-thirty, wanna meet then? You'll have to come to my side of town; all my clients are over here today."

"Sure, I can make that." I can pop back into the office and deliver the promising news, then slip out early to meet Cammie.

"Anything I should know beforehand?"

"It's easier if I explain it when I get there."

"Okay. Seeya then!" Cammie ends the call abruptly. I can't help but wonder if maybe she does harbor some hidden animosity towards me for only calling when I need something. I need to make a better effort of staying connected with her, but with work and the engagement and everything else I've fallen behind on so many things.

It doesn't matter, Cammie is here now and once I explain everything I'll at least have another opinion on the subject. Ever since college Cammie had kept me in check. I hadn't realized how much I'd missed that until right now. If Cammie had been there last night she never would have let me open that package. She would have reminded me about my triggers, would have kept me from overthinking it. If Cammie had been there none of this would have happened.

I sigh. Not much I can do about it now. I glance up at the sign hanging from the small building whose parking lot I've occupied. It reads: *The Stone Inn*. I scan the area but see no trace of an inn, just the little café that probably couldn't hold more than twenty people at a time. Strange. But I'm famished and I'm not above supporting some local businesses with my lunch order.

I step out of the car, and in the corner of my eye catch movement a few hundred feet away. But when I look around I don't see anyone. Thoughts of last night linger in my memory, but it was probably just a cat. Though I do notice just how quiet it is out here. There's only a few other cars in the lot and none driving by, probably because the site I just came from is way out on Route Six. Part of the reason the job has sat neglected so long is because there isn't normally a lot of traffic out here. But the city has put it off for a lot longer than they should have. If we get it, when we're done Route Six will have a brand-new bridge for the handful of people that drive over it per day. Which is fine by me.

I pull my coat tighter as the wind begins to pick up and make my way into the café, all my thoughts having returned to work, and nothing else. Nothing else at all.

Chapter Seven

THE LINE inside the café is only a few people long, which doesn't give me much time to pick out what I want. Their menu is larger than I would have expected for such a small shop. Do I go with the Rueben or the BLT? Or maybe a cobb salad instead? But then wait, were there sides? What about a sunshine burrito? Crap. Now I'm next and there is already someone else behind me. Why is it things like this stress me out like crazy?

"I can never decide what I want when I come here," a voice behind me says. I turn to see a brown-haired woman, maybe a little older than me with black-rimmed cat-eye glasses. Her hair is done up in a bun and she's wearing an oversized, fur-lined black coat as she stares at the specials board.

I'm not used to strangers striking up conversations with me, but I don't want to be rude. "Do you come here a lot?" I ask.

Her eyes find mine for just a second before returning to the menu board. She smiles. "I don't know why I do. Perusing this menu is worse than scrolling through Netflix."

I can't help but smile in return. "This is my first time, and I have no clue what to get. Any suggestions?"

"For your initiation?" She presses her lips together and lifts her chin slightly, apparently considering the matter carefully.

Initiation?

The man in front of me finished up and now it's my turn. The cashier doesn't say a word, just stares at me like me being here is an inconvenience to him. I've already forgotten everything on the menu and this guy's blank stare isn't helping matters any.

"I...uhhh." I scan the menu again, seeing none of it, hoping to spot some familiar word or ingredient I can fall back on. I like chicken, right? What has chicken?

"She would like the Rachel sandwich. Chips on the side."

I turn back to the woman behind me, somewhat stunned. Did this stranger just order for me?

"In fact, make that two," the woman adds, smiling at Winter. "And a couple of bottled waters." She pulls a credit card out of her wallet.

What is happening here? "Wait, um, you don't—"

"Nonsense," the woman says, cutting me off. "It's my pleasure for a first-timer. And you aided in my decision as well, so I owe you."

"I aided?" I ask as the woman hands her card over to the cashier.

"Nothing like making the decision for someone else to help you realize what you really want." The woman retrieves her card, the cashier still looking like he couldn't care less about the transaction. "As far as lunch is concerned, anyway."

"That's very kind but I can't—"

"Of course you can," she says, placing her hand on my arm. Her eyes widen in horror. "Wait, you're not a vegetarian, are you?"

I'm still fumbling over what just happened as the woman

leads us away from the counter so the next person in line can order. "No, nothing like…I…please let me pay you back."

The woman waves her hand dismissively. "Don't be so quick to repay me. You may not even like it."

I glance at the menu board again. What the hell is a Rachel?

"I've never heard of that kind of sandwich before."

"It's like a Rueben, only with turkey instead of corned beef."

Oh. My stomach grumbles in response. "That does sound pretty good." Should I introduce myself? I'm so awkward in these situations. It's only polite, right? What had I just been complaining about? The fact that I don't reach out enough to people. This is the perfect opportunity to fix that.

I stick out my hand. "I don't think I thanked you. I'm Winter."

The woman smiles again and takes my hand without really shaking it, more just holding on to it in the way a grandmother might. "Laura Blackwell. And you're very welcome."

"Do you live around here? Or work? If you come here a lot?" I ask.

"Work. What about you? New to the area?"

"Oh, no. I live on the other side of town. I'm just over here because I was on a site visit. But if my firm gets this new project I'll be over here a lot more, so maybe I'll stop in here more often." I glance at the cooks in the back, working furiously. "If it turns out to be good."

"What sort of work do you do?" Laura asks, watching me intently. Is that normal? Maybe this woman is just really friendly.

"Oh, I'm an engineer. We're bidding to rebuild that bridge down on Route Six."

Laura's lips set into a line. "The reservoir bridge?" I nod. "Well, shit. I guess I'll be finding a new way to work soon. Though I don't disagree it needs some work."

That's an understatement. If the general public actually knew the true condition of the local bridges, I doubt anyone would ever drive over one again. But that's why I'm here. "What about you? Where's work?"

"Order up!" the cook at the end of the counter yells.

"That's us," Laura says, leading me to the counter where two bags wait for us. We grab our bags and bottles of water and head out of the café.

"It was certainly nice meeting you," Laura says, pausing a minute. "Maybe I'll see you here again sometime and you can tell me about how you got that interesting name of yours."

I chuckle because I get this a lot. "It's quite the story, actually." I raise my bottle of water in a cheers gesture. "Next time."

Laura waves as she heads off towards her car parked a few spaces away.

"And thanks again!" I add, thinking of it too late as the woman slides inside her vehicle. I should have thanked her *first*. Shoot.

I can't believe it, there were still some decent people left in this world. The woman wasn't mean or petty or rude, and she'd even paid for my lunch. How often does that happen? Sure, she was a little quirky, but who wasn't these days? I make a mental note that if I ever see Laura again, *I'll* be the one paying for lunch.

I check my watch. I'll have to eat on the road if I want to swing by the office and get over to Cammie's house in time. But I feel lighter after this whole encounter, like it's lifted some of the darkness from last night away. I'm excited about the possibility of securing the contract again, and maybe this whole deal about the book isn't as big as I'm making it out to be. No matter what Cammie says, I'll drop everything regarding the book after today. It's not worth dwelling over and life is too damn short. Not *everything* is sinister or duplicitous in some way.

As I pull out of The Stone Inn's parking lot, I unwrap the sandwich and the smell of turkey and sauerkraut reach my nostrils. And as the sublime bite hits my tongue, I feel very grateful for having met Laura Blackwell.

Chapter Eight

FELTON

"THIS IS REALLY BAD. WHAT AM I GOING TO DO?"

Felton paced his small one-person office. He'd rented it from a local guy back when he branched out on his own. Back before his notoriety and success, before he was anything other than a *Byrnes*. He honestly didn't even need the space anymore with work on the house finished and the giant office there, but he'd kept his little office just in case he needed to get away. Sometimes there could be so many distractions at home, and here it was easier to think.

A couple of art prints and a few high-quality photographs were all that adorned the walls, an attempt at decorating that had never gotten off the ground. And a couple of boxes stood in the corner, full of things he'd never finished unpacking. Other than his desk and his drafting table, there was no other furniture in the room. A half-partition stood between the front part of the room and the back, a holdover from the previous tenant. And he had access to a bathroom through the back door; the only problem was it was accessible to the other tenants in the strip and often not very clean. The unit was a tiny place in the middle of strip mall facing a burger joint and a nail salon across the way. To his left a local pizza place and his right a cell phone repair shop. But it didn't matter, it was his. He stopped pacing to glance out the window. His new Mercedes looked out of place here, as if the moment he'd bought it he'd outgrown this part of town.

"You're going to keep your mouth shut," Brian replied. He'd already been there when Felton arrived thirty minutes later than he'd meant to, and was sitting in his Range Rover just stewing. Probably already berating Felton in his mind.

After Winter left for work, Felton had been almost too paralyzed to move. Someone was out there. Someone knew his secrets and they knew how to expose him. And there was literally nothing he could do about it. It was all Felton could do to keep his hands from shaking in the shower and he'd had to take something to calm himself down before driving himself over here. Something he hadn't touched in quite some time and hoped he wouldn't have to take again.

Brian flipped the book over in his hands, examining it. He wore latex gloves, careful not to press down on any flat surface.

"What are you doing?" Felton asked, noticing the gloves for the first time. He'd been so distracted that he hadn't even seen them when he handed Brian the book. It was understandable; he was doing all he could to keep from hyperventilating at the moment.

"Obviously the *author* didn't send it, so I want to find out who did," he replied. Brian set the book down on the desk and lifted the small case he'd brought with him up, laying it on the table and popping the latches. Inside were a couple of containers, a brush, scissors, tape and a few other things Felton couldn't identify.

"What is that for?

"Fingerprints. Let's see if whoever sent this was stupid enough to leave something for me."

"Where did you even get something like that?" Felton asked.

Brian glanced up. "The kit? You can get them on eBay."

"And you know what you're doing?"

Brian rolled his eyes and returned to the book. He opened one of the small containers and dipped the brush in, using it to lightly dust the front of the book. "You and Winter may have touched it too much already, but there might still be something here. Did she get a really good look at it?"

Felton shrugged. "Good enough. She knew what the dedication said. I guess that was all she needed."

"Fuck," Brian said under his breath.

Felton could relate. Why couldn't the book have come on a Saturday, when he'd been home to intercept it? And why had she been so nosy? He knew why; because shit like this was Winter's trigger and there was no escaping it.

Brian finished dusting and pulled out a roll of tape, placing it on certain areas of the book, then lifting it off gently.

"Did you get anything?"

Brian didn't respond, only placed the tape on a small card, pressing down hard. He repeated the process a few times.

"How are you going to even find out who those belong to?" Felton asked. "You're not a cop."

Brian carefully placed the card back in the kit. "If you really have to ask that question you're not thinking like a Byrnes. This is why Dad doesn't trust you to take care of this on your own."

Felton slumped down into his chair. The only chair in the office. "I really wish you hadn't told him. Does Mom know?"

Brian shrugged, pulling another piece of tape from the book. "If he told her, I guess. I didn't say anything."

"This is so fucked up," Felton said, running his hands

down his face. "This was all supposed to be over and finished! Things were finally good!"

"Aw, what's wrong? Baby's perfect little life hit a road bump?" Brian chuckled. "You have it so good, you don't even know. Nice car, by the way."

"Yeah, well, at least I bought it with my own money."

Brian shook his head. "Put a down payment, you mean. How long are your payments? Ten years?"

"Maybe I bought it outright."

Brian grinned, staring at him. "Be careful who you lie to. Don't forget I know you better than anyone."

"Let me guess, you 'checked up' on me."

"As soon as you signed the paperwork."

"What, Dad doesn't think I can even handle a car payment by myself? I'm not an imbecile. He didn't win that award." He was nearly shouting now.

"Only imbeciles use the word imbecile. You've got your issues with Dad, I get it. But don't piss all over me just because he told me to clean up your mess. Again. Work it out with him but leave me out of it. I'm just doing my job." He paused. "Which is to help you, if you haven't figured that out."

"I don't need him keeping tabs on me all the time. That's the whole reason I'm not doing what you do. It's the whole reason I never got into the family business."

"Don't remind me." Brian waved his hand dismissively. "I'm the one who has to hear about it all the time."

Felton sighed. "What do we do if the prints are hers?"

Brian packed up his kit again. "They won't be. Odds are I won't get anything except for you and Winter. But I need to eliminate the possibility."

"And then what? What happens if you don't find anything?"

Brian smiled. "Don't worry your pretty little head about it."

"I can handle it, you know."

Brian walked over to him, placed his hand on Felton's cheek and tapped it a few times. "Plausible deniability, little brother. Look it up."

Brian gathered the book and the wrapping in his arms and strode out the door.

"I know what it means!" Felton called after him. He watched as Brian climbed into his gleaming black Range Rover and drove off.

~

IT WAS DARK. NONE OF THE LIGHTS WERE ON IN THE DRIVEWAY as he pulled up. Felton wrenched himself out of the car with more difficulty than normal and made his way to the front door.

It was unlocked.

That wasn't right. The door swung open without a sound, revealing a long, dark hallway. No lights on anywhere.

Felton stepped inside, taking great care not to make any noise. The house was cold, as if someone had left the heat off for too long. He didn't dare call out. It would only reveal his location. But he headed down the hall, as if he already knew where to go. He supposed he did.

He rounded the corner, the blackness of the room before him the only thing his eyes could perceive. He fumbled for the light switch and found nothing. The switch wasn't where it was supposed to be.

"Looking for me?" a voice he hadn't heard in a very long time asked, sending shivers down his spine. He could see her silhouette clearly now against the black of the room. A slightly grey figure, too thin and wiry. Thinner than the last time he'd seen her, eight years ago. Somehow she had come back after all. Brian was wrong.

"I'll get the light," she said, her voice slightly muffled, as if she had cotton in her cheek. The figure reached out to the small lamp in the office. Felton watched, stunned as the bony hand moved towards the switch. Suddenly he didn't want the light on. All of this was very, very wrong and he didn't want to see her. To see what he'd done. Not again.

"No!" he yelled, shooting straight up in his seat. He glanced around; he was still in his office, the sun threatening to set over the hills in the distance. How long had he been asleep?

He checked his watch and saw it had been at least three hours since Brian left. He didn't remember falling asleep, but then again he couldn't remember a lot of what happened today. His mind was too frazzled. But the dream stuck in his memory. It had been her, and he'd been so afraid she'd turn on the light. Afraid of what she really might look like. He'd realized it was a dream at the last second, like the ones he used to have all the time. And now, one day after that book showed up, he'd lost eight years of progress. All that therapy, hypnotism, power of positive thinking he'd worked so hard on, gone in a matter of hours. He hadn't been prepared to see her anymore, but it was her. The voice was too unmistakable.

He hit his forehand repeatedly with the heel of his hand.

"Get...out of here."

He stood and gathered his things; another day of work wasted. He'd already been somewhat useless the past few weeks, encouraged by the promise of another award but also put off that no matter what he did he might never reach the same high. He hadn't wanted to let go of that notoriety. He didn't want to be Connecticut's next one-hit wonder. It almost seemed preferable to languish in indecision, never having to move on or take the chance to improve. Because no matter what, after each great success in Felton's life had come crushing disappointment.

Back in high school, his biggest worry had been qualifying for the golf team. And after two years of tryouts he finally made it. That was, until a new kid moved into his district and bumped him off the team—"there's only so many spots, Byrnes, and you're not one of them"—despite the fact he was doing okay. But this new kid had some sort of gift, and the school wasn't about to let him slip by. Then, in college, when he'd finally gotten a date with Allison McIntosh, he found out two weeks later she was pregnant from her old, long-time boyfriend, and Felton just couldn't deal with it. He was a sophomore and he was supposed to help raise a baby? He walked away, despite the fact that Allison was the only person he'd been interested in that entire year. He laughed. Imagine…giving Dad that little nugget of news. It was better for everyone involved that he just walk away. And then of course there had been…*Miranda.*

He shook his head. He couldn't think about her at the moment. Everything kept coming back to that damn book. He just hoped Winter was over it and didn't ask him any more questions. He really didn't want to lie to her again.

He locked the door to his office and got back into his new car. Twenty-four minutes later he pulled out of the spot and headed home.

Chapter Nine

WINTER

"CHARLIE! CHARLIE, COME HERE!"

I pull up to the scene, smiling. A thin, blonde woman wearing jean shorts and an oversized jacket runs across her yard, chasing down a very wet and somewhat soapy basset hound who is moving impressively fast despite being as low to the ground as he is.

Cammie looks up and relief washes over her face as I step out of the car. "Winter! Help me wrangle him! It's too cold for him to be running around out here!"

I cut the engine and run over, hopping the low chain-link fence without even thinking about it, landing right in front of the charging basset hound. "Hey Charlie," I coo, "come to Win-win."

Charlie stares at me a split second, then by some sixth sense feels Cammie creeping up behind him and takes off to my right, barreling through the yard.

"Dammit!" Cammie yells, traipsing after him.

"How did he get out?" I ask, doing my best to keep from laughing.

Cammie, out of breath, points at the soapy bullet now running circles in the yard. "He was my three o'clock, but his owner was late dropping him off and then I forgot to lock down the doggie door in the back, so when he slipped out of my hands he bolted. It's a good thing he's not a taller dog because I have no doubt with that much energy he could scale the fence."

"He's definitely the most hyper dog I've seen that wasn't a chihuahua."

"I knooooowwwww," Cammie exhales, coughing at the end of the word. "He's sweet, but damn he's fast."

"He just needs proper motivation." I scale the fence again and run back to the car, grabbing the remnants of my Rachel sandwich. I had planned on maybe saving the rest of it for dinner, but it seems Charlie might need it more than I do.

"Charlie! Treats!" I yell, waving the bag at him. The dog stops mid-run and locks his eyes on me, before taking off in what I can only describe as a sprint directly for my shins. He slams on the brakes just before reaching the fence and jumps up, his tiny little legs only launching him so far.

"Gotcha!" Cammie grabs him in a bear hug from behind, pulling him from the fence.

"Good boy," I say, pulling a slice of turkey from the sandwich and watching it disappear down the canine's maw as if it were a black hole.

"Get the door for me, would you?" Cammie asks. "He's a handful."

I jump the fence again and trot ahead of them, opening the side door to the house. Once we're inside, I close it back *and* the doggie door protector. Cammie sets Charlie down on the kitchen floor, but his wide eyes haven't left my bag.

"Here you go," I say, giving him a larger bite, which he takes with enough enthusiasm I'm scared for my hand.

Cammie draws a deep breath. "Sorry, I know I said between four and five-thirty, but this is going to take me a few more minutes. I'll probably have to wash him again with all the dirt he picked up outside. Then he needs a good blow-dry."

"No problem," I hold up another piece of turkey. "Maybe if I can keep him distracted he'll be more inclined to cooperate."

Cammie shoves me playfully with one hand. "I knew there was a reason I liked you."

∾

NOT ONLY DID CAMMIE RUN HER GROOMING COMPANY OUT OF her home, but she's preparing to buy a mobile grooming van so she can reach more customers. She's told me about it maybe half a dozen times, but this was the first time I've seen some of the equipment in person.

"Is this stuff going in the van?" I ask, pointing to the variety of hoses, pumps and accessories Cammie has strewn around the room.

"Yep, it's finally happening. We found the van and Mike is working with a guy to convert it to fit my needs. I want to carry my own water supply, so they have to do something to the suspension so it can hold all that extra weight. But you watch, it's gonna be awesome."

Charlie grunts as she starts scrubbing him down in the mobile tub.

"How long until it's up and running?"

"Maybe tomorrow."

"Tomorrow? So soon?"

"Yep," she says, "I've still got some equipment coming. But then I'll be able to lock this guy inside so he can't run around," she scrubs his head as I feed him another part of my sandwich. Upon seeing the food, Charlie's butt immediately hits the water, splashing us both.

"Well," I giggled, trying to wipe my face, "at least you know how to get him to sit."

"Okay, so tell me what's happening in *Winter's wonderland*."

I grimace. "Don't call it that."

"Why not? Fancy, well-to-do fiancée, living in a gorgeous custom-built home and nothing but good things on the horizon. Who could complain?"

A pit opens in my stomach. The conversation with the woman at the café had made all everything seem so trivial, but now that I have to talk about it again it feels a lot more real.

"It's not that simple. Something…came up."

Cammie stops washing Charlie for a moment. "What kind of something?"

I try to explain the situation the best I can, leaving out the part about seeing someone at the end of the driveway. I don't need Cammie thinking I'm seeing things in addition to my paranoia and obsessiveness about this book.

"And you're sure he hasn't had any contact with this Miranda lately?" Cammie asks as soon as I finish.

I feed Charlie the last bit of my sandwich and he licks his lips profusely. "I guess I just have to trust him. I don't have any real way of knowing."

"Sure you do."

I look up, surprised at her candor.

"Look at his accounts…his phone. Whatever you need."

No. Out of the question. "I can't do that. He told me what the deal was, and I need to trust him on it."

"I'm sure he's telling the truth," Cammie says, wiping her hands down and grabbing the hair dryer. "It's just to confirm it in your mind. After what you've been through, I think anyone would understand. Especially Felton. He knows everything, right?"

I nod.

"Then he probably wouldn't blame you for going through this stuff. I mean, you'll be sharing everything in a few months anyway."

Before I can respond, Cammie turns on the blow dryer, waving it over Charlie.

Maybe she's right. It would help my peace of mind if I double-check everything. But what about the next time something like this came up? Will I have to check again? Or is this one time enough? If I definitely know he's telling the truth this time, then I'd never have to check again.

Right?

As soon as Cammie finishes drying Charlie, I pipe back up. "Is that what you and Mike do? Check each other's phones and accounts and stuff?"

Cammie shrugs. "I mean not purposely, but sometimes I'll get on the computer and he'll still be logged in and I can't help but look through messages and stuff. Or when my phone dies I'll borrow his and I might sneak a look."

"And you'd have no problem with him looking at your stuff?"

"He can look at whatever he wants. If he sees something he doesn't like, I'm sure I'll hear about it." She winks at me. "But there's been no complaints so far."

"I just don't know," I say, looking down. "We keep our boundaries. Even though I don't have anything to hide, I don't like the idea of anyone going through my stuff."

"You're a private person. The point is, how does Felton feel about it? And if you don't do it, how long is this going to gnaw at you?"

"It's just all so stupid. Maybe I should just let it go."

"If you can," Cammie says, lifting Charlie out of the drying area and wrapping a thin scarf around his neck. "There you go, buddy. All pretty for mama."

Charlie looks up, wagging his tail.

Cammie rubs my shoulder. "You do whatever you think is

right. But if this bothers you that much, and you don't talk to him about it or do anything about it, is that really any different than him hiding something from you?"

The pit is growing deeper, forcing me to rethink everything.

"How did he seem when he told you the truth about it?"

Charlie marches around the kitchen, in search of another sandwich. Crossing my arms, I lean up against the counter. "Sorry. I guess." He had lied so convincingly to me. Had I not known for a fact it was a lie I wouldn't have had a second thought about it. So did that mean his explanation for the lie was also a lie? There was only one way to find out. I raise my head and stare right into Cammie's eyes.

"I know that look. You're gonna do it, aren't you?"

"I don't think I have a choice."

Chapter Ten

WHEN I ARRIVE HOME, Felton was already there. He's passed out on the couch, still in his work clothes, looking as if he'd come in the front door, barely taken his shoes off, then collapsed on the couch. He must have been wiped from getting up in the middle of the night.

I slip my shoes and jacket off, placing them in their designated places, and tip-toe past him to the kitchen, doing my best not to make any kind of sound. He's been working so hard lately, and all this extra attention from his design award has pushed an already type-A personality into the stratosphere. He's trying to do it all, take the calls for interviews, do the skype sessions and keep his regular clients happy at the same time. When did he actually get any drafting done? Regardless, most of this would die down in the next few months and he'd be able to get back to normal. At least it better, the last thing either of them needed was to be over-stressed before the wedding.

I remove the half-consumed bottle of pinot noir from the refrigerator, silently cursing myself. I didn't mean to leave it in there all night. The guy at the wine store said to put it in an hour before drinking, then remove when done. A slight chill.

Oh well.

It's not like I'm a wine snob anyway. I pull the cork and pour half a glass, not even paying attention to the taste as I drink. Thoughts of the wedding invade my mind. Of course I want to marry Felton, I love him. But the thought of going through *another* ceremony was almost too much. The first time had been such a spectacle, all of my and Thomas' families there, a huge venue, four-tiered cake, photographer, videographer; the whole works. It was supposed to be a once-in-a-lifetime event. Little did I know not more than four years later I'd be retracting all those vows I'd made in solemn oath. How could I not? And the worst part of it was Thomas had passed a pretty rigorous *smell test*. Enough so that I'd had no reservations about entering a lifetime of commitment with him. Thomas's problem was he *changed*.

As I stand there, watching my soon-to-be husband's chest rise and fall, I can't help but wonder if Felton will change too. Would he one day decide maybe I'm not enough for him and start looking for his emotional needs elsewhere just as Thomas had?

Or is he already doing it?

Cammie's voice plays through my head like a stuck record.

Look at his accounts.

Look at his phone.

Do whatever you have to do.

I drain the wine glass and move across the hardwoods, none of them creaking under the pressure. Where does he keep his phone? Still inside his jacket pocket? Or in his pants? I pat the pockets of his jacket hanging on the hook by the door—right beside mine—and find the small, black device nestled in the upper right breast pocket.

My heart rate picks up. Just a one-time thing. Once I confirm he was telling the truth then this will all be over. This is the last hurdle. And maybe it was a little farther than I want to go, but I can't live with the uncertainty. Otherwise I'll be obsessing over it every day. Look how much mental energy I've already invested and the book had arrived barely twenty-four hours ago.

I tap the screen. The image that greets me is a picture of the two of us when we were in St. John last year. My heart pangs. I can't do this. Felton is a good guy; he isn't hiding anything. He isn't Thomas. And he sure as hell isn't Scott or Sal. I slip the phone back into the coat pocket and return to the kitchen.

I'm a coward. No, I just happened to trust my partner. What is so wrong with that? The real question is can I live with never knowing for sure? As I drain the bottle in my glass I think maybe I can. Is this growth? Was this what people in normal, healthy relationships do?

In fact, I should just rid us of the entire problem. Letting Felton continue to sleep, I make my way into the office. It's time to be done with this *intrusion* once and forever. And if Miranda Maryweather shows up on our porch one day, I'll just have to tell her the truth: that we are very happy and to please never bother us again. If that doesn't work there are always restraining orders.

I reach in and open the cabinet where I'd seen him place the book last night, but it isn't there. That's odd. I check the small office trashcan to see if he's beat me to the punch, but it was still empty. What had he done with it? There's no trace of the wrapping it had come in either. Could he have thrown it in the big trash can outside? I glance around the rest of the office to make sure I'm not missing it then make my way out to the garage. The can in there only has the one bag of kitchen waste I'd put there myself the day before. If he didn't throw it away, what had he done with it?

I remind myself to take a deep breath before I get too worked up. There's a reasonable explanation for all this. I return to the living room and check Felton's satchel he carries to work every day. No trace of it in there either. Damn. Was that what he was doing last night? Getting rid of it somehow? Had he thrown it outside? Buried it? Or had he done something with it after I left for work this morning?

Either way, I don't like this feeling that's crept back into my soul. Now I really have no choice. I pull his phone out of the jacket pocket again, ignore the splash screen and unlock it easily. He uses my birthday as his code; I've seen him enter it enough times. He never made a big deal of hiding it, as a gesture of trust perhaps, after knowing what I've been through. Which means there is no way there is anything on here that might incriminate him. I'll probably have to check his other accounts on the computer to make sure. But there's no harm in just looking.

The first thing to eliminate as a possibility are the texts. I open the app to find his latest conversation with Brian. No big deal, he talks to his brother all the time. Except when I see the time stamp from their most recent conversation. It was from 2:28am. The exact time Felton had been out of bed. I open the conversation and audibly gasp.

Felton: *Are you up?*

Brian: *What do you need at this ungodly hour?*

Felton: IMG attached.

Brian: *Is this a joke?*

Felton: *I wish. It showed up in the mail today.*

The image is of the book. My hands go numb, but somehow I manage to keep tapping away. There's nothing left of the conversation, but I check his previous calls and see Brian had called him at exactly 2:30am. Brian knows about the book. And it worried them both enough to discuss it in the middle of the night. It couldn't even wait until the next day.

"I can't fucking believe this," I say aloud.

Felton groans and turns over on the couch. He still isn't awake but he's not a heavy sleeper.

My first thought is to just pack up and go. He's obviously lied to me again, twice now about the same thing. Which means something serious is going on. How is this possible? Am I such a bad judge of character that I missed the signs *again*? We've been dating for three years and not once, *not once*, in any of that time had he ever given me an opportunity to doubt him. Not until this damn book showed up. And in less than a day, it has all fallen apart.

I glare at him, my fury blooming.

Wait, just breathe Winter. You're not supposed to do this, remember?

Felton was supposed to be different. Mostly because *I'm* supposed to be different. Instead of running away from things I'm supposed to confront them head on, work through the problems instead of just saying screw it and moving on. Dr. Hobart said people were never going to be perfect, and they were going to screw up, and it was worth working through the problems.

But the betrayal. Felton *knows*. He knows what I've been through, and my triggers, and knowing all that he decided to lie to me about this. I'm so mad I almost throw the phone to the floor, hoping to smash it to a million pieces.

Instead, I walk around to the other side of the couch, and phone in hand, draw my arm back, holding it like a baseball and chuck it as hard as I can at Felton.

Damn the consequences.

Chapter Eleven

A CORNER of the phone hits Felton square in the stomach, doing a small flip and glances up over him, over the couch, landing somewhere behind in a clatter.

"What the hell?" His eyes flutter open and his hand immediately goes to his stomach, missing the phone by inches. "Winter?" He looks at me with a confused expression. "What was that?"

"Your phone, dickhead."

His eyes snap open. He looks over the couch for it, as if finding the device might erase the last fifteen minutes. It's like he wasn't even trying to hide the panic on his face.

"I'll give you one chance," I say, putting up a finger through heaving breaths, "one chance to tell me the truth or I am out that door right now. And I promise you will never see me again." I swear I'm about to hyperventilate, but I don't care.

Felton sits up, holding his stomach, as if to consider the offer, which tells me all I need to know.

That's it. I'm done.

I turn and head towards the bedroom. It's time to pack up and start over. Again.

"Winter, wait. Wait," he calls, right behind me. Too late.

I stop and turn. He's on his feet with a panicked look in his eyes.

"If I tell you, do you promise not to leave? At least not until I explain everything?"

I don't reply. He doesn't deserve it. But I *am* curious. If for no other reason than to hear whatever lie is about to come out of his mouth. Let's see how much deeper he can dig this grave. I cross my arms.

"Do you want to go sit back down?" he asks.

I don't move. He'll get nothing but the silent treatment until he starts explaining. It's what he deserved. I can't get the image of that book out of my mind. Brian knows about it! How many other people? Do his parents know too? Who *the fuck* is Miranda Maryweather?

"Okay, right. Then…just brace yourself. You saw the texts, yeah? When I told you yesterday that there was no one else but you, that was the truth. But what I didn't say, was that I've been married before."

My body feels like it's being squeezed in a vice. Married before? He'd told her he hadn't been with anyone for eight years.

"When?" I ask.

"About ten years ago. We weren't married long, only about a year and a half."

"Miranda?" I can't believe this. I'd specifically asked about previous relationships—it's one of my smell tests—and he'd told me he'd had a few serious girlfriends, but nothing more than that. I should have known better. I should have known at the time it was a flat-out lie. He was too smart, too good-looking, too many positive attributes for someone to pass him by. This explains so much.

But he still hasn't answered me.

"Was it Miranda?"

"It's complicated."

"How can it be complicated? It either was or it wasn't."

"Hon…" He reaches for me.

I pull back. "Don't."

"Miranda isn't a real person. It's a pen name."

"Your *first wife* was a writer?" I say it with such disdain. And those words feel so wrong coming out of my mouth. First wife? No, there was no way. I'll never be able to trust him again. My pulse throbs against the ring around my finger and tears well up in my eyes. I hate not being able to control it. This is all over. It doesn't matter what he says after this.

"She was trying to be a writer. She never published anything."

"Then how—"

"I don't know. We don't know, that's what has me freaked out."

I wipe my eyes. "Why? Obviously she finally got the stupid thing published and either wanted to gush or gloat. Especially with that *dedication*."

Felton lowers his head, returning to the couch. I watch him walk back, not believing what's transpiring in my own home.

But I'm determined to get answers. "Just tell me why? Why did you lie about it this whole time?"

He shakes his head. "You don't know how many times I've tried to tell you. But then every time I'd worked up the courage, I'd think about what happened to you, to all the pain you've been through and I just couldn't do it. And the longer it went on the worse it got. I kept thinking: 'tell her now, it's only going to be worse later'. Eventually it just got to the point where too much time had passed and I knew telling you would result in…this." He makes a gesture with his hand.

"You guessed right on that one."

His own eyes are wet with tears and a glimmer of pity shines through for him. "Winter, please. You're the best thing that's ever happened to me. I don't want to lose you. I was too afraid. Afraid because of what you—"

"Stop making this my fault!" I yell. "It's *your* fault you didn't tell me, not mine. Don't pin that on me!"

"You're right. It was my fault and my decision not to say anything. It was wrong and for what it's worth, I'm sorry."

I throw up my hands and turn around with every intention of stomping out of the room, but something stops me. He's just so exasperating. I need time to process this. Okay, I've confronted him, and he's admitted a plausible truth. But who knows if it's the real one? What if it's just another lie? Lies on lies. If it is, it's not a very good one because he's about to lose me anyway. The problem is, he isn't a bad person! He's kind to everyone, always helping people out, never saying a bad word about anyone…except his dad. And I know him to be trustworthy. I wouldn't be living here, getting ready to marry him if he wasn't. What if it's just this one thing? And the only reason he hasn't told me was because he knew he might lose me. There's nothing sinister about that. But it's one hell of a dark mark.

"Are you still going to leave?" he asks, his voice small behind me.

I glance over my shoulder. "I need time to think." I want to leave, find a hotel somewhere, but I've already had two glasses of wine and don't feel like getting a DUI tonight. And I don't feel like dealing with a ride share either. Maybe if he just stays on his side of the house and I stay on mine for a while I can think this through. He can sleep in the guest room until I decide what to do. My brain is too foggy and I'm too upset to think properly.

"I understand. And I'm sorry I didn't tell you about Laura."

I freeze.

"Who is Laura?"

"Miranda's real name. Her maiden name was Laura Blackwell."

Chapter Twelve

IT TAKES me a moment to realize I've been holding my breath. I'm not sure how long I stand there, stunned, but it's long enough to register pins and needles in my legs. He'd been married to the same woman who not more than four hours ago bought me lunch? Had she known who she was talking to? What were the odds of two Laura Blackwells in this town? And what were the odds it was nothing more than a coincidence?

I need to choose my next words very carefully.

"And when was the last time you had contact with Laura?" I ask with a measured breath. If this was some kind of sick prank I'd reconsider the DUI.

Felton's eyes are red and wet, with small streams falling down his cheeks. "Eight years ago."

"What happened?" I manage the words without emotion. Good. Keep it straight.

He wipes his eyes with his sleeve. Felton is not a pretty crier, and as if to send this point home, snot runs from his nose.

"Things…just didn't work out."

He's being intentionally obtuse. I'm the one who's supposed to be distraught here. But learning I've already met his first wife has focused my thoughts, sharpened me. It's obvious Laura sent the book, and then followed and befriended me. But why? To get to know me? Maybe find a way back to her lost love again? Was this all just a ploy to push me out of the picture? If so, Felton didn't know about it, or he's good at pretending not to. Though I have to imagine if they concocted this plan together, he wouldn't keep telling me I'm the only woman in his life. We're not married yet; is he too afraid to back out himself and needs help? And who better to help than his ex-wife?

I rub my temples. The only problem is none of that sounds like Felton. Neither did lying about having a previous wife, but subterfuge on this level? It just isn't in his nature. Despite what he's done I know him, deep in his core. If he wants something, he doesn't have a difficult time telling me. He's always very straightforward, something I admire and envy. I'm something of a confrontational recluse, after having so many of them blow up in my face. But Dr. Hobart said it was important to confront. It keeps things honest. I scoff at the therapist in my head. A lot of good it's done in this situation. Maybe I wasn't forceful enough with him yesterday when I first found the book. This couldn't be my fault…right?

"You swear you haven't talked to her since you two broke up?"

He shakes his head. "I swear to God. I couldn't."

I watch his eyes, looking for any trace of deception and seeing none. But now I must consider he's an accomplished liar. If the past twenty-four hours had proven anything, it was that. And if he can do it, so can I. There's no need to tell him about meeting Laura just yet; if he's still lying I don't want to show my hand. I'm going to figure this situation out one way or another.

"Where's the book?"

"I gave it to Brian."

"Why?"

"So he could find out who sent it." He wipes his eyes again. "He's got all those connections. You know."

I do know. Unfortunately. "You don't think Laura herself sent it?"

"No." His voice is small. What, did he think Laura wouldn't intrude on his life so brazenly like that? Or was there another reason? Maybe I should get in touch with Brian, tell him what I know. Bypass Felton altogether. It would be a fitting punishment, after all, as it was what his family has done to him all his life.

"Who else knows about it?"

"I assume he told Dad. That's probably it."

He was being more open, but I have the sense I'm still not hearing the whole story. That's fine. If he wants to keep lying I will find the truth elsewhere, either from Laura herself or by doing a little digging. Then I can decide how I want to proceed. Before I knew Laura was his first wife I'd been ready to let it go. But there's something deeper going on here, and just like the book itself, I can't let it go until I know the whole truth. A simple girlfriend on the side is easy enough to figure out, and I've already been down that hole once before with Thomas. Chatting on his phone too much gave him away. After that, it was just a matter of putting the pieces together until I found her. Open and closed. But this is different. This is almost a challenge. And I am not going to be made a fool.

"I'm going to bed," I say, facing him again. "I don't want to see you again until tomorrow morning."

He nods.

I turn and head down the hall, utterly spent but my mind reeling with possibilities. Should I bring Cammie in on this? After all, Cammie was the one who suggested I get involved in the first place. Without that advice I might never have found out what was going on. And Cammie had been there when things went south with Thomas. But it means admitting I've been played yet again, and I'm not sure I want to face that embarrassment. Cammie and Mike have the perfect thing going for them, and if everything holds, Felton is lining up to be just another disaster in the long string of failed relationships that's been my life. The stupid thing is I'd built a system to specifically protect against this sort of thing. A series of tests and trials to qualify potential candidates and weed out the undesirables. Cammie had no such test, none that I've ever seen anyway, and she'd hit the jackpot on her first try.

I close the door behind me and press the button to lock it from the inside. Maybe I'm just not supposed to have a solid relationship. Maybe it's just supposed to be a series of partners that don't really matter. After all, I have my job, my friends, my family. I still have a lot going for me. Maybe all this isn't worth it. Will I really be any happier with a partner?

I think back to Cammie and Mike again. How they love each other, support each other. Right now, Mike's probably spending his time working on Cammie's van so she can go out and wash more dogs tomorrow. The stupid thing is Felton is like that in his own way! Even though he has no automotive experience whatsoever, if I ask him to go out and work on my car, to improve it in some way, he'd absolutely do it even if he had no clue how. It had been very clear to me from the beginning that he was interested in making my life better. It has been the most balanced relationship I've ever had. Neither one of us ever has to do one thing all the time. If the trash needs to be taken out, he doesn't wait for me, he just does it. Or if he forgets to grab the mail, I'll go out and get it. We work on a very even schedule; it's all about getting the job done and not about who isn't living up to their responsibilities. And it had been perfect. All up until yesterday.

I flop down on the bed, but don't cry anymore. Instead, I

stare at the ornate ceiling fan above our bed. I'm done with the crying. This is about finding the truth. And that begins with finding Laura again, letting her think she can be my friend. Then, and only then, will I have enough information to find out what's really going on here.

It looks like I'll be having Rachel sandwiches all week.

Chapter Thirteen

FELTON

FELTON CRAWLED ON HIS HANDS AND KNEES ACROSS THE floor. The phone must have slid under a piece of furniture somewhere. He'd been in a deep sleep when Winter woke him. At first he thought he'd been shot, or punched really hard. That girl could throw. Even if he did find the phone, what were the chances it still worked?

How could he have been so stupid? He should have erased the texts immediately! Even though she'd never gone through his phone before it was foolish to leave any evidence at all. Another reason to get the book out of the house. Out of sight, out of mind. But now, instead of making things better, he'd made it all so much worse. There was a good chance if she'd looked on his phone and found nothing all of this would be over. But he'd been so tired it had slipped his mind. She wasn't the kind of person to let an unanswered question go unchallenged. And now...now she'd dug in.

He reached his hand under a refurbished credenza, picking up dust and debris until his hand touched something cold. Bingo. Felton examined the phone. The screen had a hairline crack that began as a spiderweb on the lower left-hand corner, but when he touched the power button it sprang to life, no other apparent damage. He reviewed the texts again and cursed himself. Could he really blame her for wanting to leave him after this? For being suspicious?

The minute he laid eyes on that book he should have come clean. But no, he'd panicked, thought up some lie and immediately tried to bury it all.

Why face the truth when a lie will do just as well?

God, he hated his dad for putting that nonsense in his head. That man, with all his secrets and all his machinations, who couldn't leave well-enough alone, had somehow still managed to permeate his life despite the fact that Felton had all but cut off communication with the bastard. And now that he knew about this book—thanks to Brian, the snitch—it wouldn't be long before he'd find a way to become involved. If for no other reason than to hold it over Felton's head as a penance for not following in the family footsteps.

Felton sighed and glanced towards the other end of the house where Winter was probably lying in bed, fuming at him. How could he have done this to her? He needed to make it right somehow. To find out who really sent him this book and why. Because if their goal had been to disrupt the best thing he'd ever found in his life, they'd succeeded.

He shoved his phone into his pocket and made his way into the kitchen, drinking two full glasses of water before taking a breath. He shouldn't have taken the Ambien back at the office; he should have been awake when Winter got home. Or at least changed the code on his phone. Or not lied about it in the first place. Or anything else other than what he'd done up to this point. The question was, what should he do now? She said she didn't want to see him again until tomorrow, so going in there would be a bad idea. But he couldn't help himself from wanting to try. If he started from the beginning, the real beginning, maybe she would come around.

Just as he decided it was a terrible idea after all, his phone vibrated in his pocket. His first thought was it was her, texting him that she was really leaving, or to tell him to go find a hotel. But when he pulled the phone out and looked at the caller ID, he winced.

"Hello?" he said.

"Son."

Felton bit his lip. "Dad. What can I—"

"Cut the shit," Lazarus Byrne replied, his voice hot. "We need to have a visit."

Right on cue. Felton was actually surprised it had taken this long. But then perhaps pops had been waiting for him to call for help. It put a smile on Felton's face to know he hadn't caved. "I can come by tomorrow afternoon."

"Now."

"It's ten-thirty at night."

"Then I'll see you in twenty minutes." Lazarus hung up.

Felton glanced down the hall again. He couldn't leave now. What would Winter think when she heard him drive off? This was the worst possible timing. He could try to sneak out, open the garage door without the motor and maybe pull the car out quietly? Damn, why hadn't he sprung for that Tesla when he had the chance?

There was another possibility. He could just not go. He considered it for a moment, then almost burst out laughing at his own stupidity. Not going would only make things worse. When Lazarus Byrne called you, you showed up. No ifs, ands or buts.

Maybe he could text Winter he was leaving, let her know Lazarus had called. She would still understand that much at least? Right?

He began to type out the message, then thought better of it and shoved his phone back in his pocket. No contact until morning meant no contact. She might just think he was going out for a drive to clear his head. Or she might think he was going to see Laura, as absurd of a notion as could be. He couldn't just say nothing.

Yanking the kitchen drawer open, Felton removed a small pad they used for grocery lists. He jotted a quick note:

Dad called, I'll be back soon. I love you.

That should do it. Sweet, simple and to the point. He laid it right on the counter where she couldn't miss it, then went into the living room and slipped his coat back on. He'd been so tired from the pills he hadn't even taken off his shoes when he got home. But after hearing from Dad, he doubted a dump truck full of Ambien could put him back to sleep.

WINTER

I'VE ALMOST DRIFTED OFF TO SLEEP WHEN I HEAR THE GARAGE door open. It isn't as loud as it normally is, like the motor has been disconnected and it's being lifted by hand. But it's still a sound I recognize. Moments later the low rumble of Felton's Mercedes filters through the walls, and then the space grows quiet again. Where is he going? Not that I'm complaining. It's better with him out of the house; I can relax a little more. Honestly, I don't care where he goes or when he's coming back. He's a big boy and can make his own decisions. At the very least it means I can leave the bedroom.

I unlock the door and head down the hallway, just catching the tail lights of his car as he turns out of the long driveway. Good riddance. Did he think he could leave without me knowing? Had that been his plan? I walk over to the garage and peer inside. Yep, he'd disconnected the motor from the chain and left the door itself open. That means he isn't planning on being gone long. He wouldn't leave it open all night to the elements.

I push the button on the wall and the motor immediately catches the disconnected chain, drawing the slack and then pushing the door back down in its place. I grin.

"Won't be getting away with that one," I say. Honestly, the longer he's gone, the better. And while he's out of the house it's a good opportunity to do some investigating. If he was married to Laura ten years ago, there must be some evidence of it somewhere. Only now does it occur to me that not only has *he* lied to me, but so has his family. Maybe not to my face, but they were still lies of omission. Never any mention of his previous wife, like she'd been completely erased from Felton's past. Knowing what I do about his father, that doesn't surprise me, but Brian and his mother Abagail aren't as duplicitous. At least they don't come off that way, but maybe they're better at hiding it. Felton made no attempt to disguise his disgust with his family at times, though he'd gone to his brother the minute he realized he was in trouble. Instead of confiding in me, he'd gone back to them. I shake my head.

I'll start in the office. He isn't stupid enough to keep something in our bedroom, where I'm more likely to stumble upon it. No, it'll be here, amidst all this crap, buried somewhere. Then again, he hadn't been smart enough to delete his own texts so maybe I'll check his side of the bed after all.

AFTER ALMOST AN HOUR OF SEARCHING, I HAVEN'T HAD MUCH luck. I've gone through folder after folder of papers, binders, and reports, finding nothing. I flipped through books and magazines, looking for anything that might be hidden in the pages inside, but they'd all been empty. There was nothing but a record of his life with me and precious little before. But that was odd too, wasn't it? I hadn't given much thought to it before now, but there seemed to be some…gaps in his life. Maybe I haven't dug far enough yet. Felton keeps records of things far longer than he needs to, something drilled into him from his daddy, I suppose. He's something of a packrat when it comes to documents, ideas, or sketches. Which means if he's telling the truth about Laura, there has to be evidence somewhere. A tax statement, a phone bill…something to prove they were once married. Once I have that, I'll feel a lot better, oddly.

I stop short. This was exactly how all this had started. With me opening something that wasn't mine. Suppose I find something worse. Can I handle it? I take a deep breath and stand amidst the papers strewn all over the floor. I'll come back to this in a minute. Right now, I'm parched as hell.

When I make it into the kitchen I nearly pass over the note without seeing it. It blends into the granite countertop in the harsh light of the overheads. But as soon as I read it, I can't help but feel just a twinge of sympathy for my fiancée, despite everything.

"Good luck, *hon*. You're gonna need it."

Chapter Fourteen

I AWAKE TO A COLD BED. I'm sure I turned the heat on before going to bed, but it's possible I forgot. With everything that happened last night I can't really blame myself. A cold snap has made its way down from Canada and even though it's insulated well, the house is probably sixty degrees at best.

I wrap the comforter around me and shuffle down the hallway to the thermostat, the wood floors like frozen concrete under my feet. Sure enough, the number fifty-nine glows bright green on the device mounted to the wall. I tap the heat button, then set it to a comfortable sixty-eight. When I turn, the door to the guest room stands open before me, the bed still made. Had Felton got up for work already?

I return to the bedroom and retrieve my phone, noting it's almost seven. He isn't normally gone this early. Unless he purposefully left before I got up. I move through the house, passing the office with all the papers strewn on the floor and head into the kitchen. Other than my wine glass and subsequent water glass on the table, nothing has been moved. Felton's note is still in its place and the coffeemaker is off.

He didn't come back home last night.

This realization sends a little surge of adrenaline through

me, but I shake it off, fixing myself some breakfast. It was probably better he didn't come back, and he more than likely just crashed at his parents' house. Though, he must have been in dire straits to beg his father for a bedroom for the night. Is this what I've driven him to?

No. It isn't my fault he lied. He'd put himself in this situation. Decided it was better to lie to me and start our life together with secrets he was too chicken to admit to. Before last night I can't think of a single time I've ever lied to him. Not a serious lie, anyway. And my lie last night was nothing but a lie of omission. It wasn't as if he'd asked me if I knew Laura.

In fact, to the people I'm closest with, I never lie. Little white lies like the one I told Janet didn't matter. But I'm always sure to never do it to those I'm closest to. Which had been—in large part—due to Daisy.

Daisy, my sister, had always been the wilder child growing up, doing all manner of drugs and getting into trouble. Going off with boys. She was a few years older than me, just enough to both attract me to her antics and repulse me at the same time. Daisy was one of the cool kids, slipping out at all hours, sneaking back into the house, causing our mother all sorts of consternation. In return, I felt like I needed to step up and be the good child. Mom didn't need another heathen running around, driving her nuts, despite how badly I wanted to be like my big sister, out smoking beside the convenience store where I sometimes saw her with her gang of friends. Or going out with Daisy when she would slip out of the house at one a.m. and get back at five, face flushed and smelling like pot. I couldn't do that; I had to make up the difference, provide the balance so the house didn't fall to pieces. With Dad out of the picture, Mom and Daisy fought almost constantly. It was better if I could be a demilitarized zone in a house of constant battle. So I never got to do the "fun" stuff. Instead, I stayed inside reading books, learning about engineering, keeping my nose clean and most importantly: not telling any lies. That was what got Daddy in trouble.

I glance at my phone, weighing if I should call Felton or not. I'm not even sure what I want anymore. I don't want to start all over again, but then why should I be the one to call? It was his screw-up, so he should be the one to fix it. I put the phone down and return to the office.

I made one hell of a dent last night, and I plan on making another one today when I get back home from work. I will find something to substantiate this whole thing or die trying. And if Felton comes home to find the office in a mess, he can just deal with it. He has his other office, he can always...

His *other* office. The one place I've only been a handful of times. The place he keeps even though he doesn't need it. I should have seen it earlier; if he kept anything secret, it would be there. Instead of wasting my time here I should focus my efforts there instead.

Yes, *now* I'm making progress. Humming a little tune, I quickly make my way back to the en suite for a shower.

∼

I CALL CAMMIE FROM THE CAR.

"Hey, my favorite leech. Whatcha need today?"

Ouch. Sometimes her jabs come off more hurtful than playful. "I wish you'd quit doing that."

"Then maybe take me out for coffee once in a while. You need to woo me a little every now and again."

I roll my eyes. "I can hang up. Do you want me to hang up?"

Cammie laughs on the other end. "Of course not. How'd it go last night?"

"You'll be happy to know your advice kicked up a shit-storm of epic proportions."

Cammie gasps. "Nooo. What happened?"

"I can't explain it all right now, it's too much. But maybe over coffee?"

"You serious? I was just joking about that part."

"I'm serious. I'm on a mission now and I'll explain more when we're in person. Are you free for lunch today?"

"You're on a *mission?*"

"Are you free or not?"

There's a pause on the other end of the line. "Uhh, I've got an opening at one."

I think back to the day before. What time had I met Laura? Two-thirty? One would be too early for Cammie to help me scope the woman out. "Do you have anything later?"

"Sorry, just that one opening today. Unless you're talking dinner."

Damn. Well at least I can fill Cammie in on all the details. I can always come back to look for Laura another day. "That's okay. Let's do one. You know that café, The Stone Inn?"

"Oh yeah, that tiny place. On the complete *other* side of town."

"That's it. Let's meet there."

"Ugh. I guess beggars can't be choosers. See ya then, lover." Cammie hangs up, leaving me feeling like I haven't been very good to her. I really need to do something nice for her one of these days.

I pull off the highway and into a large strip mall. It's been around since I was little, and I even remember coming to the Ames that was here way back when. But they ended up demolishing that and building a grocery store instead, which has also gone out of business. As a result, the largest part of the strip mall stands empty. The other tenants are small, one-door operations. It had been the perfect place for Felton to set up his business and get out from under his father's foot. A place his family would never approve of and that wouldn't flaunt the Byrnes's social status.

I scan the parking lot; no sign of Felton's car anywhere. It's almost eight-thirty. He still hadn't come back home by the time I left. If he comes straight here from his parents' house, he'll catch me in the act. But if he goes home first to shower and change, as I expect he will, I have at least thirty to forty minutes on him.

The car rumbles to a stop in the space in front of his office. "Byrnes Architecture," reads the small plastic sign affixed to the strip mall's overhang. I pull my keys out, and using the spare key I've never needed in the past three years, I unlock the front door and enter the small space.

It's just as I remember it, sparse and clean. A few pictures hang on the walls and a computer desk with a drafting desk sit off to the side. About three feet of stacked plans adorn the cubby under the main table, all rolled up and safe in their own safety containers. They're either plans he mails out to clients or vice versa, for those projects where he's picking up the slack after coming in following another architect. It's a cold space, not inviting and not particularly comfortable to work in. I need light, space and greenery if I hope to get something done. Something other than just bland grey walls and blinds covering the front floor-to-ceiling windows beside the door. I pull open the main blinds, flooding the space with light, and notice he hasn't even cleaned recently. A thin layer of dust coats the top of all his boxes.

"Now if I were a secret, where would I hide?" I ask the room. Felton keeps a series of filing cabinets tucked under his main desk. I'll go for those first.

AN HOUR PASSES WITHOUT ANY HEADWAY. IT'S TAKING LONGER because I have to put everything back as I find it. I don't care if he finds the house in a mess, but if he found out I was in here searching through his files he might think I'm too obsessive. But you know what, fuck him, he's the one who brought this on himself.

But I'm short on time, and it's either come back later or take stacks and stacks of file folders with me, neither of which is an ideal option. I've already tried to leave half a dozen times but knowing I could just be on the cusp of finding out about Laura keeps me searching through just one more folder. I glance at my watch. If he's coming into the office today he'll be here very soon. If he saw the mess at home he'd try to clean it up, which would delay him. But I can't rely on that. He's just as capable of leaving it for later. I need to leave, now.

Replacing the last file folder back in its spot, I scan the room for anything I might have missed or moved. The advantage of having such a sparse space was I didn't need to worry about upsetting a delicate balance of materials. I pull the blinds back down and check outside before exiting, locking the door behind me. What would I say if he pulled in right now? I could make something up about wanting to surprise him, but with the fight last night it probably wouldn't hold water. No, my best bet was to get out of here and avoid any kind of confrontation altogether.

I hop in the car, starting it up quickly, and pull out of the space, the whole time scanning my rearview for any sign of him. Every second that ticks by seems to resound in my gut, as if he'll appear at any moment. I take the back way out of the lot just to be sure, back behind the abandoned grocery store.

Just as I'm approaching the corner, Felton's black Mercedes catches my eye.

I gun it, trying to get out of eyesight quickly. It's possible he didn't seen me. As I disappear around the edge of the building the last thing I see is Felton getting out of the car, staring against the sun in my direction.

Chapter Fifteen

"So you don't know if he saw you or not?"

Cammie and I sit at one of the small, two-person tables at the far side of The Stone Inn. I managed to explain everything that happened the previous night, in addition to how I met Laura here yesterday, and the mad dash out of the parking lot this morning.

"I think he did. I can't be sure."

"But he hasn't called you. Or texted."

"Well. I sort of specifically told him not to. He knows it would just piss me off."

Cammie leans forward on her elbows and glances around before returning her attention to me. "What are you guys going to do?"

I just shake my head. Obviously, things can't go back to the way they were. But is there any possibility of moving forward? I turn to watch the deli chef at work. His hands move quickly, slicing and stacking, his total focus on nothing but the task ahead of him. Does he have a spouse who lied about prior relationships? What are his worries? His obstacles? I see if I can find a ring, but his hands move too fast.

"I just don't know," I finally say.

Cammie reaches out and pats my hand. "You'll figure it out. You always do."

"It's just so cliché."

"What, that you thought this one was different?"

I don't reply. Instead, I keep my eyes trained on the chef. His quick and precise movements sooth my mind. Why can't life be like that? Smooth, efficient, and without all this extra drama. How in the hell am I supposed to be this great engineer if I can't even get my own house in order?

Cammie tugs on my sleeve, bringing my attention back. "Felton *is* different. He's not Tom. You know that."

"Yeah, I know."

Cammie leans back, blowing her bangs out of her eyes. "Tell me again what this woman looks like. Who should I be looking for?"

I sigh, thankful not to think about Felton for a bleeding minute. Better to focus on the other half of this equation.

"About as tall as you. Our age, maybe a smidge older. Dark, dark, *dark* brown hair. And yesterday she had on glasses and was dressed smart. Like a lawyer."

"Someone who's got that 'don't fuck with me' look, huh?"

I smile. "That's what I thought too. I thought…why is this woman talking to me? Everything about her appearance was designed to be intimidating. I know if I wore something like that, it would be a clear signal for everyone to stay out of my way. But she couldn't have been friendlier."

"Do you think she knows who you are?" Cammie asks.

I grimace. Everything hinges on this one unknown. If Laura had known who I was, it meant she'd targeted me for some unknown reason. An idea I don't relish one bit. "I hope not. I really, really hope not."

"Well…" Cammie glances at her phone. "I have to get back. I wish I could stay longer, but I have appointments all afternoon and you know what happens when I'm late."

"Soggy dogs."

"Soggy dogs and pissed off owners."

She stands to leave.

"Hey," I say, reaching out. "Did you get the van ready?"

Cammie gives me a small smile. "Almost. Mike needs a few more days. And thank you for asking. I'll invite you over for the bottle-breaking ceremony next week."

"I'm sorry I've been kind of a horrible friend. This has me so frazzled."

She pats my shoulder. "Don't worry about it. I know you're trying your best."

"Tell Mike hey."

"And you," Cammie points at me, releasing my shoulder, "keep me in the loop. I want to know everything that's happening."

"Yes ma'am."

As soon as she's gone, I turned back in the general direction of the deli chef again without really watching him. Have I been foolish for looking for some evidence of Laura? If Felton hadn't wanted me to know that badly, wouldn't he have destroyed or gotten rid of everything that might show a prior relationship with someone? If so, the fact that he'd done so was sort of impressive, especially if it was all for my benefit. In its own way it was sweet, while at the same time incredibly deceptive. I have the urge to be just as deceptive with him. To finally unleash that part of myself I've kept inside for so long, that little kid who just wanted to open herself up and do a few not-so-nice things. But I don't want to hurt anyone. Just…ugh. I don't even have a word for it. It's as if I'm sitting on a pile of dynamite and the fuse just burnt out. I want to find out what happens when that lit fuse reaches the pile. I've been blowing it out my entire life.

I sit in the café with a cooling cup of coffee for another hour before finally giving up and leaving. I've already missed a crucial meeting at work and the partners won't be happy when I finally get back to the office.

As I reach for the car, I hear the crunch of gravel behind me.

"Winter?"

I turn, coming face to face with the woman I'd spent the afternoon looking for and I'm not prepared for it. I mentally fumble for a moment. "Oh, umm, Laura, right?" I say, feigning ignorance, as if I hadn't been thinking about this woman constantly ever since last night. Does she know I'm here for her? Did she talk to Felton already?

"You must have really liked that Rachel sandwich." She's dressed in similar clothes as yesterday, except today she wears a long black coat that mirrors the color of her hair. She smiles, but I see something behind that smile. Something I wouldn't have seen if I hadn't been looking for it. Something that might have been there yesterday, too.

"I did like it." What am I supposed to say? I'd spent all this time looking and waiting for her, hoping she'd show up with no further plan of what to do? What kind of dummy did that? Was this really the woman Felton had been married to? And what happened that caused them to get a divorce? Reflexively, I glance down at Laura's hand, noting she's not wearing a wedding or engagement ring. So either Laura doesn't believe in those things, is hiding it, or just isn't in a relationship at the moment. But given the dedication in the book, it was hard to figure out what was going on in the woman's mind.

"Are you coming or going?" Laura asks.

"I'm...um..." This is the perfect opportunity and I'm blowing it! I can't let it slip through my fingers. The partners will just have to wait. Now's my chance to learn everything I possibly can about Laura Blackwell.

"Coming," I finally say, getting ahold of myself. "And don't forget. Today it's my treat."

Chapter Sixteen

WE MAKE our way to the counter, but I hold back. "Why don't you tell me what you want and go grab a seat?" I say, eyeing the cashier who couldn't have missed the fact she'd been sitting in his café for two hours already.

"Thank you, but I can order," Laura replies, walking right up. "Give me the pastrami deluxe, no cheese and a pickle on the side. And make sure you toast the bread this time. Last time the bread was soggy."

The cashier looks slightly annoyed. "Anything to drink?"

"That stuff you call green tea will suffice."

I'm slightly puzzled. Is this the same woman who couldn't decide what she wanted yesterday? And today she rattles off an order without a second thought?

Laura stands to the side as I realize I'm up. I smile at the cashier, praying he won't say anything about me being in here so long already. He narrows his eyes, then glances to the table Cammie and I occupied. "Back so soon? What will it be this time?"

Maybe Laura will think he meant from yesterday. "I'll just have the green tea as well."

"Fifteen eighty-five."

I hand over my debit card without looking at Laura. She doesn't say anything about the cashier's remark and neither do I, instead I take my drink from him along with my receipt. This isn't how I wanted to make a second impression. Now she's going to think something's up and there will be no way for me to pretend like *something* wasn't going on. I shuffle awkwardly back to the same table I'd shared with Cammie. Laura takes her time unbuttoning her long coat, then hangs it on the seat and sits down.

I can't think of anything to say. Of all the questions I have for this woman, for all the ways I hoped this would go, I find myself dumbstruck with no way out. I can't just come out and blurt out what I know. And every second that passes only increases the tension.

"You ate already?" Laura finally asks, breaking the silence. She says it like I killed someone. Immediately I know I'm busted. What else does she know? And can I throw her off the trail?

"I was hoping to run into you again. I came over around one."

"And stayed for two hours?" Laura raises her eyebrows as she says it.

"Yeah."

"Damn." She takes a long sip of her tea. "Normally I'd be flattered. But I guess you must have figured out who I am."

My gaze and heartrate shoot up in tandem, and I lock eyes with the woman. I can just barely make out my own reflection in Laura's cat-eye glasses. I didn't expect to break this wall so quickly. But wait, is she saying what I think she's saying? In the entire time I'd been looking for evidence, I hadn't thought to Google the woman. I'd only Googled *Miranda*. How could I have been so stupid? What if *everyone* knew who Laura Blackwell was and I was somehow in the dark? How am I supposed to figure out what she means?

Laura's mouth breaks into a grin, then a laugh. "You

should see your face!" She takes a sip of the tea, then reaches over and pats my hand with perfectly manicured nails, much in the same way Cammie did. "Let me save you some consternation. Yes, I am your fiancée's first wife."

I let out a breath. It's all true.

"So yesterday wasn't a coincidence."

"I'm sorry, no." Laura's grin fades. "I didn't want to scare you off. Before yesterday you didn't know he was married before, did you?"

I shake my head. I don't like being in the dark, especially with strangers. I could try to play it off, like Felton told me a long time ago, but what good would that do? I'm trying to *gather* information; maybe the best way to do that is be upfront with everything I know. I'm more likely to get the truth out of her rather than Felton. In my lap, I clench and unclench my hands.

"Did you send it?" I ask, her voice cold.

Laura's mouth turned into a frown. "Send what?"

"Your book. Did you send him your book?" I don't mean to be so brash about it, but this woman owes me some answers.

"My book? I don't have...do you mean one of my manuscripts?"

I huff and manage not to grit my teeth. "Yes, whatever it's called. Did you send it to him?"

"Sweetie," Laura says with sympathy that makes it sound like I'm a lost child, "I haven't been in contact with him for years."

I narrow my gaze. This is too much of a coincidence to accept that she just *happens* to show up in my life the day after her book arrives on my doorstep. But I can't force it out of her. Better to just play along. "Then what do you want?"

Laura pulls a deep breath in through her nose and takes a long exhale. She reaches into her purse, removing a small mirror case. When she pops it open, a row of perfectly-aligned cigarettes stare back at her. She withdraws the first one, sticking it in her mouth.

"Hey!" the cashier yells across the small room. Everyone in the restaurant stops and turns to look at him. He's pointing at Laura. "No smoking in here." Now everyone is looking at us. I must admit it's more than a little creepy. There's no sound in the place other than something grilling in the back.

Laura already has her lighter in hand and sits frozen in place, prepared to ignite. She turns back to me. "Care to go outside? I need a smoke."

I'm *not* letting her out of my sight. "Sure."

Laura leaves her coat but grabs her purse and I do the same, following the woman out to the front. The sun is shining, but it's still on the chilly side with the wind gusts coming across the face of the building, rattling the small pennant flags on the line strung between the light post and the building.

"Aren't you cold?" I ask, holding myself.

"I've got all the warmth I need," Laura replies and lights the cigarette, the lighter disappearing back into her purse. The lenses in her glasses had darkened in response to the sunny weather and now look like sunglasses. "The reason I sought you out was because I saw your engagement announcement in the paper last week."

Where was this going? "To congratulate me?"

Laura chuckles and pushes the smoke out through her nose. "No. To warn you." She glares at me over the top of her sunglasses. "How much do you really know about Felton Byrnes?"

Chapter Seventeen

I STIFFEN. I do my best not to let it show, but from the sad smile Laura gives me I know I've failed. She takes a long drag from the cigarette and blows it out away from us, studying me, like I'm some kind of specimen. "What do you mean?" I ask, trying to sound stronger than I am.

Laura drops her gaze, kicking around some of the gravel beneath her feet. "He never told you about me. I knew that much already. But I thought it was my duty to warn you. No one else could."

"Warn me about what?" I ask, unsure of anything now. Had someone come up to me and told me I needed a warning about my fiancée before I ever found that book, I would have laughed in their face. But now I'm not so sure. What else could he be hiding?

"You guys have been together a couple of years now, right? I think I read that."

"Three."

"I was with him for less than that, only two. But I saw things in those years I never want to experience again. And he tried to convince me, tried to tell me he was going to counseling and getting himself straight, but I could never put myself in that situation again. I loved him, but once was enough for me."

Wait a second. "Are you saying…he hit you?"

Laura takes another long drag. "Maybe I let it go on for a little too long. I should have seen the early signs, the bruises when he'd grab me too hard, or push me away. But when it finally came to blows, I was done."

I'm speechless. Felton has never gotten physical, ever. Not even a hint of hurting me. He's one of the gentlest people I know. For christ sakes, he doesn't even like killing spiders! There is no way they are talking about the same person. "I…I just…can't believe that," I finally manage.

"Good," Laura replies, finally looking at me. "Then it sounds like all that work he did really helped. If he's never been that way with you, then that's great." She drops the cigarette and puts it out underneath the toe of her black pump. "But you see where I'm coming from, right? I couldn't in good conscience let anyone else get themselves into that situation without knowing all the risks."

This makes no sense. Felton wasn't like that, and I'm not about to stand here and agree with this stranger I don't know about my fiancée's behavior. "Did you file a police report?"

"I tried, but I'll give you one guess who put a stop to that."

My heart picks up, realizing that any report filed against a Byrnes could be easily squashed. "Lazarus."

"He smoothed the whole thing over. Convinced me to take a payoff if he could guarantee Felton would never touch me again. I actually made it all the way to the police station, but he was there, waiting, in that ridiculous black Escalade or whatever it is." She laughs, but there's no humor in it. "I don't even know if it would have made a difference. You know he has connections all over the police force."

"So does Brian," I say, thinking back to the thin layer of dust on the boxes back in Felton's office. The rest of the office had been so spotless, but that one area had been dustier than it should have been. As if someone had deliberately put it there. And there was only one reason I can imagine introducing dust into a room.

"Oh, don't even get me started," Laura says, pulling out another cigarette. She offers me the case. Under any other circumstances I would absolutely and unequivocally refuse, but I find myself reaching for the case and taking it. Her hand is shaking as I remove a cigarette and perch it between my lips. Laura holds up the lighter and ignites the end for me. It's time to see if these things really do take the edge off. I inhale, not too deep, as I don't want to scorch my lungs the first time, and a little jolt of electricity surges through me. I don't cough, but it burns all the same and I hold the smoke for a moment before blowing it out.

"How do I know you're telling the truth?"

Laura looks taken aback. "I guess you don't. You believe what you want to believe, but I don't really have anything to gain by telling you all this."

"You do if I leave him. Revenge."

Laura blew her smoke away and I copy the gesture. "I worked too hard in my own therapy sessions to fall back into the revenge spiral. Make no mistake, I was mad for a long time. But I got over it. If you guys are happy, then that's great. But if something ever happened to you and I hadn't said anything…well…"

I take another drag, and this one comes a little smoother. "I just don't know."

Laura exhales. "I get it. If some random lady came up to me and told me things about my husband, I'd probably tell her to fuck off."

"You're married?"

She nods. "Five years now."

"But you don't have a ring."

Laura stares at her ring finger. "We don't really believe in them." Then, after a beat, "Yeah, we're those people. No rings, no hyphenated last names or anything like that. Just two people who love and live together. And get all the tax benefits."

I take another drag on the cigarette. It warms me from the inside out; I can see why people do this. Despite my anger, I'm also slightly euphoric. Like I just discovered some long-lost secret. If only Daisy could see me now. I smile at the prospect and relish a few more pulls on the cigarette without saying anything. Can I trust this woman? Her accusations about Felton were terrible, but what if he had really done those things? It wasn't out of the realm of possibility that his family could cover them up; as far as I've seen, they could cover almost anything up. Lazarus's influence extended far and wide beyond their little corner of Connecticut. But I need evidence. And none of this answers my initial question: who sent that goddamn book?

"Who else knew about your book? Who else would have a copy?"

"Oh." Laura removes her glasses and pinches the bridge of her nose before replacing them. "That was so long ago, I don't even know. I never got serious about it, you know? I mean I tried, but they just never went anywhere. I'd actually forgotten about them until you said something." She pauses. "So someone sent you my book? Which one?"

"*Simple Desires*," I reply, doing my best to keep the vitriol out of my voice. I take another pull from the cigarette. I have to admit I do feel a little better.

"Ugh," Laura says. "My first novel. It was so bad." She smiles. "So, so bad. You didn't read it, did you?"

"Just the first few sentences."

Laura hides her face in her hands and suddenly I feel the embarrassment for her. "It's so terrible." When she comes back up for air she still has the hint of a smile on her face. "That's almost more of a punishment for me than it is for you." She stubs the second cigarette out. "But I'll see if I can't figure out who might have had a copy. I sent it to a few friends back in the day to read it for me. Give me some feedback, you know?"

"I could talk to them if you want," I suggest. If Laura could connect her to people who knew Felton when he was younger, it would go a long way to filling in some of the holes of his life. And it might confirm Laura's story.

"You want to talk to my friends?"

"Well...just...it might be someone I know. Someone Felton might have known from back when you guys were married."

"Sorry," Laura replies, "we didn't really have mutual friends. I had my crowd and he had his and rarely did the two mix. Obviously, all of mine came with me when I left." She says it like they were some kind of cadre, which I find a little odd. "But don't worry, I'll touch base with all of them. Just to make sure. Give me your phone number, so you don't have to stalk me at this crappy little café again."

"Yeah. Of course." I drop my cigarette and put it out under my own shoe. So that's what that feels like. I dig into my purse and pull out my phone. Laura rattles off her phone number and as soon as I add it I hit send. A little chime goes off inside Laura's purse.

"Perfect," Laura says. "Now that the ugly business is out of the way, care to have second lunch?"

"Absolutely," I reply, following her back inside.

Chapter Eighteen

I DON'T BOTHER GOING BACK to the office. By the time Laura and I finish at the café it's nearly five o'clock, so it's better to just go home and make up the work tomorrow. I've got three missed calls from Sidhara, none of which could be as interesting or important as getting to know more about Laura and her life. She's a web developer working for a major company based in Hartford. She met her husband only a few months after leaving Felton, though it had taken them a little longer to get together. And she is understandably shy. But the more I listened to the woman, the more I found I could relate to her. We both came from broken families, both had an older sibling working out of the country somewhere, and are both highly determined and motivated. Between the two of us we'd been able to boil down Felton's type to a very narrow band. And while that was funny in one sense, it's also a little concerning. What had he done, screwed up with Laura then gone out to look for an exact replacement with me? Like Laura was his practice run? I can't be sure until I confront him.

Which is exactly what I'm prepared to do as I pull up to our home...until I see the other car in the driveway.

I don't even bother opening the garage. Instead, I ease in behind Felton's car, keeping the noise to a minimum, then cut the engine and take a deep breath. The burn of the cigarette is still back there. Some part of me can't come to terms with the fact I'd done that. I'd refused to smoke every day of my life until today, another symptom of being the "good child." But in that moment, I'd needed something, something decidedly non-Winter. If I could do that, I can get through this.

It seems spring has gone back into hibernation after all, because when I get out of the car I can see my breath in front of me. I sneak up the walk as quietly as possible, hesitating when I reach the front door. Behind it, muffled voices shouted back and forth, none of them clear enough to make out what they are saying. There are at least two people in there, maybe more, and from what I can tell the conversation isn't a good one. As soon as I open the door I'll give myself away because of that damn security system. Why it doesn't chime on the back door or garage I don't know. But the sound of the garage opening will alert them in lieu of beeps. I toy with the idea of sneaking in through the back, but when they catch me standing there, and they eventually will, I'll have no excuse. I don't want it to look like I'm the one hiding anything. I have to keep Felton thinking he's controlling the only avenue of information about his former life. That way I can catch him in a lie.

I hold my breath and open the front door, the chimes singing overhead as I toss my keys to the side table.

"Winter? Is that you?" Felton's voice comes from the living room.

"Yeah," I reply as casually as I can. Not friendly though, he hasn't deserved that. If he *had* seen me at his office I'm not about to let him turn this around. He's the one who screwed up here, not me.

"Hey Winter," Brian's voice echoes from the living room. I

suspected he was here from the Range Rover outside, but is there anyone else?

Please God, not Lazarus, please not Lazarus.

When I turn the corner it's just the two men, sitting across from each other. Felton is on the same couch where she'd chucked his phone at him last night. I breathe an internal sigh of relief.

Brian stands and gives me a brief hug like he always does. While he does all I can think of is how he's lied to me for years about Laura. "I understand this guy is being a royal shit to you lately."

I smirk, playing along. "Something like that."

"Brian...don't," Felton says.

His brother waves him off. "I wanted to tell you about Laura from the beginning. But *some people*," he stares at Felton as he says it, "thought it would be a bad idea."

"I appreciate that," I reply, surprised by his candor. Could that be true? Could Felton have been the one who kept the rest of his family quiet about his ex? It would make sense and makes me feel just a little better about Brian being here.

"And now that you know, I want you to know I'm working on finding out who sent this book to you. Or him. I've got some of my best people looking into it."

"Your best people?"

"Private detectives, a few beat cops on their off time. You know, nothing serious but enough to make some inquiries."

I frown. Should I tell them I've met Laura? With Brian involved, what's the point in hiding? Other than the fact it might upset Felton. Not that I care very much about that at the moment. But I also like having Laura all to myself, like my own personal secret. And now that Brian has informed me of his investigation, it has lit something deep within. I need to beat Brian at his own game. Not because I don't like Brian, but because it's not his job, or his life. The book had been sent to *my* house, to *my* fiancée, and it wasn't his responsibility to figure this out. Somewhere, maybe while talking to Laura, I realized the book was a message, either to me or Felton. And I'll be damned if someone else figures it out before I do.

"Do you think Laura might have sent it?" I ask, probing him. It's time to see just how much he knows.

Brian glances at Felton, then back to me. "I guess it's a possibility?"

"Brian," Felton warns.

"I'll make sure to check into it. If it is her, I would be very surprised."

"You don't think it is."

"Not at present."

Good. That confirms Laura's story as well. But it also means that Brian might be talking to some of the same people who know Laura. Should I call and warn her to hurry up, or at least mention that my soon-to-be brother-in-law is on the case? So she won't be surprised if he or one of his underlings shows up at her house one day?

"So that's it then?"

"That's it," Brian says. "I just wanted you to know, so you wouldn't worry that someone out there might be stalking you. We've got this thing covered."

"I thought I heard you guys arguing before I came in."

"Oh, that was just my stupid brother telling me he didn't think we should tell you yet. I explained to him that you can't keep things from the woman you love, because that gets you into deep, deep trouble." He stares at Felton again.

"Sounds like sage advice," I reply. Felton's doing the smart thing and staying mostly quiet. That tells me he knows how serious this is.

"I like to think so," Brian says.

The room falls into an uncomfortable silence.

"Okay, I'm outta here." Brian grabs his jacket and heads

for the door. "Hey Win, if he keeps giving you trouble just send him back over to the house. Watching him ask Dad for a room last night was one of the best moments of my life."

"Would you just leave already," Felton says, his head still down.

Brian smirks. "Night, you two. Try not to kill each other while I'm gone." A moment later the door chimes, signaling his exit.

"So," I say, slumping down into the chair Brian just vacated. "How *is* your dad?"

"Winter, I am so, so sorry," Felton says, looking up. "The last thing I wanted to do was hurt you."

"Then you should have told me the truth from the beginning. All of it."

"I know. It won't happen again."

"You're right, it won't." I'm still not quite sure how I'm going to manage this, but for the moment I have the upper hand I'm not about to let it go.

"Tell me what you need me to do."

I ponder a moment. It's in these moments I find being mad at him difficult. And yet on some level I suspect it's an act to get back in my good graces. He always goes into this supplicant mode whenever he's royally messed up, and he's never done anything this bad before. Which means he'll be compliant for a while.

"Is there something you were looking for in the office?" he asks. "Something I can help you find?"

"No. I was just going through some stuff," I reply. "But you can clean it all up."

His lips form a line and he nods like he knew that was coming. "Sure," he replies, pushing himself up from the couch. "Guest bedroom tonight?"

I nod absently, my thoughts drifting to Laura. If there wasn't any evidence of a previous marriage here or at Felton's office—something of which I'm still not one-hundred percent sure—then it must exist somewhere. The county records office should have records of marriages and divorces; it would be the easiest place to look. Despite the fact now three different people have told me Felton was married before, I need to *see* it for myself. But there is something very strange about all of this. No one mentioned a previous marriage over the past three years and I saw absolutely no evidence to ever suggest there was one, and now in less than two days I've found out this massive secret everyone has somehow kept from me. Okay, so maybe part of this has to do with my pride. But that's understandable, nobody likes being the one person in the dark all the time. So the first order of business is to confirm both Felton and Laura's stories. Then I can move on to the more important work of finding the sender of the book, which in turn would lead me to the ultimate answer to the ultimate question: why.

I glance up to find Felton has moved right beside me, and I recoil slightly, startled. Conjured images of him lashing out, hitting Laura flash through my brain.

"Is it all right if I hug you?" he asks.

It's both pathetic and endearing at the same time. But I need to be careful. I stand. "Sure."

He wraps his arms around me and holds me tight, pulling me into him. Am I just now realizing how strong he is? Could he have hurt Laura and not meant to? Was she even telling the truth about him?

Felton sniffs. "Have you…have you been smoking?" He lets go and holds me at arm's length.

"I just had one."

"Where did you get a cigarette?"

"I borrowed it from someone at work."

"Who?"

"Just one of the interns, jeez. What's with the third degree?"

Felton casts his eyes down. "You hate smoking."

"Yeah, well, I'm a little stressed at the moment. I think any reasonable person would understand."

He doesn't say anything, just stands there. But I can still feel his judgement seeping through his skin.

I push him away. "Don't you have some cleaning to do?" I try to make it sound forceful but instead it comes out shrill. Too much panic behind my voice.

He turns and leaves the living room, allowing me to breathe a sigh of relief. Okay, the cigarette had been a one-time thing, but it might not hurt to get some breath mints tomorrow.

I listen to him rustling around in the office for a few minutes, picking up and restacking everything I poured through the previous night. On one hand I almost feel sorry for him, but that was exactly what he wanted, wasn't it? He wants the sympathy so I'll forgive him and things would "get back to normal". I'm not about to make it that easy for him. He's committed a serious error, and if this relationship has any chance of making it, he needs to prove himself to me all over again.

Dead tired, I head for the bedroom, only to have my phone beep from my purse. It's a text from Cammie.

WTF is going on? Haven't heard from you all day. Find her?

I grimace. I promised to keep Cammie in the loop, but with everything going on I'd forgotten again.

Not ignoring you. Call you tomorrow with details. Big developments.

I wait a moment for a response, but none comes. I'll have to smooth things over with Cammie tomorrow. I figure I should check my voicemails from Sidhara while I'm at it. The first two are Sidhara hanging up, but on the third she actually left a message.

"Winter. Where are you? We have to get this second proposal done or we are going to lose these bridge contracts. Call me as soon as you get this."

Shit, the bridge contracts. I'd completely forgotten. How could they have slipped my mind so easily? That never happens to me. I'll have to go in early in the morning to do some damage control there too. It seemed like it only took the tiniest push to start all the dominoes falling in every aspect of my life.

Chapter Nineteen

FELTON

FELTON LISTENED CAREFULLY AS WINTER RUSTLED AROUND THE living room for a bit and then all went quiet. He was taking as much time as he could re-filing everything she'd pulled out. It was obvious she had been looking for some evidence of Laura, perhaps a picture he'd carelessly left behind in a random file or a stray note somewhere. Maybe even a trinket or gift from Laura he couldn't bear to part with.

But no. All of that had been destroyed. He and Brian had gone through everything he owned, top to bottom, and removed any possible remnant of her years ago. Anything with her name on it, anything she'd owned, anything she'd ever even touched. Gone. Even things that meant a lot to Felton he hadn't wanted to get rid of, like their pictures from traveling to the Grand Canyon. He'd never been before and probably would never go again. And the painting she'd given him on their first anniversary. It wasn't anything anyone would recognize; she'd done it herself in sort of a Jackson Pollock style and it had hung above the mantle in their old house for most of the time they were together. Brian had insisted it be destroyed, along with everything else. There could be no trace, he said. Nothing that could ever lead back to Felton. The process had been excruciating. It was both surprisingly easy and remarkably difficult to erase someone from your life.

But was it really Brian, or were those his father's words coming to him through the avatar that had become his brother? Enforcing Dad's decrees had become Brian's way for the better part of his adult life. The path Felton could have chosen but didn't. He supposed he couldn't blame Brian too much—he was as much a victim of circumstance as a willing participant—but that didn't absolve him of everything he'd done since. All the cover-ups, all the lies and deceits. Felton had hoped to avoid it all, but somehow it had still come back to haunt him no matter what he did.

And what was all that crap he'd told Winter tonight? That it could have "possibly" come from Laura? Felton almost laughed despite himself. And why had Brian told her he was investigating it? Didn't he know Winter at all? Now she would only be more interested. This was precisely why he should have just thrown the damn book away. Or at least made a better case to Brian why they should tell Winter he threw it away. When he'd returned this morning and seen the papers strewn everywhere, he'd known immediately she wouldn't give this up. She wasn't one to let things go, not until they had reached her satisfaction. He'd hot-footed it over to his office to see if his theory was correct, and there she'd been, pulling out of the parking lot at the very last moment. He was sure she'd seen him, considering the speed she was going, but that didn't mean he needed to reveal he had seen *her*. He had all the information he would need. But no, despite all this Brian thought it was best they tell her at least some of the truth. And Felton wasn't even sure that decision hadn't come from Dad somewhere along the line. Brian said she needed an ally at the moment, someone she could trust more than Felton. And it was better that person be Brian—a person who could control the narrative—rather than someone out of their control, like Cammie, putting ideas in Winter's head.

Felton sighed, replacing some binders up in one of the office cabinets. He supposed they'd never know what Winter would've done had she not suspected they were investigating the origin of the book. Maybe Brian was right; telling her they'd just thrown it away and forgotten about it might have made her even more ravenous for information. And after he revealed he'd been married there was no pretending anymore; they'd had to come up with a new story. The fact was they still had no clue who sent the book, but whoever did had some very damaging information on the Byrnes family, Felton in particular. And Dad, for all his faults, would never stand for that. Felton was sure they would get to the bottom of it; whether his relationship would survive was the real question.

Chapter Twenty

I AWAKE EARLY, INVIGORATED. THERE'S A SMALL TINGLE IN THE back of my throat, probably from the smoke. What had I been thinking? A lifetime of healthy lungs and I probably just cut four or five months off of my life. Doesn't matter. When I'm ninety, another four months won't make a difference. Plus, it isn't like I'm going to do it again. The first order of business is to get work squared away and then head down to the county courthouse.

I pass the guest room; listening to Felton's soft snoring permeating the closed door. How late had he been up cleaning? Upon reaching the office I no longer have to guess. Everything is back in its place, almost as if I'd never done anything at all. He's trying to prove he's willing to do anything to get back in my good graces. I certainly didn't expect him to finish overnight, and for the first time a bit of guilt gnaws at me over how I'm treating him. This is the man I love, after all. But that doesn't excuse his behavior. And as much as I want to believe he isn't capable of those things Laura said, as much as I want to go into the guest room and embrace him, I just can't do it. There have to be consequences, otherwise he'll just do it again. I'm not going to be pushed around by anyone, especially not the person I plan to spend the rest of my life with.

I fix myself a quick cup of coffee and head back into the bedroom for a shower. As soon as I'm ready I'm out the door before Felton even shows himself, which is how I prefer it. I have too much on my plate to deal with that awkwardness this morning.

As I pull out of the long driveway, I wave to Janet, who is out getting her morning paper. The older woman blows me an overly-compassionate kiss and smiles. I pull onto the main road and grab my phone, quick-dialing the second number on my list.

"Hello?" Cammie says.

"Hey Cams. I'm sorry about yesterday. A lot happened."

"Oh, hey Win. Can I give you a call back? We're elbow deep in engine parts and I—"

"Laura showed up yesterday," I say hurriedly. "She knows I know who she is. She said Felton hit her and that's why she left."

"Holy shit." Cammie pauses. "Do you believe her?"

"I don't know." I speed up and pass a slow truck on the two-lane highway. I need to get into work as soon as possible.

"What are you going to do?"

"I figured out how to prove he was married before. I'm going to go pull the county records on my lunch break. Get the marriage and the divorce records."

"That's...not a bad idea."

"But I wanted to give you an update since I didn't get a chance to call you back yesterday. When I got home, Brian was here. He said he's personally investigating the book."

"That's good."

"I guess. It just makes me itchy. You know Lazarus has his hand in this somehow and I want to find out everything I can before he does. I've never had a good feeling about that man and I certainly don't want to be indebted to him. That doesn't ever seem to go over very well."

"You think he'd actually believe you owed him?"

I grimace. "If he puts a bunch of resources into finding out who did this, including his other son, and then comes back and tells me it was all for me, so I could have a happy, stress-free marriage—which, think about it, he would have no qualms about doing—then yeah, I think he would think I owed him a favor. And from everything Felton has told me, I do not want to owe that man anything."

"You make it sound like he's part of the mafia."

"You may be hitting the bullseye closer than you think."

"C'mon, Win, that's kind of ridiculous." A metal clang rattles through the phone. "Shit. I gotta go. I'll call you back later. Don't do anything rash."

I hang up and shove the phone back into my purse. Don't do anything rash...like what? I'm not putting myself in danger. All I'm going to do is head down to the Clerk's Office. But I can't help think that perhaps I'm picking at a scab that should not be disturbed. Someone had gone to a lot of trouble to conceal Felton's first marriage and people don't do that without a reason.

"WHAT THE HELL IS GOING ON HERE? I THOUGHT WE HAD THIS thing locked down! That's what you said, wasn't it? 'Locked down'? Of course that was two days ago, the last time either of us saw you, and now I'm getting calls from the city asking if we're still putting in a proposal!"

Henry paces his office while Sidhara and I sit in the other two chairs, facing his desk. We usually meet in here because he's got the biggest office, despite the fact it gets hot as hell in here in the afternoon. It was a compromise he said he was willing to make. I take a deep breath, trying to figure out a way to explain myself out of all this.

"What the hell could have been so important that you completely forgot to tell us about the site visits?" he screams before I can even answer his last question.

"Henry, calm down. Let her talk," Sidhara says. She's a much more reserved person than their colleague, but even I can see storms brewing behind her dark eyes.

"Well, I can't wait to hear it!" Henry adds, falling with a *thump* in his own seat behind his desk.

I lean forward. "I had planned on calling you. But I've had a bit of a family emergency the past couple of days and it slipped my mind." It's the best I can do without getting into the minutiae of the book and everything else. The truth is I *had* forgotten. If I tried to explain it all now they'll think I was losing my mind.

"Everyone is all right?" Sidhara asked.

I nod. "More or less. It's just been…a stressful few days. Which is why I came in early this morning to get some of the new drafts done for the proposal. I'll have them all finished before I leave today."

"That's just great, as we were supposed to submit them this morning."

I turn to Henry, doing my best to keep my temper under control. I'm not the only one who can finish proposals, even though I was the lead on these jobs. "I know, and I said I was—"

"Do you not want to do this anymore? Is this how you go off on your own? This was your idea, if I might remind you. Bring the three of us together, become the most respected engineering firm in the state. Because right now it looks like you have more important things on your plate."

"I told you I was sorry," I say through gritted teeth.

"No." Henry shakes his head. "No, I don't think you did. You gave us a half-assed excuse about a sick family member and then justified it. What was so important you couldn't even call Sid back? At least let us know you hadn't done any of the proposal work? At least let us know we were still in the running for the jobs!" His face has gone all red.

I don't respond well to men screaming in my face. So I'm not about to give him the satisfaction of a response.

"That's enough," Sidhara says. "It doesn't matter anymore. Do we still have the time to submit our final proposal or not?"

I glance at the clock. Henry isn't wrong; it was due at the city this morning, something else I've forgotten. I completely neglected everything yesterday. It was as if the day had existed outside of time and I somehow thought I could come and go as I pleased, without any consequences. Why had I thought that? Was it because this mystery had become so compelling? Or was it just the surprise of seeing Laura again, of learning about this bombshell that had turned my life upside down? It's a puzzle to be deciphered, one in which the stakes are higher than anything I've ever faced at work. Perhaps that's why everything else had seemed—and still did to some extent—less important.

"If I work through lunch, I can get it done in time." I won't have time to get to the Clerk's Office, but I don't have much of a choice. We can't afford to lose these contracts. And if I can get it done quickly enough, I might be able to swing by before the courthouse closes for the weekend. I glance at Sid. "Can you double-check my work? I need a second pair of eyes to make sure I don't miss anything."

"Of course."

The two of us stand, leaving Henry still slumped in his chair.

"Great. What am I supposed to do?" Henry asks.

"Call the city," I say. "Make something up about why it's

late and let them know they'll have it before three p.m. today."
I leave the room with Sid on my heels.

"What am I supposed to make up?" Henry calls after us.

"Whatever your tiny brain can come up with," I say under my breath.

Chapter Twenty-One

THE DRAFTING TAKES LONGER than I expect, and by the time we're done and have actually sent it off to the city it's already 4:15.

"I gotta go," I tell Sid. "I have people to attend to."

"You sure everyone is all right?" she asks again, that calm demeanor never betraying her.

"Everyone's fine. I just worry. You know how I am," I reply, shrugging my jacket on.

"Listen," Sid says, pulling me aside. "Whatever is going on with you, it's affecting all of us now. I need to know you have a handle on it. We can't afford to sacrifice jobs, not right now."

I glance down and retrieve my arm from Sid's grip. "I know we've had a bit of a slow slump lately. But I'm sure we're getting at least one of these jobs. They'd be foolish to hire anyone else and the site manager seemed agreeable with me the other day."

"You know how much can change in two days."

Tell me about it.

I want to say it out loud, to try and explain how my home life is falling apart before my eyes, but Sid and Henry don't care about any of that. And it isn't their problem. "It will be fine, I promise. If they don't like the proposals I'll go down to the office itself and make the case in person." I glance at the clock. 4:20. "I really gotta go."

Sid doesn't say anything else, only presses her lips in a line as I walk away. This is all a matter of resource allocation, and I just need to make sure I don't forget anything else. I pull out my phone and type in a reminder to check on the contracts first thing Monday with the site manager. A little follow-up might push things in our direction, even if we are slightly more expensive than the competition. GWH is all about quality and reputation, and the site manager knows it.

I brush out the doors, my stride quick and purposeful. The Clerk's Office is only about ten minutes away, but will they still process my request before they close? If only I hadn't been so frazzled yesterday, I could have planned all this out. Not that waiting until tomorrow for the certificates will hurt anything, but I need to get out in front of this and find out what is really going on before Brian comes back and feeds me some bullshit Lazarus crafted. Brian is a nice enough guy, but he's too loyal to the family, something I don't see in Felton, and part of what I admire about him. It wasn't easy to say no to a comfortable, all-your-needs-taken-care-of life. At least I assume it wasn't.

The Southerland clan hadn't exactly struggled, but things hadn't been easy either. Especially after Dad left with his new girlfriend in tow, something I still haven't forgiven him for. We see each other at Christmas and sometimes Thanksgiving, but that's about it. And maybe Lucille really is a nice person, but I don't care to find out. I'm just grateful she and Dad don't have any kids. I can't imagine a stepbrother or sister more than ten years younger than me and, what, twelve years younger than Daisy? And Mom would have a fit. No, it's best to leave Dad and Lucille in their nice little fantasy world where they don't have to worry about raising anyone and can go off on their vacations.

I slip behind the wheel and crank the heat as soon as the

car is on. I wish this cold snap would move on already. It's supposed to be spring for heaven's sake.

Pulling out of the parking lot, I push the speedometer above normal on Highway 6. I'm not normally a speeder but this is an emergency. And if I get pulled over, then so be it.

I push the accelerator harder. The speedometer inches up to forty-eight. Forty-nine. Fifty. Fifty-two.

Adrenaline pumps through my veins. It isn't the speed, but the fact the cops are vigilant on this stretch of road and speeders get caught all the time. I've never needed to get anywhere fast enough to justify a ticket. But now I get it. Maybe it isn't about getting somewhere fast but challenging and beating the system. I push the accelerator a little harder. Fifty-six and blowing past other cars on the four-lane highway. I almost want to whoop with exhilaration but stop myself.

The Clerk's Office comes up quickly on my right, a two-story nondescript building which, from the look of it, was built sometime in the 1960s with its thin windows and mix of brick and masonry construction. Most of the parking spots in front are already empty, so I yank the car to a stop in the closest one to the door and hop out, trotting up to the doors.

"Hi," I say to the woman manning the front desk. "I'm looking for some public records."

The woman makes a point to check her watch and then returns her gaze to me. "Type?"

"Marriage and divorce."

The woman sighs and pulls out a form from one of the filing cabinets beside her. "Fill this out and we'll mail them to you in four to six weeks."

"Four to six weeks? I can't wait that long."

The woman sits, unmoving. Just staring at me with her small black eyes and silver hair done up in a tight bun.

I compose myself. I have to remember I need this woman's help. All she needs is to go home away from this job. "Is there any way to speed that up?"

The woman stares at me for longer than necessary and I can't help but feel like she's intentionally stalling. Like the records office is this one woman's domain, and no one's getting past her if she doesn't approve it. Finally, she opens her mouth. "We process in-person requests Monday through Friday, nine a.m. until four p.m."

Is that a smirk on the woman's face? They don't have Saturday hours? With it being Friday, I won't get back here until next week, which means an excruciating weekend in the house with Felton, both of us tiptoeing around each other. I can't live like that.

The other option is to accept everything I've learned and drop it. Felton told me; Laura told me. Even Brian told me. Why was it so hard for me to believe he'd been married before? Felton had nothing to gain anymore by lying about it. It just…didn't seem possible. Maybe the real reason I was here was because I needed to know if my instincts really were that dull. If despite everything I've been through, I still can't see a giant red flag waving at me. Because if I can't, if Felton really has managed to lie convincingly to me all these years, I don't think I'll be able to trust anyone ever again.

And what if there were other records? What if he'd been married more than once? Maybe I needed to prove he wasn't lying about anything else; that there hadn't been anyone else before Laura. Because right now, I'm not sure.

I need access to those records. Today.

"Is there anything you can do?" I ask, already knowing the answer.

"Winter?"

I look up, past the silver-haired lady to a figure emerging from a small office off to the side.

"Janet?" The sight of my neighbor anywhere but her own house catches me off-guard. In fact, didn't I see her just this morning, getting the paper? "Do you…work here?"

The woman at the desk harrumphs.

"I do. Part time. Do you need help with something?" Janet asks.

I glance back and forth between the woman and Janet. "I do. I'm trying to get some marriage and divorce records."

"We process in-person requests Monday through—"

"Oh, can it, Mary," Janet interrupts. "I'll take care of her; you go back to your solitaire."

Mary purses her lips, then turns so her back is to us.

"Come dear, you follow me."

"Are you sure?" I ask, falling in step behind her. "I don't want to be an inconvenience."

"It isn't. What am I going to do, go home and knit?" She lets out a brief laugh.

"If you don't keel over from a coronary first!" Mary calls out from the desk, now a good eight or ten feet behind us.

"Go home and drink your medicine, Mary!" Janet calls back. Then, whispering to me, "She always gets pissy around five o'clock. If you come in the mornings she's bright as a bluebird."

I'm in awe of Janet a little bit. She has more bite in her than I'd expected. I'd always just seen her as the kind lady next door.

She leads us into a different office. It only has one small desk with a computer, but three of its walls are covered with stacks of filing cabinets.

"Are these the records?" I ask.

"Only the last ten years. Everything else is in the basement." Janet sits down behind the computer. "Who do you want to see?"

I hesitate. I thought I'd be looking through the files myself, or at least telling someone I don't know personally. But Janet knows Felton. She's been his neighbor ever since he bought that house and started refurbishing it. This is all so embarrassing. But if I want answers I don't have a choice.

"Umm. Byrnes and Blackwell."

Janet glances up briefly, then returns to the screen. "Marriage or divorce?"

"Both."

"Do you have the dates?" she asks, her voice completely even. I hope she knows how much I appreciate her not giving me any accusatory stares or lip service.

Shit. The dates. I didn't think to ask. "Do you need them?"

"Nope," Janet replies. "It will just take me a little longer. Give me a few minutes if you don't mind. Within the last ten years, right?"

"Right." I take a moment to look around the room, not that there's anything to look at except for filing cabinets, but I don't want to stare or look like I'm inviting further discussion. The best thing I can do is examine the typography on the labels affixed to the cabinets themselves until she's finished.

"Okay, I think I got it," Janet says after a few minutes.

"Really?" I turn, trying to keep my voice even. This is it. Until this moment I wasn't completely convinced the marriage had actually happened.

"Looks like the wedding date was…oh, just under the cutoff. August 29th, 2008."

An eruption of air escapes my mouth. So it's all true. He really had been married. It doesn't bother me as much as I thought it would. After all, I've been married and divorced as well. Now comes the hard part. The question that has been on her mind since she came up with this idea. "Janet, can you see if there are any other marriage records for Felton Byrnes? Other than this one?"

"Sure." Janet typed a few keys and studied the screen some more. For a second I'm sure my arm is going numb and I shake it out. Just nerves.

"Looks like this is the only one. I don't see any other records attached to his—" She corrects herself, "—*that* name." Janet stands and opens the bottom drawer of one cabinet.

After a moment she pulls out a plain-looking document. "This is it. Do you want a copy?"

I nod, taking the paper in my hands, trying to keep them from shaking.

"Let me pull the divorce record first and then I'll copy them both for you."

"Thank you," I say quietly, struggling to get the words out. My eyes scan the page. It's real. Everything matches, and that is definitely Felton's signature at the bottom. August 29th, 2008. Almost ten years ago. Which actually makes me feel a little better. It wasn't as if he'd been married only a few months before we met. Laura had said they'd only been married two years, which meant there was at least a five-year gap between when they got divorced and when he and I met. Five years is a long time. Maybe he really did change. Especially without any other relationships. Of course, just because there are no marriage records didn't mean he hadn't dated, though that wasn't a big deal. It isn't like I expected him to abstain for five years.

"Here we go," Janet said. "Divorce shows October 21st, 2010." She stands and heads to another cabinet, pulling on a different drawer and withdrawing another, thicker set of documents. "Let me get these copied for you," she says, her eyes all business as she takes the marriage certificate from me.

I have the proof. I should be furious, but in reality I feel better. Knowing that he actually came clean and there aren't any other secret marriages goes a long way to helping me regain some small amount of trust in him. Maybe we can work this out after all. It isn't hard to believe he'd hidden the truth from me; I know I can be harsh about that kind of thing. Haven't I been in similar situations? Wanting to tell someone something important and waiting too long? And then it becomes too late and you just look like an ass for never saying anything. So you keep quiet. And that's exactly what Felton had done. It just happened to involve the one thing he knew would trigger me. Things might just be okay.

Janet comes back into the room, one set of papers in each hand.

"Win, I don't mean to alarm you but I think we might have an issue."

I look up. I hadn't even realized I'd been staring at my own shoes. "An issue?"

"Look at this," Janet says, placing the marriage certificate and the divorce filing beside each other in front of me.

It takes me a moment to see what she's talking about. On both pieces of paper Felton's signature is nearly identical. But Laura's is not. On the marriage certificate it has clean, swooping lines in a very script-y style. But on the divorce filing it doesn't quite look right. There is a messiness that isn't present in the other document. Like someone tried to copy her signature and hadn't done a very good job.

"What does it mean?" I ask, all sense of relief now gone, replaced by fear and trepidation.

"It means I don't think the same person signed both of these documents."

Chapter Twenty-Two

I TAKE a deep breath and examine the documents again. Giving them both a close look might change things. Maybe if I squint hard enough, I can make the signatures match.

"I don't mean to intrude," Janet says softly, "but how important is this, dear?"

I draw a second breath, trying to work out the implications. Maybe Laura had been drunk, or high? Or incapacitated in some way so she couldn't sign properly? Maybe she'd just been nervous? I mean, how many times have I tried to sign the stupid little pad at the grocery store only for it to come out an unintelligible mess?

I lay the documents on the desk and rub my hands down my face. Am I making too big a deal out of this?

"I...don't know," I finally reply.

"Listen," Janet says, still whispering. "I have a friend who used to work for the FBI doing handwriting analysis. I could get him to take a look for you. This might not be anything."

"And it might be something." I scan the rest of the divorce signature page. There's only one lawyer listed, the Byrnes family council himself, Jackson Willoughby. Wasn't it customary to have two lawyers present in these types of proceedings? There had definitely been two lawyers when Thomas and I went through our divorce. Had Felton forced Laura into something she hadn't wanted to do?

FBI agent. Janet said FBI agent. One who could decipher handwriting styles. "Do you think he could look at a few things for me?" I ask.

"I don't see why not."

"Does he live here in town? Is he close?"

Janet nods. "He's retired. Doesn't live too far from us, actually. Jack's got himself a small farm out there, keeps a few chickens. I think he's got a goat now."

I'm out of my chair and hugging Janet, almost knocking the older woman off balance. "You have no idea how helpful you're being to me."

"I don't want to see you hurt," Janet replies. "I mean, I don't want to see anyone hurt, but I have a feeling you've been through more than your fair share."

The sudden empathy makes my eyes prickle. "You don't even know."

Janet pats my hand, not unlike my mother used to do. "We'll get you straightened out. I'll make some more copies of these and drop them by Jack's on the way home. What else do you want him to look at?"

No one else knows about the book, but this is a safe bet, right? I am *sure* Janet didn't deliver it and this guy is FBI. "I received an anonymous package in the mail, but it was hand-addressed. I wonder if he can compare it to these two signatures."

"He's thorough. I had a landlord once who'd forged my signature on a rental agreement. He'd written up something that said he was no longer required to pay for the water utilities and signed my name to it. So when they shut off my water due to lack of payment, I took it over to Jack—he was still working back then, field office—and he ended up writing me a four-page report on why my signature didn't match the one on the landlord's document. One look from the judge and the jerk had to not only pay three months of utilities, but a reconnection fee, and punitive damages to me for putting me through it. All to save twenty bucks a month." She grins, her straight teeth a brilliant white. "He'll do a good job for you."

"Will he…" I begin, not quite sure how to phrase the question.

"He doesn't have to know it's you if you don't want him to," she replies, reading my mind. "Nobody else has to know. As far as I'm concerned, it's your business and no one else's."

"Thank you," I say again. This woman is a lifesaver.

"Do you have the package with you? I can drop it off at the same time."

"I…" Damn. Brian took it. Which means there's no way I can get hold of it. Odds are he's stashed it away or given it to one of his father's cronies by now. Why didn't I just take a picture of it when it was still at the house?

"No, and I'm not sure I can get it back."

Janet gives me a look that's full of sympathy. "Well, if you happen to find it, let me know. I'm sure Jack will be happy to take a look."

"Thanks," I say, though I can't help but feel defeated and out of options.

WE LEAVE THE CLERK'S OFFICE TOGETHER, JANET LOCKING everything up. Mary must have slipped out unannounced sometime while Janet was pulling the files, for which I'm grateful. I don't need anyone else sticking their nose into my business. After agreeing to get back in touch if I get the picture, we say our brief goodbyes and head off in opposite directions. Presumably Janet is off to drop the documents with Jack while I'm left to wait for…what? Someone to tell me the signatures are or are not from the same person?

Wait a minute. I can find out myself. I don't have to wait on Jack. Without the package I can't even prove someone sent the book to our house anymore. But I do have access to a resource who can tell me what happened when the divorce was finalized: Laura.

Since I already know who she is and that she was married to Felton, there's no reason I can't ask her about the divorce records. The only problem is I have very little reason to trust her. But maybe I can catch her off guard, we could meet for dinner and I could just casually ask about it, maybe she'll open up about what happened there at the end. I fumble for my phone and dial Laura's number. The other end rings longer than I expect and I'm about to hang up when she answers.

"Winter?"

"Hi, good afternoon." I glance at the clock on the dash. "Or I guess it's evening. I can't wait for daylight savings time to end; I hate these long nights." God, I'm rambling because I'm nervous.

"What can I do for you?" she asks, her voice guarded.

"I was hoping we could meet again. I have some more questions."

There's silence on the other end. "What else can I tell you that you don't already know?"

Well, so much for a casual dinner. "I found your divorce records in the courthouse. I wanted to ask you about them."

"You did?" She sounds surprised.

"I have a friend who works over there. She pulled them all for me." There's a long pause on the other end.

"Okay," she says. "Let me look at my schedule and call you back." She ends the call without another word and I'm left there holding my phone, surprised at her sudden abruptness.

I sigh. I'd hoped to get something on my schedule as I really don't think I can wait very long, but what choice do I have? It isn't like I know where she lives. I grab my copies of the marriage and divorce records and stuff them into my purse. That way I'll have them when we meet and she can tell me immediately if that's her signature or not. With any luck she'll be able to tell me what happened at that last meeting that had her so distraught that the County Clerk thinks they aren't the same signature.

I start up my engine, the car rumbling against the cold and try not to make any assumptions about what any of this means. But I can't help my mind from drifting. Immediately my mind goes to my bank accounts. If things don't work out with Felton I'll be back on my own, which means renting again for a while until I can find a place. I've saved some money not needing to pay rent or a mortgage, but it might be difficult finding my own place for cheap. When we'd first moved in together, I was more than happy to pay half the mortgage, until I learned Lazarus had already paid for the house outright. Apparently it had been a gift of some kind to his son. But Felton told me that his name was on the property, not his father's. I hadn't been able to relax until Felton had showed me the title which confirmed it. Just the possibility of Lazarus owning the house we live in is enough to put my nerves on end. There is just something about that man.

I pray I never find out what that something is.

Chapter Twenty-Three

WHEN I PULL into the driveway, I realize something is different.

Felton's car is already in the drive. For some reason he's decided to come home early for once. But I don't understand why he didn't pull his car into the garage like he normally does. Why is he here already? I was looking forward to a little time by myself before facing him again. He usually works late on Fridays then takes the weekends off. Can I really stay in the house with him for two whole days wondering what he did to his ex-wife to screw up her signature on their divorce papers? Maybe some people wouldn't think that's a big deal, but it's often the little details which reveal the most about the secrets we keep. It means something, and I'm not letting go until I know what that something is. I sigh, getting out of my car.

When I get inside, Felton is in the office, working on his drafting table. That explains why he's here; of all days, he's decided to work from home today.

"Hey," he says. "How was work?" Like everything is normal.

"What?" I ask, having forgotten all about the proposals until he said something. "Oh, fine." He's awfully calm for everything that's happened the past few days. I head into the kitchen. I need something to take the edge off.

The fresh smell of body wash drifts to my nose. He's taken a shower and cleaned up, which is better than the alternative I suppose. But it also means he's feeling more confident. Maybe he thinks this is all going to blow over. I pull a bottle of wine down from on top of the fridge. It's a white, but I don't feel like waiting for it to chill. I grab a tumbler and fill it with ice, then pop the cork and pour it over ice.

The ice sours the taste and I pour the glass in the sink and shove the bottle in the freezer. Fifteen minutes ought to do it.

He appears in the large opening to the kitchen, leaning against the frame. "How are you?"

"I'm a little frustrated, to be honest." I busy myself with putting away the dishes that are still in the dishwasher.

He's silent for a moment. "I'm frustrated too."

I stifle a laugh. As if he has the right. "What do you have to be frustrated about?"

"I just feel like you're pushing me away. Like you don't want to talk about any of this."

"Felton, it's been three days! Three days in which my entire world has been turned upside down!" I can't help it; the words come fast and hard. "You knew! You knew this was the one thing I had a problem with. And yet you kept it from me." I throw a pan into the sink, which makes an awful, harsh clang. "You're lucky I haven't left already. How would you like it if you found out I'd been lying to you for three years? For our entire relationship? How do you think you'd cope with that?"

"I don't—"

"Shut. Up." I say, cutting him off. I don't want to hear his excuses. But I can't help myself. It's like someone has opened a pressure valve. "You don't have the right to defend yourself. Not right now. You want to talk, fine, *I'll* talk. You knew I was married once before. You knew I found out Thomas was cheating on me and was keeping his relationship with that woman secret for *years*. You knew the day I found out was the day I called a divorce lawyer. And yet you decided to do the exact same thing. You have been lying to me the entire time we've known each other, Felton. The ENTIRE TIME. And whether you meant to do it or not, it still hurts just as bad. And I can't keep from thinking, 'What would have happened if that book had never shown up?' Would I have ever known about her? Or was that just a secret you were going to take to your grave?"

His eyes meet mine, but he doesn't respond.

"Your silence speaks volumes. You never were going to tell me, were you?"

He finally breaks eye contact. "No." And there it is. The truth.

Despite being mad as hell, I need to know more. He's finally opening up and I'm not going to let this opportunity pass. "Why?"

He furrows his brow and opens his mouth to say something before closing it again. "I just couldn't," he finally says.

"That's not a reason." Tears form in my eyes. I turn and finish putting away the dishes. I wish he'd had a better reason. "And it's not enough."

"I can never tell you how sorry I am."

I close my eyes and let out a long breath. Despite the rage of emotions flooding through me, I've at least been given a glimmer of the truth. Part of me wants to try and work this out with him, the other part just wants to leave and be done with him. "I need some time alone." My hands are trembling.

"For how long?"

"Jesus, Felton," I say, both out of frustration and anger. "The rest of the evening. Just…" I reach into the freezer and grab the wine again, even though I can feel it's still warm. "Just stay in the office, okay? I don't want to see you again tonight." I push past him and head down to the main bedroom.

"Fine," he says, hurt in his voice. I'm not used to seeing that much determination on his face as he turns and disappears back into the office.

His absolute refusal to tell me his reasons is not only infuriating, but incredibly hurtful. Does he just think I can't handle it? Does he really think that after what I've been through I'd just shut down? I hoped I've at least proved him wrong on that point. But I can't deny that part of the reason I'm still going strong is my own pride. I have to figure out what I've missed. That way, in my next relationship (if there is one), I'll know what to look for and how to avoid it. It's all a matter of refining my process to find someone by design instead of by chance, like Cammie. I can't rely on luck; a lifetime relationship is too important. One way or another, I will find a way to make my system work.

AN HOUR LATER HALF THE BOTTLE IS GONE AND I'M STUCK playing a stupid game on my phone. I don't even perceive time anymore, the only reason I know the time is because it keeps staring back at me from the top of my phone. How am I going to make it an entire weekend with him? Maybe I should go stay at a hotel until I get some answers. I also realize that I might not be entirely lucid at this point. Between the proposals this morning, everything at the courthouse and the fight we just had, I'm exhausted. But every time I try going to sleep I can't seem to get images of him with someone else out of my head. I grab the bottle and take another gulp.

My phone rings at exactly the same time, causing me to sputter and spray part of the comforter with wine. "Shit!" I say.

I replace the bottle on my nightstand and tap my phone. "Hello?"

"Hi." It's Laura.

"Hi," I reply, my heart picking up. "Did you look at your schedule?"

"Yes. Unfortunately I'm booked through the weekend. I've got some family visiting and I don't think I can get away."

"Oh," I say, sitting back on the wet part of the bed. "I understand."

"What was it you wanted to ask me?" she says.

"You're going to think I'm crazy," I say, laying back on the bed.

"Try me."

I take a deep breath, feeling the fuzziness from the wine. "Okay. I went to the county courthouse today and pulled the records for your marriage to Felton. But your signatures on the marriage certificate and the divorce agreement don't match."

Silence on the other end. Shit. I've gone too far. She must think I'm a full on psycho.

"Huh," she finally says.

"Laura, I'm sorry. I shouldn't have been so nosy. It's just, I can't get Felton to tell me anything and I don't have any idea what's going on. I kind of feel like I'm going a little crazy."

"What do you mean?" she asks.

"I can't find anything about you!" I say. "There's nothing. No pictures, no documents, records, bills, mementos, nothing. It's like he's wiped you from his life."

"You think I'm lying," she says.

I sit up, alarmed. "No, no. Not at all. I saw the papers; I know it was official. It's just...weird. There's nothing of you in his life."

"Well," she says, and I'm sure she's about to hang up on me and never talk to me again. "Have you looked in the crawlspace?"

"The what?" I ask.

"The crawlspace. There's a trap door in what used to be the house's kitchen, back when it was built. In the middle of the floor. If he's got something to hide, I'd bet it's down there."

"I've never seen any trap door," I say, adrenaline clearing my head.

"Have you ever looked under the rug?" she says and part of me wonders how she knows we have a rug.

"No..." I say.

"It's probably still there. It was the last time I saw that house, back before he began renovations. I'd check there; it's the perfect hiding spot."

"You think he hid stuff under the house?" I ask.

"It worked, didn't it? You never would have thought to look under there."

I can't help but be curious now. Is she right? Now that I think about it, I don't believe I ever *have* seen under the rug in our living room. The house has always been furnished, ever since I moved in. "I guess so."

"Well," she says. "Good luck. I hope you find what you're looking for."

"Wait!" I say before she can hang up. "What about the divorce? What happened? Why is your signature all messy?"

"Oh," she says. "I was probably a little drunk. It's not every day you leave the man who assaulted you. I remember being nervous because I thought they might try to stop me from going through with it. That his dad would find a way to keep me in the marriage. So I might have had too much."

This god damn family. Pushing her to the edge just because she wanted to leave. I'm not going to give them enough of a chance to do that to me. "I'm so sorry," I say.

"Thank you. Good night, Winter."

"Night," I say, hanging up. I stand, realizing my pants are wet from the wine on the bed. I quickly change into another pair before cracking the bedroom door. What if it's true?

What if there's a hidden compartment under the floor? Do I dare look with him still in the house?

The more dominant part of me, probably propelled by slight inebriation, says yes. That no matter what I find it's my right to search. This is my house too, after all. Another, smaller part of me, says this might not be the best idea.

I shut that part down and make my way down the hallway toward the living room.

Chapter Twenty-Four

I CREEP AS QUIETLY AS I possibly can. Though the room is tilting slightly and I have to catch myself from toppling over. Had I known Laura was going to drop this bombshell on me maybe I wouldn't have downed half a bottle of warm pinot Grigio.

Felton is still in his office, typing away. Good. I'd half expected to come out here to find him sprawled on the couch. But thankfully my chastising seems to have kept him where he can't see me. I just need to be inordinately quiet.

I stop at the couch, looking around the edge. Thankfully it's not one of those monsters that takes an entire moving crew. It's much more understated and mid-century. Though now that I think about it, I'm not even sure who chose this couch. It was already here when I moved in a few months ago. Did Felton buy it, or did he have someone decorate? I'm sure we've talked about this in the past, but for the life of me I can't remember.

Screw it. I move over to the edge of the carpet, wondering what's the best way to do this. I have no idea where the door could be, so I'm not sure which side of the carpet I need to roll up. I lift up one edge, trying to peer along the floor into the darkness but I can't see anything. I want to sigh in frustration but I stop myself before I can make a sound. I don't want to alert him.

Okay. So no matter what I do, I'm going to have to move the couch out of the way. There's really no way it can stay where it is. I get up under one side and walk it over until its legs are no longer on the carpet and set it down as carefully as I can. I wait a second to see if the typing in the other room stops and when it doesn't, I creep over to the other side.

Once the couch is off the rug I get in the middle and begin rolling, revealing the polished wood floor beneath me. I never really noticed before but it looks like the floor has been refinished, like it could be the original, just with a new sand, stain and lacquer.

I only get the rug about half way before it runs into one of the side chairs. What if she was just screwing with me? It isn't like she's seen this house since it was finished; he might have had the trap door removed from the revised plans. I mean, this place has had some major work on it. You can't even tell this room used to be the kitchen. The only reason I know is because it has the fireplace and Felton once told me that was where they used to cook all the food back when the house was built.

Once the chair and a small side table are out of the way, I continue rolling, until I uncover a small metal hook embedded in the floor itself.

I stop rolling, my heart pounding as I look down at what could very well be a door. I look back over my shoulder, still hearing the sound of light tapping away on keys. It only takes a few more rolls to completely uncover the door embedded in the floor, the antique hinges on the other side mark where the door ends.

"Son of a bitch," I whisper then clasp my hand over my mouth. Did he hear that? I still, and the tapping of keys continues. A long, slow breath escapes my lungs. I know I should wait until he's not here to open this door, but my curiosity is getting the best of me. I've come this far; I'm almost there.

I hook my finger under the clasp nearest to me, giving it a quick pull. There's no catch, it's just held down by gravity and the door lifts open without resistance. The smell of dankness fills my nose as I open it all the way, peering into the pitch black beneath me.

I can't believe this has been here the entire time and I've never known about it.

Pulling out my phone, I activate the flashlight and shine it down into the hole, anticipating finding a treasure trove of hidden memories. But instead I'm greeted by only a single white banker's box. I reach in and pull the box out, setting it on the floor in front of me. Screwing up my face, I lean back into the hole, shining the light all around the crawl-space, but I don't see anything else. Just the one box? What the hell?

Still, my heart threatens to break through my ribcage. This is it. This is exactly what I've been looking for. He wouldn't keep any of his sensitive documents at his office, where he couldn't get to them at a moment's notice. He'd keep them here, right under his feet. Where they're safe. Whatever is in here, he never wanted anyone to find. Probably most of all not me.

I glance back toward the office again. Does he know? Does some part of him sense that I've found his secret hiding spot, that I'm about to uncover all of his secrets?

Steeling myself, I remove the lid and almost cry out.

At the very top, bound together by a piece of metal spiral, is a stack of papers with a neatly typed title: *Simple Desires* by Miranda Maryweather.

"It's the book," I say, removing it and holding it up. But this is an earlier, less refined copy. It isn't double-printed, professionally bound and doesn't even have a cover. This looks like what someone would have printed out from their home computer and bound themselves.

I'm not sure what to do. I just sit there, holding the manuscript in my hand, reading and rereading the title over again.

He has the manuscripts. This entire time he's had them. Underneath the top one sits another one, and another under that one. Had he made copies? And why had he kept them? It meant he could have had the book printed up, and Lord knew he had the technical ability to complete a layout—however incompetent—and mail it to himself. But why? Maybe as a test? To see if I would open it? Is this all some kind of sick game to him?

The very fact he keeps them buried beneath the home we share unnerves me. Why keep your ex-wife's unpublished works? Unless there's some deeper meaning to them, something I could only learn by reading them. Could it be the text itself?

I set *Simple Desires* down and pick up the one under it. *Two Dudes 'till Midnight*. I want to groan at the title, but instead I turn to the dedication page.

To my Dearest F, you make all things possible.

WAS *THIS* WHY HE'D KEPT THEM? WHY HE'D HIDDEN THEM SO thoroughly? There was no way I would have found this door by myself, not until we replaced the rug anyway. And when that day came, Felton would surely have had time to move these. I peer down into the opening again, shining my flashlight around, despite my shaking hand and find nothing but the blackness of the crawlspace staring back. This box is the only thing he's hidden. I thought there would be more, pictures of their life together, mementoes, anything that might remind him of her. But all he'd kept was this box of "books." I check the stack, and five different manuscripts are present. In a way they almost remind me of movie scripts in the haphazard way they're presented here. They almost reek of desperation.

Some dust from the crawlspace finds its way to my nose and even though I try to hold it in, I can't help myself and sneeze into my sleeve. It makes an echoing sound through the room and down into the crawlspace.

The sound of typing from the office stops. "Win?" he asks, coming around the corner. As soon as he sees me, he freezes in place, his eyes as wide as saucers.

Chapter Twenty-Five

I HAVE the brief feeling of floating, as if gravity has turned off somehow, when in fact all I've done is stand up to face him. My whole body has gone numb and I have to look down at my hand to make sure I'm still holding the manuscript. My eyes travel slowly across everything. The couch pulled out of the way, the rug rolled up haphazardly, the trap door open to the darkness beyond, and the white box full of writings—née, love letters from my fiancée's ex-wife.

It's as if I'm outside my own body. I have time to wonder how this all must look to him. His treasure of secrets, exposed and out in the open. The one person he's tried to keep everything from finally learning the truth. He doesn't move, he only glances from the hole in the floor to me and back again.

Despite everything he said, he's betrayed me over and over again, and now I have proof. It isn't enough that he never told me about his previous marriage, something that, in time, I may have forgiven. But to discover he's hidden her writings right under our feet? Those times when we'd made love on the couch, had he been thinking about these *things* only a few feet away? I drop the manuscript in disgust. He jumps slightly as it hits the floor. Suddenly I'm furious. I bend down, grab it, and slam it down again. He doesn't jump a second time, only stands, as if in disbelief.

All I have to do is get him to admit he sent the book and this will all be over. I can put all this behind me and move on, just like before.

"What are those?" he finally asks.

My eyes widen at his brazenness. "You know exactly what they are." I consider picking it up again and throwing it at him.

"Winter, I don't. Was…was that in the *floor?*" He takes a cautious step forward.

"No, sir. You're not going to play dumb with me. I finally caught you." I say it with such conviction, I have found all the evidence I need. He's not going to weasel out of this.

"Those aren't…" he steps closer. "Her books?" His breath hitches. "Were they in the crawlspace?" He's almost yelling, as if he can't believe they're real.

"Right where you hid them," I say triumphantly.

"Shit. Shit!" Felton's hand goes to his pocket and he withdraws his phone. "You didn't touch any of—dammit, how many did you touch? Don't move!" he yells, frantically dialing.

"Of course I touched them. I had to read her lovely dedications—"

He holds up a hand to cut me off while he speaks into the phone, which only infuriates me. I can feel my anger bubbling up. "Brian. Get over here now. Winter found something. Yeah. I think it's all of her books." He pauses. "Under the house! What? I don't know, just get over here right now! Yeah…yeah, I know. Hurry." Felton hangs up and turns back to me. "Don't touch anything else."

He *has* to be joking. "What are—"

"Winter, I didn't put those there," he says, staring directly into my eyes. "I don't know who did, but whoever it was has access to this house. *Our* house. It isn't safe for us to stay here, okay? Brian is on the way over. He's going to bag all this stuff up."

Bag it up? Just like the first book? "Oh no," I say, grabbing the dropped manuscript. "This is my evidence! You're not taking it away from me!"

"Sweetie, please! It might have fingerprints, you're contaminating—"

"Don't sweetie me!" I roar. "You have been hiding this behind my back the entire time, don't you dare deny it."

"Winter, I swear to you, to everything I have, I did not put that there. I haven't seen that box in eight years. I destroyed it. Along with everything else."

Why does he have to do this? Why make this so difficult? I've caught him red-handed. Why can't he just admit it and move on? Wouldn't it be easier for everyone, instead of going through this entire charade? "Stop. Lying. To. Me."

"What do you want me to say? It's the truth!" He turns away for a moment, then faces me again. "I made a mistake! I should have told you about Laura from the beginning. But I couldn't. She's gone, out of my life now. I want nothing else to do with her. If a machine existed that could erase memories, I would wipe her in a millisecond. I *don't want* to remember her. Do you understand? I don't want anything to do with her, so why would I keep something like this? Do you think I'm so shallow I can't let go of some stupid books from ten years ago just because they have a dedication to me? Do you think I need love so badly?"

His chest rises and falls with each tortured breath. I've never heard him so intense before; something about all this has struck a nerve, but not necessarily the one I thought. What if I just consider the possibility he hadn't put these down there? It would mean someone else had entered our home and planted evidence against him. There are only two people I can think of who have the motive. Laura, of course, as she pointed me right to them, and Lazarus. He would know about the trap door, having financed this house, and he would also know about the manuscripts. But what would he gain from framing his own son? Laura's motivations were clear, she wanted revenge for…okay, maybe they weren't so clear. But Lazarus, if he had done it (or more likely had one of his cronies do it, possibly even Brian), what would his reason be? Humiliation? An attempt to sabotage our relationship?

He'd never been very happy about Felton going off on his own, leaving the family as Felton sometimes describes it. Was this some kind of punishment? Some way to break his son down? If I'm out of the picture would that force Felton back home somehow? Brian said Lazarus had taken particular pleasure in Felton asking for a place to stay the night I kicked him out. Could he really be that cruel with his own son? I don't know for sure.

"You can't let Brian come over here," I say, resetting my gaze.

"Why?" Felton asks, still intense.

"Because if your father planted this to frame you, Brian will destroy any evidence."

"My father?"

"If what you say is true and you didn't put that down there, which I'm not saying I believe, then someone is framing you. Can you think of anyone better than your Dad?" I'm still not ready to tell him about Laura. If it was her, I'll handle it on my own. But Lazarus was the big boss. I'll need Felton's help to figure out if it was him.

"He wouldn't do that to me. He wouldn't go that far."

"Then who would? Who else wants to see you suffer?"

Just say her name, just do it and admit to it.

Felton shakes his head. "I don't know."

This is how I know he's lying about some part of this. Any reasonable person would suspect their ex first. But Felton seems incapable of the idea. But it still doesn't make sense. Why would he do this to himself? To drive me insane? If so, he was doing a good job. I need to keep the evidence. If Brian decides to take everything, I'll be right back to square one.

"Do you really think he would do that?" Felton asks, oblivious.

"Don't you?"

Felton knits his eyebrows, staring past me. Lost in concentration. Despite all the anger I feel for him in this moment, I realize he's not trying to come up with another lie, he's trying to understand. I can see it in the way his mouth turns down like it does when he's working a problem. I've seen that face often enough. Maybe he didn't put these here after all.

"If he did do it, what are the odds Brian knows about it?" I ask, rethinking my options.

"High." He turns away from me and curses. "Why did I call him? I should have seen this. Who else would do this to me?" He shakes his head in disbelief, then turns back to me. "How did you find them?"

A tremor shoots through me. I can't tell him about Laura, not yet. Not until I rule her out as a suspect. Plus, I'm still not sure I can trust him. He might be covering for her in some way. If all the blame is focused on Lazarus, no one will be looking at Laura. And if Felton still loved her, maybe on some deep level he doesn't even realize, he might be inadvertently protecting her.

"I've been looking for evidence," I say, defiant.

"Of what?"

"Of your prior marriage."

"I already told you…everything. It wasn't like it was something I was proud to admit."

"I wanted to make sure there wasn't anything else. No other secret relationships." I clutch the one manuscript tight. Or something more nefarious, that could lead to a mismatched signature. I'm not quite sure I buy Laura's explanation, though I can't figure out why she'd try to cover for him now.

"I guess I can't blame you." He looks down at the hole in the floor. "Though I'm surprised you found this. I'd almost forgotten about it. They used to use it to store canned goods back when the house was first built. It's a lot cooler closer to the earth and the dirt acted as…" he trails off.

"Acted as what?" I ask.

Felton bends down, staring at the side of the box. "Look at this."

I lean over, his hand points along the bottom of the box. "Little to no dirt. If it had been in that hole any amount of time it would have gathered dust and the bottom would be filthy. Plus, you remember when we had that storm a few months ago and it was raining like crazy?"

I nod.

"The bottom of the box should have some water damage, but I don't see anything. It hasn't been in that hole long."

He's right. There are no signs of the telltale water damage normally found on cardboard after it gets wet, and the box is relatively clean. Had he kept it under the house for years it should be a lot dirtier. Which means either he moved it here very recently, or someone else did.

"What do we do about Brian?" I ask, now very unsure of the facts. "He's coming."

"If this was Dad, he'll cover all this up. Hang on." Felton runs into the kitchen and returns with a box of gallon-sized ziplocks.

"Here, put the one you've got on the floor, and grab one of the ones you haven't touched yet, but grab it by the edge if you can. We'll put it in here."

"You think you can pull fingerprints off it?"

"Maybe. Right now we just need to preserve it and keep it out of Brian's hands. At least until we know his agenda."

I can't argue with the plan. I just have to make sure to keep those manuscripts in my sight and not let Felton take them. I shouldn't have touched any of them, but I'd been so shocked I couldn't help it. I lay down the already-crumpled manuscript and reach into the box with both hands, removing two manuscripts at once by their edges. "I want them both. Just in case."

Felton nods and holds out a gallon bag. The first one doesn't quite fit all the way, but it is in enough that we can handle it without risking contamination. He holds out a second bag and I deposit the second manuscript into it.

"Okay, leave the rest. We'll tell him this is all you found," Felton says, gathering the two together and wrapping them in a plastic grocery bag.

"Wait, what are you doing with those?" I ask.

"Hiding them. Just until he leaves."

I hold out my hand. "Give them to me, I'll hide them."

Felton stops. The tension is palpable. He'd been doing so well, and now that prickle in the back of my brain is back. What was he really going to do with them? Get rid of them? Is he secretly working with Brian?

"Felton," I repeat. "Give them to me." I urge my hand forward.

"I was just going to hide them in the kitchen," he says.

"Now." My outstretched arm trembles.

He hands the bag over, staring at me. "Just hurry up. He'll be here any minute."

I retreat to the bedroom and slip the bag in the back of my closet, behind a large pile of clothes I never bothered to pick up off the floor.

When I look up, shadows move across the back wall, announcing the arrival of a car in our driveway.

Chapter Twenty-Six

"You found the jackpot!" Brian announces, entering the house.

I barely have just enough time to get back in the living room before the door bursts open. He didn't even knock.

"I did!" I reply, trying to keep the conversation light.

"Jeez, how did you uncover this?" Brian asks, approaching the disheveled room and hole in the floor.

"Accident," I say. "The vacuum always catches on this one part of the carpet and I guess I just finally got fed up with it." I point to the top of the trap door. "Turns out it was that little ring." While it was obvious the ring sat flush in the wood, it was plausible the vacuum could have caught it.

Brian eyes me for a minute, and I can feel the scrutiny of his gaze. Will he look around for the vacuum? I remain steadfast until he turns his attention back to the box. "What did you touch?"

"I pulled the box out, so the outside of it, and the lid. And the top manuscript. That's it."

"Okay," Brian replies, pulling out a pair of blue latex gloves from his back pocket.

"It hasn't been here long, Bry," Felton says.

"Doesn't look like it. And I have to ask this to be thorough: neither of you put it there?"

"Of course not," Felton replies, anger in his voice. If he's not genuine it's a good act.

"Have either of you let anyone in this house recently? Anyone you might have taken your eyes off for a minute?"

"I think we would have seen someone hauling a big box in our house."

"It's not that," I say. "He thinks someone might have copied our house key."

"You are too sharp, sis. Have I ever told you that?" Brian winks at me, then bends over to inspect the box.

I don't feel like being winked at. It had to be someone who is familiar with the house. Someone like Brian, who no doubt had a spare key, probably given to him by Lazarus.

"What about the security system?" Felton asks.

"They must have the code," Brian says. "I suggest you change it immediately."

Felton groans. "I don't even know where the manual is."

"But you haven't given anyone access to the house that you know about?" Brian repeats.

"I haven't," Felton says, turning to me. "Have you?"

I shake my head, trying to look innocent.

"And there's no other maintenance access under the house? No outside door or anything for the crawlspace?"

"Not unless someone made their own door," Felton says. "I specifically didn't install an outside door because we have this access if we ever need to get under there."

Brian nods. "Then we need to inspect your locks and windows. Someone got in here recently to do this. We need to determine the point of entry."

Not if it was you, I think. "Should we call the cops then? If we're dealing with a breaking and entering?" Not that I necessarily want to involve the police, but this has grown beyond the scope of just family matters. The police wouldn't know what to do with an errant book delivered to their house, but a burglar was another matter. Then again, who ever heard of a burglar bringing something *into* the house?

"Don't worry," Brian says. "I can handle it. I'll let a few of my friends down at the station know and they can help me do a full inspection tomorrow. For tonight I can at least check your locks."

I furrow my brow and glance at Felton. He looks worried. Neither of us likes it when Brian circumvents the police. It doesn't help that Lazarus has so much influence with the local boys in blue, but Felton used to tell me about how Brian could sometimes get problems to go away with the family connections down at the station. It's one of the reasons he never wanted to work for his father. I can't help but wonder just how deep Lazarus's power goes.

"Trust me," Brian says. "It will save you guys a lot of headache." He pulls out some large black bags from his coat pocket and begins the process of placing the manuscripts inside them. I find it odd he just happens to carry gloves and black bags with him wherever he goes.

"What are you going to do with those?" I ask.

"Find what I can. Maybe I can grab a match on one of these."

My heart jumps. "Did you find something on the book?"

Brian smiles that stupid placating smile. "Don't worry. When I have something substantive I'll let you know. You just take care of each other."

I can never tell if Brian is genuinely concerned for us or if is all some elaborate ruse to cover up his true purposes. Like the other night he seemed normal. It's almost like whenever there's a crisis, a different Brian emerges. One who answers to one person only.

"Are you both planning on staying here tonight?" Brian asks.

I exchange looks with Felton. "We're not sure yet."

"For your own safety, I'd suggest you move somewhere secure."

Felton gives him a hollow laugh. "Where? Dad's house I suppose?"

"Or a hotel."

"Is that really necessary?" I ask. I don't want to leave the house. My mind flashes back to the figure I saw at the end of the driveway Tuesday evening. I'd almost completely forgotten with everything else going on.

"I may have something," I add before anyone can respond to my question.

"What?" Felton asks. He's grown indignant and grumpy. The mere mention of his father's house has put him in a sour mood.

"I might have seen someone. The day we got the book. I think I saw someone at the end of the driveway. At first I thought they might just be looking at the house. But now I'm not so sure."

"What did the person look like?" Brian asks. "Man or woman?"

"I couldn't tell. Too far away. I called Janet but she didn't see anything. I'd completely forgotten about them until now." Another lie.

Felton shakes his head and turns away from me. "That's it," he says after a pause. "We're not staying here. Something is going on, and I'm not about to be one of those people who gets killed in their sleep because they didn't pay attention to the signs."

"Normally I'd call you a wuss, but I think you're right on this one," Brian says, bagging up the box. "Someone is deliberately stalking you and the sooner we find out who it is the better."

I exchange glances with Felton again. He's clearly distraught, and now that I've planted the idea that this could all be an elaborate ruse from his father, he won't be able to let it go. At the very least I've made some progress in eliminating him as a suspect. I now think Brian might have more to do with this than Felton. Felton is the kind of guy who would have locked this box up in a safety deposit box if he really wanted to keep it secure. Under the house just isn't his style. He isn't that careless with his precious things. I'd been so ready to crucify him without thinking it through logically. For the moment, I'm willing to consider he might be innocent in all this. A victim, just like me.

Maybe I can recruit him to help me. To do some reconnaissance on Lazarus, find out what was going on up there in his *castle*. No, that's a step too far. Things are still precarious, and I don't want to risk it. I'll have to do this myself.

"Fuck it, I'm going to a hotel for the night," Felton says. "I won't be able to sleep here anyway." Felton's words pull me out of my thoughts. "Do you want to do that? We can do separate rooms." He doesn't look at me.

"Okay," I reply without really thinking about it. Part of me wants to stay in the house and see if I can catch someone breaking back in. But that's foolish; I'm in no way equipped to fight a burglar, and honestly, I might be in over my head here. The minor confrontation with Laura proves that.

"Let me just go get some things," I say absentmindedly, realizing no one else is saying anything. Maybe a hotel is a good idea, that way I can think all this through. This is like information overload; I need to go somewhere I know I'm safe.

Ten minutes later, I have my duffel packed. "Ready?"

Felton hasn't bothered to grab anything but his toiletries. Brian glances between us before declaring a hearty "okay" and leading us out of the house. He's already transferred the black bags to his car, but I watch his body language for anything that might give him away. "I'll be back here in the morning with a few uniforms and we'll do a thorough check.

Until then, I'll get out of your hair," he says, climbing into his Range Rover.

We watch him back out of the long driveway before Felton says anything. "Do you want to take one car or two?"

"Where are we going?"

"There's that motor lodge a couple of miles away."

Ugh. The motor lodge. I guess it will do, though it doesn't strike me as the safest place. I give him *the face*.

"Or there's a Doubletree out past Bristol," Felton adds, checking his phone.

"The whole idea is to go somewhere safer, right?" I ask. Not the *Connecticut Chainsaw Massacre Inn*.

He nods.

"Doubletree," we both say simultaneously. I have to suppress a grin. This is the old Felton I know. The one I fell in love with.

I indicate my car. His is already in the garage. "We can take one car. No reason to waste gas."

He gives me a grateful nod, and heads to the passenger side of my car.

As we pull out of the driveway I check the growing darkness for any shadowy figures, seeing nothing.

WHEN WE ARRIVE AT THE DOUBLETREE IT'S ALMOST NINE AND pitch black out. The only person working is a young woman who looks bored more than anything.

"Last name?" she asks as we approach the counter.

"We don't have a reservation," Felton says, bracing himself against the counter. He looks exhausted. "We'll need two rooms for the night."

"Wait," I say, reaching out for him, but stopping just from touching his hand. Is this a good idea? I still can't believe he would actually hurt me, and if he was faking all of this it had been one hell of a performance up until now. What was his end game? To get me in a hotel room alone with him so he could beat me up? It doesn't make sense. I've been sleeping in the same bed with this man for years. And right now he's the closest thing I have to an ally.

He turns to me.

"We'll be fine with one."

"You sure?" he asks, surprise in his eyes.

"Yeah, no need to waste the money." I turn to the counter lady. "Two queen beds?"

The lady's eyes flick between us for a minute. "I'll need a driver's license and a credit card."

While Felton provides the necessary credentials, I take a moment to breathe. I don't want to keep pushing him away, especially if he's innocent in all this. We are in this together now. For the first time since the book showed up, I'm glad I didn't walk away immediately. In fact, I'm quite proud of myself. This might be the most difficult relationship hurdle I've ever faced.

"Ready?" Felton asks.

"Room 425. Elevators are there, breakfast is from six until ten," the woman says lazily, no longer looking at them. She's become engrossed in whatever is on her phone.

The room is a standard hotel room, nothing fancy. But when I walk through the door it looks like the most comfortable place I've ever seen. After all the ordeals of the day—the proposals, the courthouse, the fight with Felton, my strange phone call with Laura, capped off with finding the box and the manuscripts—I'm ready to plow face-first into that pillow.

"Closest one to the window is yours," Felton says, setting his toiletries in the bathroom.

"You know me too well," I reply, smirking. Had it been one large bed I would have taken the side closest to the window. I always do. Not that there's any particular reason, it just feels more natural. He's sweet to remember.

Felton plops on the other bed. "This is all so stupid," he says, hanging his head. "What is happening to us?"

"I don't know. But we're going to figure it out."

"Do you really think it could be Dad? Or did you just say that because you don't like him?"

"You're no fan of his either, last time I checked," I reply, setting my bag down on the lone small chair in the room.

"C'mon. Seriously."

"Yes. I do. If anyone has the resources and the desire to see you screw up, it's him."

Felton lets out a long breath and falls back on the bed. "I hate to say you're right. But...you are." He pauses a minute, then lifts up to look at me. "Are we going to be okay?"

"I don't know." I play with the zipper on my bag. "But we're okay for right now."

"You know I love you more than anything, right? I would never put you through this, not on purpose."

I take a deep breath, and the affirmation is like a bright sunbeam breaking through heavy clouds. Felton isn't perfect by any means, but I know he wants the best for me. I have a hard time believing the man I love would do this to me, purposely. Sometimes I just can't help myself from thinking the worst about people. And every now and again, it happens with someone I love. Maybe I shouldn't be so quick to judgment. "I know."

"If we can't trust Brian, what do we do? How do we move past all this?"

I think about it a minute. "We can't until we know who sent that book."

"And how do we find that out?"

I lay down on the other bed, staring up at the ceiling.

"Winter?"

"We take matters into our own hands," I finally say.

Chapter Twenty-Seven

I can't say the thought of climbing into Felton's bed in the middle of the night doesn't cross my mind. As much as I need to sleep, it only comes in broken bouts and I toss most of the night. It would have been so easy and comfortable to slip over there, to slip back into what had once been a beautiful thing, but we're not there. Not yet. Still, the idea of returning to something comfortable and safe is almost too much to resist. Even though he doesn't say anything, I hear him turning over again and again in frustration. But as dawn breaks, I haven't moved from my bed and he hasn't moved from his.

We go about our morning routine silently, Felton putting on the same clothes as the day before. I can't say sleeping in the hotel did either of us much good, other than the fact we didn't have to worry about someone coming in during the middle of the night. We grab a quick breakfast before heading back home.

"And what was the point of that exactly?" I ask as we drive back.

Felton shakes his head. "I don't know anymore. It seemed like a much better idea last night. But now I just feel stupid."

"Me too. Are we going to have to do that every night?"

"If Brian thinks it's necessary, maybe. Do you feel safe staying there?"

I shrug. "Do you feel like Brian has our best interests at heart? And I can't live out of a hotel for a week or however long it takes for him to catch this person."

"That's true. But if you're right and both Brian and Dad are involved, isn't it better we keep him happy? He tells us to go, we go. That way he doesn't suspect anything."

I relent. Keeping them off guard is the best plan. But my brain is foggy from lack of sleep and stress. "Maybe."

I put my head against the headrest but keep my eyes on the road. If someone wants to harm us, wouldn't they have done it when they broke in the first time? And if Lazarus really is behind all this, Brian is playing his part perfectly. Making it look like we are in danger, getting us out of the house for the night. Had he come back last night after they left to plant more "evidence"? All of this weighs heavily on my mind. At least I don't have to be at work today. We have the weekend to figure this out.

I pull in the driveway, recalling how mad I was at him last night. First for the lies, then upon finding the box and now... now I'm just too exhausted to care anymore. "Can we go in or do we need supervision?" I ask, the sarcasm seeping from my voice.

"Just go in. He said he'd be by later anyway. I don't see any need to rush him."

"You sure? There might be someone waiting on the other side of the door for us. Ready to murder us with our own knives."

Felton laughs. "Then you go first."

I smile and grab my bag from the backseat, and head towards the door. As soon as I put the key into the lock, Felton lays a warm hand on mine. I look up at him, wondering what he's doing.

"Just in case," he says, moving me out of the way and

opening the door. The security system beeps and Felton punches the code into the pad. I'm touched, though I didn't really expect anyone to be inside. But the fact he's thinking about me like that is refreshing.

"You need to change that code," I say, dropping my bag in the foyer and shedding my coat.

"It's probably easier to buy a new system than find the manual for this one," Felton says, tossing his shoes across the stone entrance. They tumble across the floor until they reach the rug, coming to an abrupt stop. For a moment I don't realize anything is wrong, until I remember we didn't put anything back last night before leaving. The entire living room has been returned to normal. The trap door is closed and hidden by the rug. The couch is back in its original position, the feet back in the indentations they'd spent months burrowing.

And there, on the coffee table, sits a small brown package with our address handwritten on the front.

Chapter Twenty-Eight

"Don't!" I yell as Felton reaches for his phone. "Just...don't do anything." I hold my hand outstretched, as if I can keep him in that position by some nonexistent telekinetic power. Another package, just like the first one. Does this one contain a book as well?

"Brian was right," Felton says, his voice dropping to a whisper.

"For all we know, Brian put it there," I reply. "He had access, didn't he? Does he know the security code?"

"I've never told him."

"Does your Dad?"

Felton shakes his head, as if he can't believe it. "Maybe. I may have given it to him at some point, in case of emergency. I...I don't know."

"But it's possible."

"Yeah, it's possible."

I swear but keep my feet planted in the foyer. Part of me thinks any kind of movement will set off an invisible trap. I imagine a smattering of faint red lines crisscrossing the room. Should we stay? What if the person who set this up was still in the house? Are they in one of the bedrooms, just waiting for us to be stupid enough to go in there by ourselves? Or is this nothing but a message, something to show us we're not safe in our own home? Regardless, I won't be a prisoner here and I won't be a victim.

"Stay here," I whisper, taking a few steps forward.

"What are you doing?"

"Searching the house."

"Win, we should leave. Call Brian, tell him what's going on. Or hell, screw Brian and just call the police."

If the police come we'll lose any control over this situation. They'll confiscate the package and I'm not about to have that. But just in case...

I step forward with my phone in hand and snap a picture of the front. I'm not making that mistake again. I don't think Janet has the kind of phone that can receive pictures, which means I'll need to print this off and deliver it to her. But more than that, I want the package itself for my own evidence before it disappears into the black pit that seems to appear anytime Brian comes around.

"What's that for?" he asks.

"We're taking care of this ourselves," I say, moving to the office and giving it the onceover. "No Brian. No police. Whoever did this wants to send us a message. I don't think they're still here," I say. "We can't get a message if we're dead."

"A message that says what?" Felton asks.

"They want us to know they have access to our home, to our schedules," I reply, returning to the living room. "Whoever is sending these things is taunting us."

"To what end?"

I shake my head. "I have no idea. To screw with our heads?" I step over to the table and pick up the package. Maybe I can learn more from it now that I know what's coming.

"Don't touch it! What about fingerprints?"

"Whoever left this isn't stupid enough to leave fingerprints. That's why Brian doesn't have anything from the first one yet." I turn it over in my hands. Except for the postage, it's identical to the first one. Same brown wrapping, same light, scripty lettering. I can't tell if it's the same as what's on the divorce documents or not. That writing looked a lot dirtier, less flowing. Then again, I'm not an expert. I realize I've never seen Brian's handwriting. "Assuming he's not in on it." What better way to throw us off than to make it look like a woman wrote it? "I wonder which one it is?"

Felton comes up beside me. "I bet I know."

I raise my eyebrows, prompting him to continue.

"If the first one was her first book, this is probably her second."

"What was the name again?"

"*Two Dudes 'till Midnight*." He shudders.

Right, how could I have forgotten a title like that? I stifle a laugh before an uneasy feeling wells up in my stomach. "You remembered," I say, quietly.

"Yeah, you pulled the manuscript out last night. I'm surprised you didn't. It's one of the worst titles I've ever heard." He's right. The rough version of *Two Dudes 'till Midnight* is currently under a pile of clothes in the bottom of my bag.

"Are you going to open it?"

I stare at the small package. The last time I opened one of these it completely unraveled my life. What if opening this one does something worse? I already know what's inside, what if I just left it sealed? But what if whoever left this here buried a clue inside? Someone is playing a sick game with us, and obviously wants us to do *something*. As much as part of me doesn't want to open it, I know I have no choice. Not if I want to find out who is doing this to us.

I take the package to the kitchen and grab one of the

knives out of the block, using it to cut every piece of tape on the package. Then I carefully unwrap it, taking care not to tear or crease the smallest piece. Once the wrapping is off I turn the book over to reveal the cover.

Felton was right. It *is* the second book.

It's immediately clear someone printed this cover on their home computer. Much like the previous book, the spacing is off, the colors aren't blended right, and none of the figures look like they belong there.

Felton stares at it over my shoulder. "Jeez," he says.

"What the hell is this book about?" I ask, unable to tear my eyes from the insanity splashed across the cover. One man with a cowboy hat stands on the left, in what looks like a pixelated field of wheat or maybe corn? It's hard to tell. And he's looking off to the right, where another cowboy stands, though he's much closer to the viewer, but his feet have been cut off in a deliberate attempt to make it look like he's standing *in* the grass. And despite both of these figures being lit by full sunlight in whatever original media they came from, there hangs a bright white moon between them, with a starfield behind everything. Are they looking at the moon? At each other? Past each other? She can't tell.

"Um, from what I remember it was supposed to be like a sexy version of *Brokeback Mountain*."

I tear my gaze away from the cover. "What do you mean sexy?"

"Graphic," he says, shifting in that way he does whenever he's uncomfortable.

I raise my eyebrows in surprise. "Oh?" I guess I get that from this cover, but honestly this looks like one of the worst books I've ever seen. "Wasn't the first one a mystery?"

Felton nods. "She was trying lots of different things. The one after this was horror, I think, but I don't remember what the last two were."

"Did you ever read them?"

He takes a deep breath. "I tried. I really did. I wanted to be a supportive husband, but they were a little…rough around the edges."

I flip the book back over. Nothing on the back but an empty starfield. If there's a clue, it will be inside. I open the inside cover—no copyrights, no printing information. Which means whoever printed it didn't do it professionally. That left local printers. There couldn't be that many around town, right? I could take the book to each of them, ask anyone if they recognize it and they remember who had it printed. They might even have receipts. I mean, who could forget a cover like this? But if it was Brian, would he have paid off the printers not to say anything? Or even rented the space to do this in private?

I glance at my watch. It isn't even ten yet. But it's Saturday, which means some places might open a little later, but that's okay. I can still make the rounds.

"I'm going out," I say suddenly, grabbing the wrapping along with the book.

"Where?"

"To track down some leads." I pull my phone back out and send the picture of the cover to the printer. Even though I have the original, it won't hurt to have a copy for Janet. I can drop it by on the way.

"Track down some leads? You're not a private eye."

"That doesn't mean I don't know what I'm talking about. I've made more progress in two days than your crack shot of a brother has, even with all his police sources." I say as the printer in the office warms up to print the picture.

Felton furrows his brow. "Progress? What are you talking about? What have you found?"

I slip my coat back on and grab the picture from the office. "You'll know when I can start piecing it together. Stay here, check the rest of the house for anything else and call me if you find something."

"Winter, you have to tell me. Don't leave me in the dark like this."

"I'm not." I smile. "There's not a cloud in the sky today." Before he can protest further, I'm out the door.

Chapter Twenty-Nine

FELTON

FELTON SLUMPED DOWN ON THE LIVING ROOM COUCH. WINTER hadn't been gone ten minutes, but he needed to wait a little longer. He drew his hand up through his hair. A shower would be good right about now, but there was business that needed to be resolved. A second book? Was this mysterious person going to send him all five? And then what? What was the endgame?

He glanced at his cell. Twelve minutes since she left. He couldn't hold it in any longer.

He dialed.

"Morning, brother," Brian said on the other end.

"We received a second package." Felton registered a pang of guilt at the thought of going behind Winter's back, but he couldn't leave this up to her. She might suspect Brian, but he knew his brother would never stab him in the back like this. Not after everything they'd been through together as kids.

"Another what?" Brian paused. "*What?*"

"It was on the living room table. They got in the house,

past the security system again, and laid it out for us. And they put everything back the way it was. You didn't come back here last night, right?"

"Jesus, no. Of course not. I wanted to leave everything as it was for when I came back with a few uniforms. I spoke to my contact this morning and he said it was a busy morning, but he could get someone out there this afternoon."

"Brian, what am I going to do? Winter's out there chasing leads as she calls them, and yet these things keep happening. Oh yeah, and you've been a big help, so thanks."

"Winter's what? She's investigating? Why didn't you stop her?"

"Oh yeah, Bry. What am I going to do, tell her not to? Have you met Winter? The minute you tell her to keep away from something it only drives her further."

"What sort of leads is she talking about?"

Felton rubbed his face with his free hand. "She wouldn't say. She just took the book and left."

"Oh hell. She's going to get herself killed. I told her to stay out of this for a reason."

Felton sat up straight. "Killed? What do you mean? Did you find something?"

"Everything I've found points to this person being unstable in some way. They're going to great lengths to torture you, psychologically."

"Winter thought it might be Dad."

Brian laughed. "I think if it were, I'd know it."

"Would you, though? You know how cagey he can be. How many secrets he keeps. He doesn't tell you everything. He doesn't tell anyone everything; that's the whole deal, remember? Compartmentalize so no one person can screw over everyone else."

"I remember those breakfast-table discussions just as well as you do. But I have access to most of his stuff. If something were going on, I'd know. I'd see changes in personnel. He'd never do it himself, he'd get someone else."

"That's true," Felton said, sitting back. "Do you really think Winter is in danger?"

"I think if she digs too deep she will be. So far this person seems fixated on you, but she might accidentally make herself a target."

"Brian, I have to tell her. I can't keep lying to her."

There was a muffled noise on the other end of the line. When he came back, he was much closer to the receiver. "Are you crazy? What do you think she'll do? And I can guarantee you, if you do tell her, Dad *will* get involved. And I'm not sure how he'll react. You might not be safe."

"He doesn't have to know."

"You think she won't go to the police? Or worse? You saw how she reacted to just the book itself."

Felton rubbed his forehead. There had to be a way out of this. Why couldn't anything in his life just be normal? That's all he'd ever wanted. Nice, quiet and normal. "You have to find this person before she does."

"What do you think I've been doing?" Brian yelled. Clearly, his anger was getting the better of him.

"You haven't done anything! You come over and tell us not to stay—"

"Which might have just saved your lives, by the way," he interrupted.

"—but you're still no closer to finding out who this person is, or why they're doing this to me."

"I'll find them. I'm close. But if you think I'm doing such a shitty job, why don't you come with me? I'm not just sitting over here, whacking off."

"Don't put that image in my head. Come with you where?"

"I might have something. There was a strange car parked close to your neighborhood last night. One of your neighbor's surveillance cameras picked it up. It might belong to the person who broke in."

"How did you get access to that?" Felton asked.

"You don't need to worry about that. I've been keeping a running tally of all the cars coming and going from your neighborhood and matching them to their respective houses. Some are visitors, I can't find any connection for this one. And it was parked far enough away so as to not look suspicious."

"Then how did you find it?"

"Like I said, I haven't just been sitting on my ass over here. I have resources, you know. Do you want to come or not?"

Going with Brian might help this go faster. And it would allow Felton to keep a closer eye on his brother. Even though he didn't suspect him, he couldn't help but feel something was going on, given how easy it would have been for Brian to set all this up. If for no other reason than to prove his brother's innocence, he'd go. Whoever was sending these packages obviously knew about Laura, and no one knew more about Laura than Felton. Maybe he'd see something Brian might miss. As much as it hurt to remember everything they'd been through, if doing this would put all of this to rest, it would be worth it.

"Okay," he said. "I'll be right there."

Chapter Thirty

I WATCH FELTON PULL OUT OF OUR DRIVEWAY AND DRIVE OFF. Before heading off to investigate the print shops I stopped by Janet's to drop off the picture. I figured now was as good a time as any to drop it off and thankfully she'd been home. She's still as worried as she was last night, telling me not to get into too much trouble but also promising she'd get the image to Jack so he could compare the samples. I was walking back to my car when I see him pull out of our driveway through Janet's high hedge. It and her curved driveway blocks anyone from being able to see my car from the road, so I know he has no idea I'm over here.

Where could he be heading? I expected him to stay at the house, maybe take a shower, but instead he's off again. That old familiar feeling creeps back up my spine and I push it away. I feel like we've made progress in the past twelve hours; I don't want to go backwards. Especially when I don't have anyone else. We're supposed to be on the same team, if he needed to go somewhere, he should have told me before I left.

Or texted me. I check my phone, but there's nothing from him. Part of me wants to send him a quick note asking him if he's still at home.

No, I won't do that. We've established a small amount of trust since yesterday and I'm reasonably sure he isn't the one sending the books. Especially considering he was with me the entire time while the second one showed up.

But still.

I slip into the car and back out of Janet's driveway, anxious to catch up with him. I gun it for longer than I should, pushing the needle past the thirty-five in a twenty-five until I see the black form of his car ahead of me, taking a left on Keegan Road, heading towards town. As I'm thinking about what I'm going to say to him when I catch up, he takes a left onto a residential road and I slow to keep my distance. I'm about to make the turn myself when my phone rings in my purse, startling me.

"Shit," I say, my heart racing. I fish it out of my bag. "SHIT," I yell again, recognizing the number as Cammie's. I haven't been keeping her up to date like I told her I would. There was so much to go over, the divorce documents, the trap door, the manuscripts, *and* the fact of a new manuscript showing up this morning.

"Hello?" I say meekly.

"Winter! Where the hell are you?"

"Cammie, I am so sorry. There's just been so much—"

"Are you even okay? I almost did it. I almost called the cops. Where are you?"

"Thank God you didn't," I say. "I'm in my car…tailing Felton." He's about a quarter of a mile ahead of me, keeping to the speed limit. I have to do the same to stay far enough back.

"I should have. I'm worried about you! The only reason I didn't is because I figured you forgot about me again. Ever heard of the boy who called wolf? This is like the reverse of that. I haven't heard from you in almost two days, Win. Two days when you're dealing with this woman who may or may not be sending you strange packages. You could be in a cellar right now for all I know."

I wince, thinking back to the trap door in the house. "I know and I'm so sorry."

"I can't do this anymore. I've got a business to run, clients to deal with and I can't be worried about you all the time if you're not going to call me back. It's not fair. To either of us."

Felton makes another turn down a side street, but it's going to take me a minute to get there. I'm only half-listening until I realize what she's said. "Wait, what do you mean you can't do this anymore?"

"Whatever it is you feel you have to do with this, I'm out," Cammie says. "I'm supposed to be your best friend, but I've been thinking about this—"

"No, Cammie, hang on. Just hang on a second." I put the phone down on my seat and survey the road. I made the same turn, but there's no sign of him anywhere. It's just houses here and he's not in any of the driveways. Could he have seen me following him? And if so, did he just come down here to lose me? I pull over to the side of the road and pick up the phone again.

"I'm sorry, I just lost him. What were you saying?"

There's no answer on the other end. I hold the phone up, but it's gone dark. She hung up on me. I redial her number, but she doesn't pick up and it goes to voicemail.

"Hey, it's me." I know I've been shitty to her, but I try to play it off. "We got disconnected. Call me back, okay? I'm really sorry I haven't kept you in the loop. So much has happened. I'll tell you about it when you call. Okay. Bye."

I put the phone back in my purse and stare out the windshield. Had she meant that she was done helping me with this, or she was done with our friendship entirely? I can't believe she'd go that far, but maybe I've pushed her too far.

I snatch up the phone again and punch out a message: *Please call me back. I will make this right.*

I think about sending another one but that will probably just piss her off. Cammie has every right to be mad at me, but I can't believe she'd destroy our friendship over this. Plus, I don't do well when I'm isolated like this, she knows that. She knows when I'm alone I often forget to keep those connections, because I feel like I'm on my own island. It's always been that way, ever since I was little. Daisy wasn't the most supportive big sister and Mom was always off in her own little world. My problems were my own.

Maybe I should go over to her house instead of hitting the printing shops. They'll be open all day, and this is something urgent. Felton is my first priority, but there's no way I'll find him now, especially if he knows I was on his tail. I don't relish that conversation when I get back home, but honestly, he's on shaky ground as it is. He obviously doesn't want me to see whatever it is he's doing, going to all this trouble to get away from me.

I reach into my purse and pull out the package with the writing on it. To my eye the address on the front doesn't look very much like either of the signatures on the marriage and divorce documents. But that doesn't mean they weren't made by the same person. I have no idea how people manage to compare handwriting, I just hope it leads to something. Because if I can eliminate Laura as a suspect, then I'll *know* it's Lazarus and probably Brian too. Even though I won't have hard evidence it's them, it will be enough for me to know. And then I can sit back and wait for one of them to screw up. Felton said Laura wrote five books. We've only received two. That gives me three more chances to catch them in the act.

But first, I need to make things right with my friend. I put the car in drive and pull a U-turn, exiting the neighborhood. If she won't answer the phone, maybe she'll answer her door.

～

"CAMMIE!" I POUND ON THE DOOR. "C'MON, JUST LET ME explain! I know you're mad and I'm sorry." It's been almost ten minutes and my hand is starting to get sore. Her van is still in the driveway, along with Mike's car. She must be really pissed.

Finally, through the glass, a shadow moves across the hallway.

"Oh, thank God."

When the door opens, it's Mike. "Hey Win," he says with a sheepish smile. "She doesn't want to see you."

"Can I just come in and explain? Five minutes."

Mike stands firm. He's a large guy, at least six-foot-two with the muscle to match. He'd never hurt me, I know that, but I don't have the strength to get past him and it seems Cammie has anointed him her personal bouncer.

"Can you at least give her a message for me?"

"She really doesn't want to hear from you. And I don't want to get in the middle of it." He drops his voice. "You really had her worried. And you hurt her. It was a pretty shitty thing to do."

"I know!" I say. "I just wanted to tell her how sorry I am. She's like my rock sometimes—I just don't know what I'd do without her. And I'm sorry I've been taking advantage of our relationship."

"Again, I'm not saying anything because I'm not getting into it with her," Mike says. "Maybe just give her a few days to cool off."

I peer around the mass of a man, trying to see if Cammie is visible anywhere in the hallway, but she's not there. More than likely she's hiding out in one of their bedrooms. Well, I can't say I didn't try.

"Okay," I finally relent. "Sorry for bothering you."

Mike gives me a sympathetic nod before closing the door.

It's like she's being shut out of my life, and it's all my fault. I know that. I had all these wonderful people and now they were falling away, one by one. First Felton, then I pissed off the partners and now my best friend and her boyfriend. Soon enough I won't have anyone left.

Maybe Mike's right. The best thing I can do is give her time. I should have done better by Cammie, I should have kept her in the loop the entire time, especially after what I learned from the courthouse. I'd tried, but then so much had happened I'd just...forgot. Now I'll be lucky if I don't lose her forever.

All I can do is keep moving forward. I have to work the leads, find the evidence. Moping around won't do me any good. With the book in my possession I finally have something to work with. I head back to my car, opening the maps app on my phone and searching out all the printing shops within a thirty-mile radius of the middle of town. There are thirteen different locations. I sigh, slipping back into the car. Thankfully my gas gauge is close to full. I'm going to need it.

THE CLOCK ON MY DASHBOARD CLICKS TO 4:27. I'VE BEEN driving for what seems like days, when it's really only been a few hours. I managed to get to twelve of the shops so far, but no luck from any of them. Two told me to come back on Monday when the managers would be there, but there's no telling if any of these is even where the books were printed. It's possible they were printed in some town out in California then mailed here.

I sigh and stare up at the plexiglass sign bolted to the front of the strip mall. It says *Printing Services* in large, faded yellow letters. Not even a logo. Coincidentally this is the same strip mall where Felton's office is located. I saved this one for last in case he happened to be here, but when I pulled in he wasn't anywhere to be seen. Hopefully my luck holds and this doesn't take very long.

I sigh and grab the book from the passenger seat, exiting the car. "Lucky number thirteen," I say quietly to myself.

Upon entering, I find a small older man sitting at a computer at the end of a long counter that runs parallel from front to back. It splits the space into two long hallways, him on one side with all the shelves, computers and stacks of paper and me on the other with the copy machines, printing machines, and work desk for trimming and finishing projects.

"Help you?" the man asks without looking up from his computer.

I hold up the book. "I'm trying to find out if this was printed here. Do you recognize it?"

The man glances up. "Hang on," he says, pushing himself from his chair with a grunt and slipping a pair of glasses down the bridge of his nose from their previous perch at the top of his head. He walks over to me, gently taking the book with old, weathered hands.

"Oh." He laughs. "This one." He looks back at me and removes the glasses from his face. "Kinda hard to forget the sexy cowboys."

My heart does a double-skip. "You recognize it!"

"Yeah, the lady who printed it tried to do it all herself, but the machine got jammed and I had to come over to help."

"A lady? What did she look like?"

He shrugs. "I'm not sure; she had on a black hoodie and kept it pretty tight around her face. But she was here forever getting that thing printed, cut, and then binding it. She printed the cover on one of the printers over there." He indicates the bank of chest-high printers along the side wall. "Took at least an hour."

A woman. That eliminates Brian. Which means it *has* to be Laura. "When was she here? When did she do this?"

The man glances at his feet a moment before looking back up, his face twisted in concentration. "Two, three weeks ago?"

"Did she print anything else?"

"Yeah, this wasn't the only one. She did another one but I forget the name."

"*Simple Desires?*" I suggest.

He shrugs again. "Could be. My memory isn't too reliable these days." He points at the cover again. "But that I wouldn't forget."

"It was definitely a woman," I ask, wanting to make sure.

"Yep."

"Can you tell me anything else about her? I need to find her. Did she pay with a credit card?"

"I don't think so, but I'll double check the accounts." He heads toward the back. "What do you need her for, if you don't mind me asking?"

Well, I think she might be sending these books to torture my future husband. "I'm…a fan…of her work," I managed to stutter, trying my best to make it sound genuine. I don't know if he'll believe it or not, especially if he read any of her stuff.

"Oh, she wrote them too? I suppose that makes sense."

I nod. There's no question in my mind anymore. Part of me is relieved, but at the same time I'd hoped maybe it *wouldn't* be her. I have such a hard time connecting with people and she seemed like someone I could be friends with. Obviously now that I know she's the one torturing us I can finally go to the police, they can take a statement from this old man and all of this can finally be over. She'd broken into our house in order to leave this, that had to be some kind of punishable crime, even if she didn't take anything, right? Or stalking, harassment, mental anguish; there's a whole host of things we can charge her with. It doesn't really matter what's going on with the divorce documents anymore. She's obviously the person who signed all three, but she was probably trying to disguise her handwriting. Little does she know I know someone who knows someone who used to be in the FBI. Take *that*, Felton! I knew I could do this private investigation stuff.

"I'm sorry, it looks like—what's wrong?" the man asks, returning from the back room.

"Oh," I snap to attention. "Just thinking. She paid cash?"

"Yep. Sorry I can't give you anything else. Don't authors usually put some kinda contact information in the books?"

"I think she's still pretty new at this," I say, tucking the book back into my purse.

"Well, good luck to you."

I thank him and head back to my car. As I'm opening the door, my phone rings in my purse. Maybe it's Felton with an explanation as to what the hell he was doing this morning.

"Hello?"

"Winter? It's Janet."

"Oh! Great timing. I was just about to call you to let you know I don't need the samples compared anymore. Did you already send them to Jack? I don't want to waste his time."

"That's why I'm calling," Janet replies. "He just finished inspecting them. I'm sorry, Winter, but none of the samples are a match. Each was written by a different person."

Chapter Thirty-One

FELTON

"YOU NEED A SHOWER," BRIAN SAID AS FELTON WALKED IN through the side door.

"She was following me."

"Who was?"

"Who do you think?"

Brian rubbed his temples with one hand. "Didn't I teach you anything? You shouldn't have left while she was still at home."

"I didn't! She'd been gone at least ten or fifteen minutes. I thought I was good. But then she just appeared in my rearview. What was I supposed to do?"

"I knew this was a mistake. You should have stayed home." He paused a moment. "I assume you lost her."

"Yeah, but I wasn't very subtle about it. I started to panic."

Brian shook his head. "You gotta get your mind straight, little brother. This is eating you up, and if you're not careful everything you care about is headed to that big swamp in the sky."

"I can't help it! I love her! This was all supposed to be finished a long time ago. All this Laura business was wrapped up and in the past. I wouldn't have even dared to date anyone seriously if it weren't completely buttoned up. For this exact reason."

"Hey man, I know. And it sucks." Brian stood and put his hand on Felton's shoulder. "But it's out there now and we have to deal with it."

Felton sighed. "What did you find?"

"I ran the plates off that car," Brian said, turning and pulling a sheet of paper from the kitchen table. "Got an address to check out."

"Why not send any of your police buddies to do it?"

"Because if they find something, I don't want them digging too deep. We've still got a couple on our side—well, Dad's side—but I don't trust some of the newer ones. You know how they are, full of integrity and zeal. They don't have any black marks yet, nothing to sway them."

Felton shook his head. "God, I hate this. I hate what you two do. This whole business."

"This whole business kept you out of jail eight years ago, don't forget that," Brian said, suddenly intense. "Would you rather Dad hadn't been there?"

"I sometimes wonder if things would have been simpler."

Brian scoffed. "Really? Okay then. I guess I'll just go let him know…"

Felton grabbed his arm. "No. I didn't mean it. I'm just under a lot of stress at the moment."

The lone kitchen light above them flickered once. Brian's eyes considered the light for a brief second before returning to Felton. "I know you are. And I'm just trying to help. But it means Dad has to be kept in the loop."

"Yeah." Felton sighed. "Yeah, I know. Let's get this over with."

Brian nodded and disappeared into one of the back rooms

for a minute, returning holding his 9mm before stuffing it in his belt.

"You really think you'll need that?"

"All I know is the one time I really need it and don't have it I'll have wished I carried it everywhere. So I carry it everywhere."

Felton couldn't argue with that logic. He gave Brian a resigned look and they both left through the side door, Brian locking it behind them and letting the screen clap shut.

Almost thirty minutes later Brian pulled his Range Rover up to a small crest, just off the side of the main road.

"Is that it?" Felton asked.

Brian consulted the GPS. "Says it's that development right down there."

"I'd say 'development' is being a bit generous."

"You're a stuck-up little snot sometimes." Brian smiled. "Everyone's got to live somewhere."

They stared down into the community of mobile homes, each one identical to the next. It was one of the nicer mobile home neighborhoods, with each plot clearly marked and most tended and kept well. Some even had miniature white picket fences.

"Which one is it?"

"Address just says 1805 Salem Drive. It could be any one of them. We'll just look for the one with the car."

"And then what?"

"Wait until they leave and take a look around."

"You mean break in."

"I mean do whatever we have to do to find out who is threatening you. If that means breaking into a mobile home, then yes."

"What if they have a family, other people living there?"

Brian shook his head. "No way. My psychological eval tells me this person is a loner. Most likely very isolated from everyone else. He's probably a hermit, only leaves when he absolutely has to."

"Which means?"

"Which means we may not be able to wait. His next venture out could be to leave another book at your house. And that might take days. We may have to go in while he's inside."

"Fuck," whispered Felton.

"See? Now aren't you glad I brought this?" Brian smiled and patted the gun in the wood-paneled console between them. But somehow it didn't make Felton feel any better.

THEY TOOK A FEW MINUTES TO DRIVE AROUND THE neighborhood. It was a series of two concentric circles, a smaller one inside of the larger one, connected on both ends by long lanes providing two entrances and exits out of the development. They found the car on the outer circle, sitting next to a light-blue mobile home. It had no personal decorations outside and the grass had grown too long.

"Yep, that's him all right," Brian said as they passed. "Might as well have a big bullseye on that thing."

"What do we do?"

"We'll wait him out for a few hours. If he doesn't come out by the time it gets dark, we'll make our way inside."

They left the park and took some of the smaller roads off to the north. Brian used the GPS to swing them back around so they were parked in an adjacent neighborhood (one with slightly nicer houses) with a perfect view of the mobile home.

Two hours later, nothing had changed and Felton had grown anxious.

"Let's just forget this. Let's go back home, and—"

"And do what? Forget all about it? What happens when the third book arrives? Then the fourth and the fifth? What then? You think he's just going to stop? He's building up to something. He's building *himself* up to something. The first one was on your stoop. The second in your house. Do you want to wait around and find out where he puts the third one?"

"We could leave. Winter and I. We could just leave for a few months. Until things calm down."

"And how do you think she's going to feel about that?" Brian asked. "Leaving her job, her friends, and an investigation you yourself told me she's hooked on, to go off with the man she was tailing this morning because she doesn't trust him anymore. Tell me again how that pans out."

Felton didn't reply. Brian was right, there was no way around this now. Things were getting serious, and if he ever wanted a chance at a normal life, he'd have to see this all the way through.

Brian elbowed him. "Look."

Felton squinted to see through the twilight. A dark figure emerged from the mobile home and promptly got in the car and drove away.

"Perfect."

"Should we follow him? What if he's going back to my house?"

"I think we'll learn more by checking the place out while he's gone. It's better this way. We don't have to get our hands dirty."

"It always makes me nervous when you say that because it never ends up working out."

"Whatever."

Brian exited the vehicle and closed his door without a sound. Felton tried to do the same but ended up pushing it too hard. Brian gave him a sidelong glance as he stuffed the gun in the back of his belt.

They made their way across the small field separating the two developments. There weren't many trees out there, only a few at the edge of each property. Most of it was overgrown grass and muddy earth. When they reached the mobile home, Felton noted that lights were on in both neighboring units.

"It's fine. If anyone asks, tell them we work for the property owner and are checking for gas issues," Brian said.

"How many times have you done this?" Felton asked.

"I thought you didn't want to know about the business." Brian made his way up the three stairs to the door and pulled a small black piece of plastic out of his pocket. From this he pulled an even smaller piece of metal, shaped in different ways. It was in the lock less than a minute before he had the door unlocked.

Brian put his ear to the door, listening before nodding to Felton and turning the doorknob.

The door opened into a dark space, and Felton couldn't see anything other than the dark outline of shapes against what little light filtered in. The windows were covered by standard blinds, mutating the light into long parallel beams. Brian closed the door behind them and flicked on the light.

The room was surprisingly bare. To their right was the modest kitchen, missing an oven and with a refrigerator that had to be at least thirty years old. Beside that, almost in front of them, sat the couch, a ratty, plaid specimen from another era. Off to the left was a hallway and doors to what Felton assumed were the bathroom and bedroom. The place was completely void of any personal touches.

"Kind of looks like your house," Felton said. "Just smaller."

"I'll decorate when I get a day off," Brian replied, taking a close look at what little was in the room. "Look for anything that you might recognize. Any papers, manuscripts, anything of Laura's." He tossed Felton a pair of latex gloves.

Felton took a deep breath and began his search. Not that there was much. The house looked like it had been cleaned out. Or hadn't been lived in for a while at least. He made his way into the kitchen. The countertops were all Formica with old, wooden cabinets underneath that were not much thicker than MDF. The lack of stove was odd, leaving the disconnected gas line hookup and scuff marks on the floor where the old one had been removed. Whoever was taunting him apparently didn't need an oven for meals.

Felton opened the fridge to find very little: a carton of old milk, a half-used bottle of ketchup and a Styrofoam container with some soggy fries. The freezer contained a couple of microwave dinners.

"Anything?" Brian asked, returning from the bedroom.

"Not much."

"It's been more or less vacated as far as I can tell. No clothes. No personal effects. Not even a toothbrush."

"So what does—" Felton began to ask until Brian put his finger to his lips. Felton listened. Footsteps and rustling outside.

Brian drew the gun from his belt and flipped the safety off. He started to creep towards the door when the voice came from the other side.

"Get out of there, now!"

The voice was rough, but there was something odd about it. It didn't sound like a police officer or anyone who was threatening them. It was more urgent than that. Felton exchanged looks with Brian.

"Hurry up!" the voice yelled.

Brian held the gun in one hand and the door knob in the other. He pulled the door open with a yank and pointed the gun into the darkness.

There was no one there.

"What the hell? You stay here, I'm going to check it out." He stepped out onto the porch. Felton hadn't liked the urgency of that voice. It was like a warning. He pushed past

Brian and ran outside, no longer wanting to be anywhere near the mobile home.

"C'mon! Get away from there!" Felton yelled, running at top speed.

"What the—Felton! Felton!" Brian ran down the steps after him.

It happened in slow motion.

There was a small pop in the air, like someone bursting a balloon a few feet away, and then sound disappeared for a moment. A gust of air hit Felton, knocking him forward as an eruption exploded in his ears. He looked back to see the roof of the mobile home launch itself up into the air while every window in the home exploded. A giant fire followed the shattering glass, pouring out of every opening, including the door they'd just run through. The roof reached its maximum height and fell back to earth, smashing into the mobile home and enraging the fire.

"Brian!" Felton called. "Brian!" There was no answer.

In the edge of his vision he thought he saw the dark form of someone running from the scene, but the figure was too far away to be Brian. He glanced down and saw smoke rising from a body on the ground. He crawled over, the heat from the flames making him shield his eyes as he inched closer. He was vaguely aware of people running and yelling all around him, yelling at him. But he had to reach Brian. The gun was still in his hand.

He grabbed his brother by the shoulders, pulling him away from the flames while another smaller explosion came from somewhere inside the structure. The entire area was awash in flame light.

Once he'd dragged him a suitable distance—just beyond the trees and into the tall grass where they'd come from—he flipped Brian over.

He was breathing, but unconscious. Second degree burns had scorched his face and had melted the gloves to his hands.

He'd been too close to the explosion. Felton tapped his burned cheeks as lightly as he could.

Brian jerked his eyes open, trying to scramble away from Felton, waving the gun at him.

"Whoa! Easy, it's me. Easy!"

Brian stared at him a moment but didn't move, keeping the gun outstretched.

"Here," Felton said, his own hand shaking. He put one hand on the barrel of the gun. As soon as he did, Brian's grip relaxed and he let go. Imitating his brother, Felton shoved it behind him in his belt. The last thing he wanted to do was get shot tonight.

"Brian. It's me. There was an explosion."

"Explosion." His voice was rough, like he'd been smoking his entire life.

"Yeah, you got burned. Can you walk? We have to get out of here." Already the sound of sirens filled the air.

That seemed to rouse him. Brian blinked a few times, took a look at the burning husk that was the trailer, then looked back to where they'd parked the car. "We have to go." He looked down. "My hands." It was as if he could comprehend it, but couldn't feel the pain.

"We'll get you fixed up."

Felton helped him to his feet. Brian stumbled twice but made it to the car on the other end of the field.

"Keys?" Felton asked.

"Right pocket." Brian closed his eyes and leaned on the car, moaning slightly. Across the way, the first fire trucks had arrived.

"Here." Felton unlocked the doors and helped him into the passenger seat. "Don't touch anything until we can get those off you." The gloves were one thing, but the burns on his face were another. And there was no telling what other injuries he might have suffered. If he went to the hospital, it wouldn't take long before they put two and two together and connected them to the mobile home. It wasn't like there were a lot of fires around here. Felton only knew one place he could take Brian and get him the help he needed without a bunch of questions.

It was time to see Dad.

Chapter Thirty-Two

WINTER

I DON'T UNDERSTAND. HOW COULD NONE OF THE SIGNATURES match?

"Wait, are you sure?" I ask Janet.

"I made sure he went over it twice. He said there is no way the same person did any of these."

But that doesn't make any sense. Laura signed the marriage certificate, but she hadn't signed the divorce papers? And it completely blows my theory about Laura sending the books to our house. Could she have had someone else address them for her?

"What if someone was under duress? Or if they were drunk or on drugs or something?"

"Win, honey, he's been doing this a long time. He was very sure they were all different people. He tried to explain it to me, but I couldn't keep up. It's a very meticulous process."

"No, I don't mean...I'm sure he knows what he's doing. It's just...it doesn't make any sense. It doesn't fit."

"Then you need a bigger box," Janet says. "Is there anything else I can do to help you?"

"No, no. I don't want to bother you any more than I already have. You've been a big help. You can just...can he give me a notarized copy or something of his work? I'm happy to pay for it."

"No, don't you worry about that. I'll make sure he gets you something in writing and you can pick it up anytime. I'll be home all day tomorrow or you can always find me at the courthouse. I work most weekdays." She pauses. "I'm sorry it wasn't the answer you were looking for."

"That's okay."

I hang up, deflated. How could none of them match? At the very least, the marriage and divorce signatures should be from the same person! Something must have happened at that divorce proceeding. Something no one wants to talk about. That's where I need to turn my focus, and just as I thought I had this figured out. Should I call Laura and ask her? Especially when she's still my prime suspect? Will she even be honest with me? I don't know the woman at all, and there's no telling who is behind all of this.

I also have to consider Laura has nothing to do with it. I was so sure a few moments ago that she'd been orchestrating this whole thing as a way to get at me or Felton, or...I don't know. I can't figure out the motivation if it is her. Now I have to consider Brian and Lazarus are still involved somehow. Brian would have been there eight years ago when Felton and Laura got divorced, so he knows what happened. But he'll never tell me, he's too loyal to his father. He's the only one I can see who is smart and capable enough to do all of this if it isn't Laura. But why? Does he really hate me that much that he wants to break me and Felton up to get his son back home? Or is he hiding some family secret, something that Felton threatens by being out of his control? That makes more sense to me, but the chances of me finding out what it is are slim to none. The way that man holds secrets, he probably knows more about Felton than Felton knows about himself.

Lazarus has always been suspicious to me. Closed off, cold and not particularly happy about our relationship. Every time I've met the man he's lorded his power over people like he's some kind of king. Felton has told me on more than one occasion he has dirt on everyone, because he never knew when "it might become useful." On the outside he runs a successful logging company. He'd been one of the first innovators to start importing wood from Russia, Brazil and—most profitably—Canada, selling them at premium prices here in the states. But it's his business *behind* the business that really brings in the money. The enforcement jobs, keeping the competition out of their small corner of Connecticut and keeping the cops fat and happy. Not to mention all the "imports and exports" coming and going with the logs. But I'm not supposed to know about that. Maybe that was the problem, Lazarus was afraid Felton might reveal too much to me, and with his independent streak, he can't keep tabs on his son like he does Brian. Felton could probably bring his father's entire operation down if he wanted to, but as far as I've seen he wants nothing to do with it, good or bad. He just wants to make his own way in the world and leave his father to his own machinations.

Felton had spent so much time trying to get away from his father's reputation and everything that went along with it. And maybe the logging magnate wouldn't be so good at his job if Lazarus's own father and grandfather hadn't built all those longstanding relationships back when the town was new and small. But today, just like the town, Lazarus's reach has grown further and deeper than ever. And Felton sits at the end of a long line of power.

All of which contrasts deeply with my own past. A moderate life, regular parents, regular sister, right up until the day Mom found out Dad was cheating with Lucille Touffey and kicked him out of the house. They separated for a few months at first, while they "worked things out." Then he moved back in with promises it was all over, and everything was okay again.

Unfortunately, it didn't last.

Dad came back *with Lucille in tow* to pick up his stuff before I finally overheard what really happened. After his first round of affairs, Mom had convinced Dad to come back despite him not wanting to. She said it was the best thing for us girls and we needed our father around, like she didn't want him there to help take care of things for her too. I hated how she always tried to pin that on us. But of course he just kept on cheating behind her back. He hadn't even been back in the house a year before it started up again.

After that, I decided I was no longer going to be the reason anyone split up. And I made damn sure anyone I dated had none of my father's hallmarks. Everything had to line up, everything had to fit. That was the entire reason I made the system. I could evaluate guys, make sure everything was compatible before moving forward. And if it wasn't, I was gone. Like when I found those text messages between Thomas and his coworker. There hadn't been any question about it, I was on the phone with the divorce lawyer that day. I made sure there would be no last-minute begging to come back, or any tearful goodbyes like with my parents. He'd made his choice clear and I wasn't about to stick around for it.

It took less than a day to pack up all my stuff. Had Thomas slept with his coworker? No, not to my knowledge. But the texts were intimate, more intimate than he'd been with me in a long time. It wasn't difficult to see the writing on the wall.

Which was why when I met Felton I'd gone through the entire checklist. Entire history, history of his family, old girl-friends, everything. What I hadn't counted on was his ability to lie to me so convincingly for so long. But now that I think about it, he was practically groomed by a master manipulator, so should I be surprised he's good at it as well?

I grit my teeth. I'm tired of this song and dance, it's time I get some answers. If Lazarus is the one who sent the books, then he'll know Brian never recovered the one we found this morning. And if Brian doesn't have it, he'll assume either Felton or I do. But he won't know about Janet or Jack. He doesn't know I know about the divorce papers, which I might be able to use to my advantage. Someone as smart as Lazarus must know what happened with his son's first marriage all those years ago. And maybe I can leverage what I know to get him to reveal enough to give himself away. I don't expect him to come right out and say it, but I'm tired of being jerked around here. I have to at least try.

If I'm going to have any chance at a happy, normal life, I need to deal with this now and stand up to the man. Otherwise he'll be dogging me for the rest of my life. How would the wedding even go with his continuous attempts to sabotage our relationship? Maybe he's torturing Felton or maybe his son is nothing more than collateral damage and I'm his real target. There's no way to know until I look him in the eyes and find out. Maybe all of this is nothing more than my trial, to confirm I can't handle the pressures of being in this family, with its secrets and power struggles and shady dealings. It's meant to scare me off because I've aligned myself with his ostracized son, and no one says no to Lazarus Byrnes.

I smile as I pull out of the parking lot. I can't wait to see his face when I march up to the house and announce I won't be scared away by a little book. It's going to take something much, much worse. And perhaps that challenge will finally earn me enough respect to be left alone.

Chapter Thirty-Three

I GLANCE at the clock on my dashboard. It isn't much past six and the sun is already disappearing behind the tree line as I pull up to the giant wrought-iron gates. Will I be interrupting their dinner? Do I even care? Hell, I'm mad enough to knock the bowl of gruel right out of his cold hands if I have to.

The black orb on the small metal pad beside the gate stares at me as I press the button. "Winter Southerland," I say clearly.

"Welcome, Miss," a formal voice answers. Was that Jakoby or Warren? I can't tell. "I don't see you on the schedule for this evening."

"I need to speak with him. It's important."

"I'm sorry, Miss Southerland, but you know the rules. You'll have to—hold please."

I sit back against my headrest. Lazarus isn't a coward; if I'm right and he knows why I'm here, he'll let me in. His pride won't let him hide or be intimidated by a woman half his age.

"Please park near the west wing of the house," the voice says before promptly cutting off. I'm about to ask which side is west when the iron gates screech open in front of me. They're at least ten feet high, attached to stone walls on either side. It's as if I'm entering the gates of hell.

Not too far off, I think, steeling myself.

The driveway is all gravel, and I have to drive slowly to avoid kicking anything up that might damage my car's paint. This is a deliberate choice on Lazarus's part, I'm sure of it. To intimidate people by making them literally crawl up to meet with him, with his imposing house looming in the distance. Or else risk damage to their expensive vehicles.

The last vestiges of light fade from the sky as the property lighting clicks on. I pass giant Italian cypress trees on my right, a light on every other tree to highlight the height of them all. The view on the left is reserved for a wide expanse of well-groomed grass, with a huge three-tier fountain, complete with its own lighting. Lazarus is nothing if not ostentatious. Of course, his wife was sure to have input as well. It's their way of showing off their tremendous wealth.

I've only been here twice before, but it isn't the type of house you forget. When I first saw it, I would have described it as a modern-day castle. A giant monstrosity done in the French Revival style, though updated sometime in the past twenty years so it has all the modern amenities. Made completely of stone, it includes a giant, two-story arch show-casing the front door. The entrance is flanked by a three-story turret on the right and a large bump-out on the left, supported by columns underneath. The rest of the house flows away from the center naturally. I can't understand how people live in places like this. They always seem so cold, so impersonal and so cut off from reality. It was as if the Byrnes' had walled themselves off from everyone and everything, hiding in a jail of their own design.

As I pull up, I try to discern which side of the house is west. It's not like my car has a compass built in. I make good money, but not *that* good. Screw it, it doesn't matter. I drive up to the front entrance and park underneath the giant portico, the kind I assumed only existed at fancy hotels. The ten-foot oak doors accentuated with iron details are all that stand between me and the answers I need. I saunter up to them, but before I can knock, the latch clicks and the door opens to reveal Warren, looking slightly annoyed.

"This isn't the west wing, Miss."

"Sorry, Warren. Tell him he needs to put signposts out there. There are too many driveways."

Warren doesn't respond, only closes the door behind us.

"Winter. How nice." Abagail Byrnes approaches me, her light grey hair tied up in a bun and her long white robe dragging on the floor. She reaches in and gives me a half hug and kisses each cheek. "What brings you to visit? How is my son?"

I manage a smile. My fight isn't with her. "He's…good. Busy, you know. I came to see your husband. I hope I'm not interrupting anything."

Abagail scoffs, rubbing my shoulder lightly. "If he didn't want you here, you wouldn't be here," she says in that cold way I've never encountered with anyone else. It was as if she tries to be friendly, but behind it all exists someone who doesn't understand the basic concept of empathy.

"He'll be in his study. We were just in the middle of dinner."

"Oh, I'm sorry, I should have called—"

Abagail smiles. "Yes, you should have. You're here now. Go see him." The smile doesn't quite reach her eyes. She turns and disappears into some corner of this maze of a house. Great. I've already pissed off one of the two occupants of this house, might as well make it two for two.

Which way is the study? Considering the last time I was here was six months ago and this house has more doors and hallways than a city block, I can't exactly be chastised for not remembering. I look at Warren, hoping for some help.

"This way," he says, somewhat exasperated. Warren isn't what anyone would call a typical butler—I don't even know if he *is* the butler—but he wears a smart suit and has the most penetrating blue eyes. Felton told me he's been working for his family since before he was born and still he doesn't know much about the man's personal life. Was it possible he did jobs for Lazarus? Could *he* be the one who left the book in our house? Or is Warren nothing more than a glorified handyman, taking care of the house and nothing else? I admit, I have no clue how many people Lazarus keeps on his personal payroll.

Warren directs me to a large wooden door on the same floor, full of ornamentation and molding. Something much too opulent for a normal house, but it fits here. Still, it's cold and foreboding. No wonder Felton doesn't like coming here. This whole place is impressive, but it's also obnoxious. Give me a warm throw and a soft couch over this any day.

"He'll be waiting for you in here, Miss." Warren opens the door but does not step inside. My heart picks up an extra beat. I've never been in this room before, only passed it once. The floor is a dark cherry hardwood, covered in opulent carpeting that doesn't reach the walls. Floor-to-ceiling antique bookshelves line every wall that doesn't have a window, and those are flanked by dark-red curtains. Lazarus isn't a hunter, but if he had been, I'm sure a couple of animal heads would look right at home in here. In the middle of everything sits a ginormous desk, complete with green-shaded work lamp and a high-backed chair containing the man himself.

Except that it doesn't.

The chair tries to contain him but fails miserably; the presence of Lazarus Byrnes could not be constrained within one piece of furniture alone. As I survey the room, I doubt ten rooms of this size could contain him.

"Good evening," he says, staring me down, his dark grey eyes matching his wavy hair. As a younger man he'd probably been impossible to resist, at least until people got to know him.

"Evening," I reply, doing my best not to let my voice

waver. Everything about this room screams intimidation, but I'm not going to cave. Not when I'm this close.

Lazarus continues to watch me, picking up a glass half full of brown liquid and taking a long sip before putting it back down, his eyes never leaving mine. "Can I offer you something?"

I shake my head. "I just need a moment of your time."

Lazarus sits back in his chair, his hand still on his glass. He gestures with his other hand to a chair in front of his desk. "The rest of my evening is yours," he says, his voice dripping with sarcasm.

Internally I wince, but I take the seat anyway. Now that I'm here, I'm not feeling as confident as I had been driving up here. I'd been so sure about my plan all the way up until this moment when I'm in front of this man who has power I can't even comprehend.

"It must be awfully important to come at a time like this." He takes a sip. "Outside of business hours." His voice is low, measured, every word carries his gravitas.

"Are you…" I falter. I'm about to accuse the most powerful man within fifty miles of harassing his own son and future daughter-in-law. Maybe not the best idea.

"Am I what?" he asks. "Annoyed? Inconvenienced? Upset?" With each word his voice grows deeper. "Spit. It. Out." Any trace of a smile has disappeared from his face.

"Are you the one sending the books to Felton?" I somehow manage to ask.

Lazarus narrows his eyes. "No."

I bite the inside of my cheek. He's so damn direct. I need to ask in a better way. "Do you have anything to do with the books? With what happened between Felton and Laura?"

Lazarus sits very still, considering her. He's not going to answer. He'll just sit here and deny everything. Why had she thought this could work? She'd been stupid to ask. Stupid to come.

"Those…are two very different questions," Lazarus finally says.

"I want an answer to both," I reply.

Lazarus's face turns into a sneer. "What makes you think you deserve one? Just because you are marrying my son? You think you can come into this family and dictate terms to me?"

"I deserve them because they affect me. And they are tearing your son apart."

Lazarus leans back again. "I can't say I'm surprised. He never was good under pressure." He takes another sip.

"I have the divorce papers," I blurt out, having lost all my composure.

He eyes me. "Divorce papers?"

"From the county courthouse. The ones that were filed when Felton and Laura got divorced."

"And?"

"And I want to know what happened. Why is her signature different? Felton's is the same, but Laura's is different."

"I can't say," he replies, taking another sip.

"You bastard," I whisper. "I know you're doing all of this. The books, all of it. To get back at him for not being part of your little mafia up here. Whether you admit it or not. And you're not going to wedge us apart." I stand to leave.

"Stupid little girl," Lazarus says, his voice deep and resonating. "If I wanted to torture my son, I wouldn't send him some flimsy books. I'm much more creative than that. And if I didn't want you to be part of his life, trust me, you wouldn't be."

A chill runs through me, but I stand my ground. "Is that a threat?"

"You'll know when I'm making a threat." The smile returns to Lazarus's face. "Unless you're dumber than I gave you credit for." He takes one last sip, draining the glass, but his eyes are still on me.

"No, I'm pretty smart," I say, having found my voice.

"Smart enough to know that rich people like you make sure you have insurance on everything, including your family. And whatever this has been, whatever you're hoping to accomplish, you're only going to tear your family further apart. If you're too much of a coward to admit it to me, at least admit it to yourself."

Lazarus shoots up out of his chair faster than I think possible. Before I realize what's happening he's leaning over the desk, his nostrils flaring. "How dare you," he says through clenched teeth. "Your generation's reputation for lack of respect is well-earned."

"I don't respect liars."

He stands up to his full height. Was his side of the desk higher? He looks about six inches taller than the last time I saw him.

"Is this what you did to Laura? Intimidated her? Forced her to sign the divorce papers?"

"You should have taken my son's advice and stayed out of this. You don't know what you've gotten yourself into," he rumbles.

"What do you mean?"

"Laura is dead, you stupid, stupid girl."

Chapter Thirty-Four

OBVIOUSLY HE'S LYING. He's just trying to rattle me. He doesn't know I've been talking to Laura this entire time; the woman has been my primary source of information. And she sought me out, not the other way around. I hadn't even known Laura existed until after I met her.

"Just another lie, another manipulation," I finally find the strength to say, my focus on Lazarus. *Don't break eye contact. Whatever you do, don't let him see you as weak.*

Lazarus scoffs. "I don't care if you believe me or not. The fact of the matter is she's dead. Believe whatever you want or need to. It changes nothing. And you have no idea what you've gotten yourself into." He sits back down in his chair. I take it as an invitation to do the same..

"You're telling me the woman I've been talking to for the past four days is dead?"

Lazarus's eyes widen, but it's very subtle. Like a fly landing on a lampshade, the movement is so small it's barely perceptible. But I can tell I've surprised him. He hasn't anticipated me talking to her. Maybe I should have kept it in my back pocket, but it's out now. Nothing I can do about it. *"Never give the man any advantage, never let him get up over you, because you'll never get out from under his boot.*" Felton's words.

"Interesting." Lazarus says. He picks up his cell phone, which acts as a paperweight for a small stack of papers on the giant desk. He types something out, but I can't see the screen. Who is he contacting? And what is he telling them?

Maybe the best tactic would be for me to indulge him. "Okay. Let's say Laura is dead, as you say. What happened to her? How did she die?"

Lazarus finishes typing and sets his phone down again. A smile creeps across his face. "I'll leave my son to tell you that story."

"Felton knows?"

"Of course Felton knows. He was there."

The room feels smaller, even though I know this is nothing more than Lazarus playing his games. I keep pushing. "Did he do something to her? Did something happen?" Laura's words echo in my head. His grip, the bruising. How he'd lost control. She'd been so adamant I thought there was no way she could be lying.

Lazarus sits silently on his side of the desk, his smile never wavering.

"Why did you even tell me if you're not going to give me any details?" I demand.

"You asked me how I could torture my son."

I draw back, disgusted. Was this how it's going to be? He's still trying to pit us against each other. I really have crossed into hell. "Why?"

Lazarus stands, taking his glass over to the small bar area on the left side of the room. It's filled with an array of bottles, all with names I don't recognize. But knowing Lazarus, they all probably cost at least five hundred dollars apiece. He picks up one with a gilded label, but all I can read is "Aged 35 Years." He returns to the desk with the glass half full.

"Oh. I'm sorry," he says in mocking tone as he notices me looking at his glass. "Did you want one?"

I don't dignify the comment.

He takes his seat across from me again, relaxing back into the chair. "The thing you have to understand about fathers and sons is their relationship is complicated. You wouldn't know, as you didn't have any brothers and of course your father wasn't the best of role models."

I bite the inside of my cheek to keep from saying something I'll regret. How did he find out about Dad? How much does he know about me? He probably used all his contacts to find out as much as he could the day Felton and I went on our first date. Still, I don't like him knowing my personal business. This man is not family to me, he's a stranger. And it's unnerving to hear such personal information come from someone like him.

"See, sometimes, little boys have trouble listening. And they won't do what's best for them. And those little boys grow up into little men, and they grow stubborn. So you have to institute what I like to call 'creative punishment.' For their own good, of course." The smile never leaves his face. He enjoys this way too much. Too much to be healthy, too much to be sane. Not that anyone will ever call him on it. Felton had been the only one to break ranks, and look what Lazarus is doing to him.

I reach up and touch my cheek; my face has grown hot and I barely feel it.

"But don't think I haven't thought about you." He holds his glass out to me in a mock salute and then takes a sip. "I actually quite like you, Winter. I wasn't sure before tonight, but it takes some balls to come in here and face me. Stronger and richer people have tried and failed, so I have to give you points for that."

"I'd hate to see what you do to the people you really *don't* like."

He considers that a moment. "No, you probably wouldn't. My actions are as much for your benefit as my son's. If you're going to be part of this family, you're not going to be skirting the edges, flitting to and fro as you see fit. Unity keeps a family strong. And strong families withstand. Don't think I'm picking on you, I would test anyone my sons bring into my orbit."

Was he saying this *was* all a test? What about what he said about Laura? Was that just to gauge my reaction? "I'm not so sure I want to be part of it anymore."

He shrugs, as if it doesn't matter to him one way or another.

"What if I decide to go to the police?"

He laughs, almost choking on his drink. "And tell them what?"

"Tell me what happened!" I've lost all semblance of civility; I just need to know what happened. This man, this criminal, is manipulating me and the man I love, all for his own personal amusement. There is no telling if what he's saying is accurate or not. It could be part of another elaborate ruse. His little game to prove I'm Byrnes material.

I level my gaze. "Who signed the divorce documents if it wasn't Laura?"

"I'm not sure I should tell you that," Lazarus replies. "Since you're not sure you want to be part of this family anymore."

So he *does* know. In not answering he's already answered my real question, and that was if he'd been involved when they got divorced. He knows who signed the papers, who tried to copy her signature. He was probably able to get it past the county clerk with a quick payoff all those years ago, so no one would take a close look. And after this much time, it wasn't as if people were out checking old divorce certificates to see if signatures matched.

"They know. Down at the Clerk's Office. They know the

marriage and divorce signatures don't match. We found out yesterday when I went to pull them," I say.

Lazarus slams the glass on his desk, causing me to jump. I can't help but wonder if Felton has that angry streak in him too. "Do. Not. Threaten. Me." He stares at me a moment and I feel like I might pass out for as fast as my pulse is. Finally, he resumes drinking. "I have fail-safes in place. It won't be a problem." His demeanor is back to normal, but these flashes of anger scare me. I need to leave, while I still can. I think I've learned everything I can.

"Are you going to let me leave? Or am I trapped here?" I ask.

"We're all trapped," Lazarus says, his eyes finally leaving me. He leans back in his chair, staring behind me. "By our decisions or our mistakes. One way or another, we're all trapped."

Great. Cryptic platitudes. Really helpful. This has obviously been a mistake. What was I thinking, assuming I could get anything but lies from this man? I'll need to go back to Laura. After all, she led me to the trap door and the manuscripts. And maybe *she'll* actually tell me the truth. As I prepare to stand, the door flies open to reveal Warren, his face flushed, and his breath ragged.

"Sir!"

Lazarus looks up, and within seconds he's on his feet and out the door behind Warren without giving me a second glance. I'm momentarily startled, not sure what's happening. I stand to follow, only to realize I've been left alone in this man's study. Is there something in here I can use? Something that might give me answers?

I scan the bookshelves, and my eyes land on the drawers beneath, each punctuated with small metal locks in the center. The keys might be in here, might even be in his desk. But as I round the desk to open it I stop short. Is Lazarus really that foolish to keep records that might implicate him? And if he comes back in here to find me going through his personal belongings, I might find myself at the bottom of the Farmington River. I'm impulsive, but I'm not stupid, at least, not *that* stupid. I'll have to make do with Laura.

I leave the office and retrace my steps back out to the main atrium, following not only my original path, but a cacophony of voices coming from the front entrance. I turn the corner to find Lazarus yelling at two men I don't know, while Abagail stands, her hand over her mouth.

When I peer around the corner, I'm surprised to see Felton standing beside Warren, both of them tending to a man seated, with his back to me.

And from the looks on their faces I can tell something is very wrong.

Chapter Thirty-Five

"FELTON?" I ask. "What are you doing here?"

Abagail looks up, tears in her eyes as Felton turns away from the man slumped in the chair. "What are you waiting for?" Lazarus roars. "Get him downstairs immediately!" The two men hoist the figure in the chair up between them and help him down the corridor. As they turn I gasp, realizing it's Brian. His face is covered in burns and his eyes are closed. I can't tell if he's breathing or not.

"Oh my god," I say. "What's he doing here? He needs to go to a hospital!"

"There's a medical area downstairs," Felton says, approaching me and leading me away from the crowd. "Dad has a surgeon on retainer, they're on their way."

"On retainer? For what?" I'm practically screaming. "What do you need a surgical center for? In a house!"

"Trust me, you don't want to know." Felton wraps his arms around me, dragging me away from his parents and Warren who are following Brian and the others down the corridor. "Let's go. You don't want to be here for this."

"What happened to him?" I sniff the air. It smells of sulfur and ash, and it's coming from Felton. "What happened to *you?*"

"Brian thought he'd found the person sending the books. It was a trap. It almost killed both of us."

I pivot, grabbing him, struck with the possibility that he might be hurt. "Are you okay?"

He waves me off. "I'm fine. I was far enough away. Brian was a lot closer. He lost consciousness in the car on the way over."

"Thank God." I wrap my arms around him. "You're sure you're not hurt?"

He nods again. This is the closest we've been physically since the book arrived. But at the moment I don't care. I can't believe he was almost killed. Everyone else has already gone with Brian, leaving just the two of us. But I can hear the opening and closing of large doors in the distance. "Can they help him here? Wouldn't he be better off—"

"We can't risk it. I seriously thought about it, but then they'd start asking questions and anyone who saw the house explode would figure out we were there. That's information we don't want going around."

I pull back from him. "It's your brother's life. Who cares if anyone knows if you were there or not?"

"Dad doesn't want to get emergency services involved. There's paperwork and we can't chase down this person and deal with an inquiry as to why we were in someone's house when it exploded."

"You're saying 'we' a lot." I don't like how much he's already ingratiated himself back into the family. "And a house explosion?"

"Mobile home. If someone hadn't warned us, we would have both been inside when it went off. We were lucky."

Warren returns to the hallway, his face somewhat flushed. He doesn't say anything, only stands by the hallway where they took Brian, his hands clasped in front of him.

I return my attention to Felton. "Someone warned you?"

"Brian thought it was the owner or something, like they'd caught us. But I knew better, I know panic when I hear it. They said get out, so I got the fuck out."

I flick my gaze to Warren. He's watching both of us. "Who was it?"

Felton shakes his head. "I don't know. I didn't see them. I only saw someone dressed all in black, running away from the explosion. I assume that's who it was, but I could be wrong. My ears were ringing and I was more concerned with getting to Brian."

"I need to sit down," I say. I find an ornate chair by itself, against one of the walls of the massive foyer. I reach it just in time to feel all the strength leave my legs. This is getting serious; could this explosion be connected to the books? "I don't understand," I say. "Why did the house explode?"

"I assume it was set in case someone that wasn't supposed to came snooping," he says. "Brian had a lead on the person living there. We saw them leave then went to investigate."

"And you give me shit about snooping around," I say, unable to believe he'd been so reckless. At least I'm not out there almost getting blown up.

"Don't worry, Brian will be okay. Dad knows some of the best doctors around."

I scoff. "I bet he does." What sort of business doesn't have surgeons on retainer for when employees or family members almost get blown up?

Silence fills the air between us as I try to process everything. Part of me wants to go back into Lazarus' study and search it now, knowing he definitely won't be coming back for a while. The other part just wants to give all this up, to leave Felton and this insane family behind. I don't need this.

"What are you doing here?" Felton asks, bringing me back out of it. "Was this where you were planning on coming when you left this morning?"

His tone is accusatory, and I don't like it. Maybe I should ask him why he tried to lose me this morning as well. I shoot a look at Warren. He stands impassive and as still as a Roman centurion. I don't want to get into this with Felton right now, not here where Lazarus's henchman can relay everything we say back to him.

"Let's talk about it on the way home." He's watching me, his eyes suspicious. "Do you…need to check out or whatever?"

"Win, I don't think I can leave."

Right. Have to stay close to the family and all that. "Yeah, okay. I don't think I can stay here. I'm going back home."

"You can't," Felton says. "We don't know if it's safe. Whoever broke in is still out there. Stay here, and let dad debrief you. He'll know what to do."

"Debrief me?" I ask, incredulous. "I don't think so." Wasn't this the same man who just a few days ago wanted nothing to do with his father? And now he's willing to stick around and let daddy take care of everything? "What happened to not wanting to be part of this madness? Of this life?"

"Winter, I *am* part of it. Whether I like it or not."

"Oh. I see." I stand, the strength having returned to my legs. "So rejecting your father, rejecting this life. That was all another lie for my benefit?"

"What? No! I tried, I really did. But someone just tried to kill me and my brother. I can't ignore that."

"I'm not asking you to," I half-shout. "But that doesn't mean you have to be a lapdog to that monster you call a father."

It doesn't escape my notice that Warren visibly tenses.

"I'm not a lapdog. I don't even want to be here. But I *have* to. At least right now. At least until this is sorted out."

"So you'll reject your father, but only when it's convenient. Is that it?" I make my way towards the door.

"Hey!" he yells after me. "That's not fair. What do you

want me to do? Just ignore it? Pretend like it all never happened?"

I spin on him, the full fury of everything I've felt the past four days coming to a head. "I want you to stop lying to me! I want you to give me a straight and clear answer. That's all I've ever wanted."

He hesitates. Here it is, the crux of everything. He's still keeping secrets from me, despite his promises to be honest. For whatever reason, he can't make the right decision. Why can't he just stop lying and tell me? What's he so afraid of?

I don't think he's going to say anything but he drops his head. "Then ask. Ask whatever you want and I will tell you the truth."

My eyes are already wet, but I don't bother wiping them away. I want to leave him standing here, looking foolish, but he's laid down the gauntlet, which means I need to pick it up. There's only one way to tell if he's really ready to be honest with me or not. After this, I'll know for sure if this relationship has any chance of a future or not.

I steel myself. "Then tell me. Is Laura, your ex-wife, really dead?"

Felton lifts his head, stares directly into my eyes, and nods.

Chapter Thirty-Six

AT LEAST NOW I know what he thinks of me.

I shake my head and laugh, heading back towards the door.

"What's so funny?" he asks. He's close to tears. Is it because he knows his lies are driving me away? Or because his father will punish him for not getting me to believe this bullshit story they've concocted?

"You," I say, turning again, no longer caring that Warren is still there in the background. "You're what's so funny. But make no mistake. I'm laughing *at* you, not with you. You're a joke, Felton. You obviously don't think very much of me and part of me just thinks you're lying to drive me away. I tried to make it work, I really did. But I'm done. Have a nice life."

"It's not a lie!" he insists. For a moment I pause from the intensity of his voice. He shoots a glance at Warren who looks like he wants to step forward and say something, but he remains rooted to the spot.

"It *is* a lie," I fire back. "I've met Laura! I've had lunch with her twice! She's the one who told me about the hidden space in the floor of the house. And she's happily remarried, though I can't imagine why on Earth you think lying to me about her is doing anything but digging you into a deeper hole."

Felton stands there, his mouth open for a moment. He turns back to Warren, who looks similarly alarmed before looking me in the eye again. Felton sputters. "Winter, no. She's *dead*. I saw her body myself. I..." His voice hitches as tears fall from his eyes.

"No," I say again, my frustration really showing through. "She's perfectly fine. I spoke with her yesterday on the phone."

"It's true, Miss," Warren says. "Laura died eight years ago. I was there."

I can't comprehend what he's saying. This doesn't make any sense. "Then who have I been talking to?" I ask.

"I don't know," Felton says.

Lazarus was telling the truth?

I swallow, hard. Suddenly my throat is very dry. I don't know what it is, but the both of them insisting on this...something makes me consider the possibility. Felton has never shown this much emotion when he's lied before. But it can't be true, can it? "If that's true, then how did she die?"

Felton and Warren exchange glances. "Maybe you should come and sit down," Felton says, regaining his composure. His cheeks are wet, but he seems to have hold of himself again. "Come into the kitchen. I'll get you some water. You look like you're about to topple over."

I hold my hand out. "Felton, *how?*"

"She was...um, murdered," he says.

I look at him, then at Warren, then at this entire house. And suddenly it all makes sense. The veiled threats from Lazarus, the coverup, all the work this family has done to bury their secrets. Laura had come into the family and threatened them somehow, and she'd been taken care of, just like Lazarus had told me I would be. Was this why Brian never married? Because anyone who comes into this family and doesn't abide by their rules is branded a problem and removed?

I back away from Felton and Warren; I have to get out of this house, away from these people. If I stay here I'll end up just like her. I pull the engagement ring off my finger and toss it at Felton. It hits him in the chest and falls to the floor, clinking on the marble. "Stay away from me," I say.

"Winter, you don't understand," he says, reaching out for me. Warren approaches as well. This is how it's going to happen. I know their secret now; they can't let me leave, I'm too much of a security risk. "Come on, let's just…"

I shake my head. If he thinks he's keeping me in this house he's sorely mistaken. I reach behind me and feel the large wooden door, My only escape route. I manage to press the handle, the door opening at my touch. I half expected it to be locked, but they might not have had a chance after what happened with Brian.

"Miss—" Warren says as I get the door open. "Please."

I turn and bolt for my car, fumbling for the keys in my pocket, thinking any second I'm going to trip and fall face-first on the gravel. But I manage to reach my car as Felton and Warren come rushing out of the house after me. As Felton reaches my door I slam the lock button and shove the keys into the ignition.

"Winter! Wait, please, it's not—"

Before he can finish the sentence I throw the car into reverse and peel out, barely missing Warren who is on the other side. He has to jump aside to keep from my fender catching him. Felton is trying to get hold of my door handle again and I kick the car into drive and floor it, sending up dirt and gravel all over the place. Half of it's hitting my car but right now I don't care. I barrel down the driveway, not even bothering to slow. I'll slam through those gates if I have to, but I find they're already open when I get back to the entrance. I don't question it. I just need to get as far away from this place as I possibly can. I glance in the back seat; I already took my overnight bag back into the house this morning. *Fuck*. I'll have to make a quick stop by the house and grab my essentials and anything else I can't live without. I need those manuscripts. They're going to be my evidence to the police. But not here. Lazarus owns the cops here. I'll need to go a few towns over, or maybe even into Hartford. They'll have to get the FBI involved. I'm the only one who can tear this little empire down, but it's not going to be easy.

I gun it when I reach the blacktop, skidding onto the double yellow. All that matters is getting away. If it's really true and Laura is dead, then who have I been talking to? Someone impersonating her? There's no doubt in my mind now that she's the one who's been sending the books, considering everyone else thinks she's dead. But to what end?

It doesn't matter. I can't be involved in this anymore. It's going to end up getting me killed. I've stumbled into some mafia-level shit here and I'm not about to stick around to be silenced when I voice a differing opinion. But what does that mean? Do I leave my job? Leave town? I can't exactly stay here, Lazarus has people everywhere. I need to get as far away as possible, maybe California. Maybe Canada. Just somewhere they won't look for me.

"Goddammit!" I yell, rolling down all the windows in the car, feeling the cold wind whip through the car. I need to feel the cold up against my skin, to remember that I *can* feel. That I haven't been sucked into this so far that I'm not still me. This is so much worse than Thomas and my test has completely failed me. And trying to work through everything has only made it worse. If I'd just walked away the day I realized Felton was lying to me none of this would be happening to me. I might not even be on Lazarus' radar. But it was too late for that now.

A thought crosses my mind. Whoever "Laura" is, she has done me a massive favor. I never would have known about any of this if not for those books showing up. They were the key; they'd cracked this world wide open for me to see. She wasn't honest with me either, but she dropped the breadcrumbs for me to find, and they've led me here. What if what she said about Felton was true? Was that how the real Laura had died? Had he done something to her, or had Lazarus just stepped in to cover for his son? Either way, I can't help but feel a kinship with the woman. What if she found out about someone else, like I found out about her? What had they even done with her body? I'm sure there's no grave anywhere, she probably just disappeared one day and was never heard from again. That explains the signature! Someone had to forge her name on the divorce document because she was already dead!

Jesus fuck me!

Chapter Thirty-Seven

TWENTY MINUTES later I pull into the driveway, Felton's driveway. Tears sting my eyes not because I'm sad but because I'm terrified they'll catch up to me. I don't even care about my stuff anymore, but I need those manuscripts, as proof. I leave the car running and rush up to the house, unlocking the door and punching in the code as soon as I'm inside. It registers that I've been living nothing but one big lie the entire time I've lived here and I'll be happy to put this place behind me as I run down the hallway to the bedroom, grabbing the bag I took to the hotel last night. There's no time for anything else. I can replace the rest of it later. I can't replace my life.

I run back into the hallway and stop cold.

Felton stands there, breathing hard with both hands out. Christ, he must have been right behind me the entire time. And I didn't even realize. I'd pushed my car close to sixty on roads that were posted at thirty-five. And somehow he'd been right there the entire time.

I look for a weapon, seeing none. But he's still blocking me from getting out of this house. How many more of them are out there? I should have just run, headed out of town.

"Winter, please just let me explain." His voice trembles and I don't want to hear it. I've already been lied to so much, how can I ever listen to him again? The only thing that keeps me from charging into him is I don't know if he's armed or not. How did Laura die? Was she shot? Stabbed? I have no idea.

"Are you going to kill me too?" I ask, holding my bag against my chest. "Is that how this ends?"

"You don't understand, I didn't kill her!" he says. He looks exhausted, like he might collapse, but I can't let my guard down. Maybe if I throw the bag at him it will distract him long enough I can get out of here. But I'll lose the manuscripts.

"Just…" He rubs his hand against his head. "Just let me explain, okay? We'd had a fight, I—"

"It doesn't matter what you tell me," I yell. "I'm never going to believe you. Please just let me go."

His eyes fall and he nods, backing up until he's no longer blocking my path to the front door. "Further," I say. He steps back until he's almost in the kitchen. I take a few steps forward, testing him, and he doesn't move. He puts both hands up and just stares off to the side while I creep closer to the door. He's not going to actually let me leave, I know that. He's going to grab me the minute I get close enough. But I have to try. There's no other way out. I can still hear the engine of my car running outside. I just need to get there, nothing else matters in this moment.

"I didn't kill her," he whispers as I'm almost to the door. "I couldn't. I loved her. As much as I love you."

"Funny way of showing it," I say, right on the threshold. My car is right there, and he didn't block me in, which is… strange. If he was going to keep me from running, wouldn't he have pulled in behind me, or at least taken the keys out of my car? For that matter, wouldn't he have already tried to restrain or attack me? If he's trying to keep me here, he's taking a big risk by leaving all these avenues open. I'm only steps away from my car…and my freedom.

"I'd hurt her," he says as I'm on the threshold. I stop. Laura had said something about that, she said he'd been abusive to her…or to the real Laura. So she was telling the truth about that part.

"Bruised her arm?" I ask.

Confusion crosses his face. "How did you know?" He shakes his head. "It doesn't matter. I didn't mean to. I was frustrated and grabbed her and I accidentally left a bruise. I felt terrible about it as soon as it happened. It had never happened before and never did again. I was so embarrassed… I didn't think I deserved to be around her, so I…left."

"You left," I say.

"I'd hurt her. I didn't deserve to be with her. In fact, I came back the next morning prepared for her to say she was leaving me. And if she didn't, I was going to insist on it."

"Because of a bruise."

"Because I'd gotten physical, and I'd promised myself I never would. It doesn't matter how angry I get, no one deserves that. I knew in that moment she could do better than me, even though it hurt like hell to admit it."

He pauses, and in the silence all I can hear is the quiet inhale and exhale of my lungs. Why am I standing here listening to this? I should be gone by now, but part of me *has* to know. All this began with Laura's books. I need to know how it ends.

"When I came back the next morning, I found her. She'd been…someone…left her on th floor." He begins sobbing in between his words. "Her neck was practically black from where they'd crushed it!"

My heart goes out to him. Despite everything that's happened, I can't help but feel sorry for him. Maybe he really did love her. But that doesn't excuse covering up her death.

"Why didn't you call the cops?" I ask.

He shakes his head. "I wanted to. I should have. But I was only twenty-five and I still trusted him back then."

"Your dad."

He sniffs and nods. "*He* thought I'd done it in a fit of rage. And no matter how much I tried to convince him otherwise, he was fixated on it. Said that even if I didn't do it, the bruise on her arm made me the primary suspect. And even he couldn't make that go away once the police got wind of it."

I glance back at the car. Still there, still running. I can still get out.

"What happened?" I ask.

"He cleaned everything up. We got rid of it all, made it look like she'd taken off without telling anyone. That she'd hired a lawyer and left signed divorce records for me to sign. Remember I told you I burned her box of manuscripts? That was the truth." His voice is small now, so vulnerable.

"How do I know you're telling the truth?"

"You don't. That's the problem. I've told so many lies, you don't know what to believe."

I let out a long breath. "So you don't know who killed her."

He shakes his head.

"You don't think it could have been Lazarus, or one of his men? You said you weren't here, you don't know what happened."

He gives me a pained look. "No, of course not. My dad might be an asshole but he's not a cold-blooded killer."

"You sure about that?" I ask. His threats to me seemed pretty sincere.

"He didn't kill her."

"Well someone did. And I'm willing to bet it was because she got mixed up in this fucked-up thing you call a family. I suggest you have a long, hard talk with your father about it. But you can leave me out of it." I walk out into the cold, headed for my car, the bag hanging down by my side.

"Please," he says, stepping forward, which causes me to recoil back. "Please, Win. I love you. I can't go through this again."

"And I'm not about to end up like your first wife," I say. "Disappeared where no one can find me." He takes another step forward, then retreats back to the house, as if I've physically wounded him. He's holding himself so tight.

"What should I do?" he asks just before I close the door. I can barely hear him, but it's enough to stop me for a second. I close the door anyway and lean my head out the open window.

"If I were you, I'd find the woman posing as your ex-wife."

"How?"

I let out a breath. I'm losing my only resource here, but honestly, I need to be finished with this whole thing. And me contacting "Laura" any more won't do me any good. "Look for a woman, black hair, glasses. Five-foot-six. Here." I rattle off her number to him from my own phone. Once he has it, he nods in appreciation, but his eyes are still pleading me to stay.

There's no way. I don't even look at him as I back down the driveway and leave Felton Byrnes and all his baggage behind. Just like I should have done from the beginning. I'm free.

Chapter Thirty-Eight

Tap, tap, tap.

I glance up into the morning sun. A dark figure shifts in front of my window, blotting out the rays and my adrenaline spikes. I jump up, thinking it's Lazarus or one of his men.

"Miss? Miss, you can't sleep here."

I squint, blocking out the harshest light and allowing the man's features to materialize. He's a regular beat cop, bundled up in his cold-weather gear. I put my hand out to support myself while my swimming head returns to normal. I manage to get my bearings in the backseat and open the door to talk to him.

"I'm sorry, officer. I'll move it right now," I say, slipping on my flats and getting out of the car. I slept in what I'd worn all day, not bothering to change in the back of a car. If I was going to be slumming it for a while, I might as well lean into it.

"Rough night?" the cop asks.

"Something like that."

"Miss, I need you to look at me. I need to make sure you're okay to drive."

I screw up my features, but it makes sense. He thinks I tied one off last night. "It was nothing like that. I just…I had a fight with my boyfriend. Fiancée. I haven't been drinking."

The cop stares into my eyes. I hope they're not too bloodshot. It wasn't like the car had been the most comfortable place to spend the night.

"Couldn't stay at a friend's? Or a hotel?"

The answer is no to both. I have no friends left. At least none I can count on. Cammie has shut me out, and I can't exactly go to Janet, being next door to Felton. I want to go to a hotel, but I also have to consider I only have four hundred dollars in my account at the moment and if I'm going to be running from Lazarus, then I can't waste money on a hotel if I can help it. I can't access my savings because they're in a joint account with Felton, which means unless I can find a big pile of cash, I'm going to be short for a while.

"I just…got really tired. I didn't think it would be safe for me to keep driving."

The cop stares at me. "Then you probably did the right thing. Next time, try not to stay anywhere more than a couple of hours. We have regulations around here."

I nod. "Yes, sir."

He tips his hat. "Have a good day."

I watch him walk away. I parked in a parking garage, but on the first floor in case I needed to make a quick getaway. I'm still somewhat surprised Warren or someone else didn't find me in the middle of the night. I'm even more surprised Felton let me walk. Whether that was because he loves me or he really doesn't think anyone's coming after me is anyone's guess. But I can't rely on him to protect me now. He couldn't protect his first wife, why should I be any different?

I get in behind the wheel and rub my hands down my face. Am I being too paranoid? After all, I've managed to elude them this long. I'd think someone with Lazarus's resources wouldn't have let me get off the grounds if he hadn't wanted to, but the gate had been wide open, despite the fact I know they keep it closed all the time. And Felton, he'd just let me leave, no threats, no weapons, nothing. Maybe they aren't after me and it was just the shock of everything: Brian, finding out about Laura. It's more than I've ever had to handle at once.

I glance at my watch. The metal had made a bright pink indentation into my skin from where I'd slept on it. Seven-thirty. On a Sunday. Nothing was open yet so the possibility of a cup of coffee was out of the question. I can't keep going like this. I need some help. But for that, I need to make amends first.

∼

WHEN I PULL UP AND CUT THE CAR OFF IT'S ALMOST EIGHT. Still early enough to catch her. I park on the side of the road as not to appear to presumptuous. Cammie's dog-cleaning van sits in her driveway, beside Mike's truck. I make my way around the long fence and to the front door, knocking instead of ringing the bell.

I'm not sure anyone will answer, but I have to keep trying. Honestly, I won't blame Cammie if she decides to leave me out here in the cold by myself. I haven't been exactly the most reliable person through this whole endeavor.

Just as I'm about to give up, something shuffles behind the door and the latch turns. The door opens to reveal Cammie, fully dressed in her new "uniform," slacks and a collared shirt with her logo on it. Today must be the first day she's using the new van. Something else I should have known.

She stands there, waiting, and I realize she's waiting on me to start. I should be able to tell by the indignant look on her face.

I take a breath. "When you said you couldn't do this anymore, did you mean...us? You couldn't be my friend anymore?"

"I've never heard a worse apology in my life," Cammie say, crossing her arms.

"Cams, I can't lose you. I know I've been horrible this past week. Really horrible. And I've been making you worry. And you've been the only person who was there for me, no matter what. It's hard for me to reciprocate that sometimes. I am sorry. Because I didn't realize what I had until it was gone."

Her mouth forms a thin line, and her face remains stern. She isn't going to forgive me this time, I've burned this bridge and there's no way back. I drop my eyes. "I just want you to know I love you. Because if I never get to talk to you again I want it to be the last thing you remember about me. Not...not everything else." I take one last look at her, hoping for any kind of break in her stone façade. Seeing nothing, I head back down the steps.

"God, you can be so dramatic sometimes," Cammie says behind me. My heart springs because I know that voice. It's the voice of resigned indignation! She does forgive me! "I'm not going to stop being your friend just because we had a fight. This is the thing you don't seem to get. One event isn't worth throwing everything away. At least it isn't to me."

I walk back up to the door. "It isn't to me either."

"Are you sure? Because it seems to me you're ready to tuck tail and run."

"I came, didn't I? I'm trying."

Cammie's face softens. "I know you are." She pauses. "You look like shit."

"I slept in my car."

"Bet that felt awesome."

"Not so much."

She takes a deep breath. "Maybe you're not hopeless after all. I forgive you, but you owe me."

For the first time in a week I feel like some of the weight on my back has lifted. "I do. I'll do anything."

Cammie grabs me and pulls me into a hug. "Just try not to be so stupid in the future."

"I promise."

As we break apart, a smile comes over her face. "I know how you can repay me."

"How?"

Cammie pulls her cell phone from her back pocket, checking something on the screen. "You're going to be my assistant for the day," she says, scrolling on the phone.

Suddenly, everything comes tumbling back down, including the reasons why I'm here. "Cammie. I need your help."

The smile drops from Cammie's face. "Does this have to do with what's been going on?"

I nod.

"Get in here."

Chapter Thirty-Nine

IT ONLY TAKES me half an hour to relate everything that's happened. I start with the second meeting with "Laura" and conclude with waking up in my back seat this morning. At one point Mike had appeared at the doorway, keeping a respectful distance, but listening all the same, which is fine with me. I've known him for years now and trust him almost as much as I trust Cammie.

I find it's more helpful than I realized to go over it all again, just for my own benefit. So much has happened I found myself taking a second to make sure I got the sequence of everything right. When I'm done Cammie gives me a few knowing nods, then stands and heads over to the sink. She picks up a soggy sponge and heaves it right at Mike, where it smacks him on the chest, then lands in his coffee cup, spilling his coffee all over the linoleum floor.

"What's that for?" he yelled, trying to wipe the spilled coffee off the front of his shirt.

"For not letting her in yesterday! What the hell were you thinking?"

"You're the one who told me you didn't want to talk to

her!" Mike says, his face awash in confusion. I love it when Cammie gets like this. How often has she told me one thing, then turned around berated me for the exact same thing twenty minutes later? It's one of her more redeeming qualities.

"I didn't know all of that! Gawd!" Cammie comes over to my side of the table and bends down, wrapping me in an awkward hug. Over her shoulder, Mike just shakes his head and deposits his half-empty cup in the sink.

"Guess I'll change," he says, leaving the two of us alone.

"Okay. What do we need to do?" Cammie asks, pulling away.

"I'm not sure. I don't know what to do anymore. Part of me says I need to just leave all this behind—" she clears her throat. "But some other, *louder* part of me says maybe that's not what I should do."

"Do you really think Lazarus killed your fiancée's first wife?" she asks.

"I don't know," I admit. "He's intimidating, but part of me thinks that's all just part of the image. I don't know if he's a cold-blooded killer. And what's the motive? They had been married for a while already, so why destroy his son's life like that? Not to mention, Felton said he had to convince his father that *he* didn't kill her. If Lazarus had done it, would he even question it?"

"Maybe to cover his bases? Make sure Felton didn't suspect him?" she offers.

Mike comes back into the kitchen with a fresh shirt.

"Maybe," I say. Plus, I doubt Lazarus would have put his sons in any danger *unless* the person who warned them happened to work for him. Still, it's a stretch. "Everything seems to point back to this woman masquerading as Felton's ex-wife."

"You think she sent the books?" Mike asks.

"It looks that way. But I can't figure out why. If she's not Laura, and that's looking more likely by the minute, then who is she, and why is she doing this?"

"Why don't you call her and find out?" Cammie asks. "You have her number."

I look at my phone on the table beside me. "What if she's dangerous? I mean, she can't exactly be stable, right? Not after all this subterfuge."

"Then we'll just call the police. Let them deal with it. You said Lazarus knows people in the force, right? Can't he get on it?"

I think back to last night when I told him I'd been talking to Laura. "He texted someone last night when I told him who I'd been talking to, but I don't know who. If he already knew Laura was dead, he might be out looking for this mystery woman already."

"Great," Mike says. "Problem solved."

"Except," Cammie offers. "What if Felton really did kill his wife? And all of this is nothing but a cover-up? That woman, whoever she is, knows the truth. She tried to warn you."

I push back from the table. "I don't believe that. Not after last night. He might have grabbed her too hard by accident, but strangled her? He doesn't have it in him. His father does. And Brian probably does. And Abagail would kill you with a cold stare if she could. But he's not like the rest of them."

"You still love him."

I hesitate, surprised by the question. "I never said I didn't. I just wasn't sure I could live with someone with so many secrets. I'm still not."

Cammie hooks a thumb back to Mike. "If Gigantor over here had this much baggage, I'd have some serious questions myself."

"Hey!" Mike protests.

"Oh, don't worry, you big baby. I know all about your 'tawdry past.'" She uses air-quotes.

Mike grimaces until it becomes a heavy frown.

"Tawdry past?" I ask.

Cammie pulls her blonde hair back into a ponytail, using a band on her wrist to tie it back. "He shadowed a male stripper for a few months. Didn't have the nerve for the stage, though."

"Jesus, Cams! That's private!" Mike sputters.

"I know, honey, I know. But it's a good thing. See, Winter has more respect for you now that you abandoned the pole life." She motions to me, and whatever expression is plastered across my face makes her crack a huge grin. I can't imagine Mike as a stripper, but as soon as I think about it, I form a mental image and begin giggling. I guess I can imagine it after all. It feels good to laugh again. I can't remember the last time. Mike, for all the ribbing, has crossed his arms, but he's wearing a bit of a smirk behind his grimace.

"What do you want to do?" Cammie asks, once we calm down.

I can't just walk away. I need to find this woman, learn who she is and figure out what she wants. Maybe then I'll get some answers. "I think we have to find her. I could try setting up another meeting, maybe confide in her some more. You guys can be my backup, in case she's dangerous."

Mike squirms. "I don't know. What are we supposed to do if she tries to hurt you? Tackle her?"

I'm wondering that myself. Even if Lazarus is out looking for her, there's no chance he'll find her. Even if Felton tries calling, she might not be willing to talk to him. For whatever reason she approached me. I might be the only one who can interact with her. "She's not stupid enough to try anything in public. We can just talk. I'll confront her, tell her I know she's not Laura. Maybe she'll open up. You never know. It's better than doing nothing and letting things escalate. She sent the second book yesterday, so who knows when she'll deliver the third."

"And you think once she delivers all five, the countdown is over and she…" Mike trails off.

A shudder runs through my back. I hadn't considered what *her* endgame might be. "I don't know. But it probably isn't good."

"Call her." Cammie says. "Make up some excuse about work."

I grab the phone and dial before I can chicken out. It rings five times. "No one's picking up."

"Let it go to voicemail." Cammie says, watching me intently.

The message comes on, but it's automated. "It just goes to a generic voice message," I say, hanging up.

"It's probably not even her real phone," Mike says, taking a seat at the table with us.

"What I don't understand is how she could know about Laura in the first place," Cammie says. "From what you said about Lazarus, I doubt he'd ever let anyone talk about it."

"So…what? You're saying she was there?" I ask.

"I don't know. But somehow she knows these things, and no one knows her. It doesn't make sense."

"*Someone* knows her. They have to. But until we have a name or at least a picture, I have no way of telling anyone. I guess I could go to a sketch artist…" I trail off.

"What about Laura? The real Laura, I mean. What did she look like?" Mike asks.

I shrug. I've never seen the woman, and Felton certainly didn't keep any pictures. He said his father had made him destroy all evidence of their time together. "I'm not sure, why?"

"I'm just curious. He couldn't have erased her completely. She had a life before Felton, right? Family? Friends? A job? Where do they think she disappeared to?"

"I don't know. But…"

"What?"

"I'm just thinking back to what Warren said last night. He said he was there too, he saw her. So he knew. And presumably so does Brian. But what if there were other people there, people who worked for Lazarus?"

"Like a clean up crew?" Cammie offers.

"Yeah. People to come in and make it look like it never happened. I doubt Felton would have been much help that night. And Lazarus isn't the kind to get his hands dirty. Warren and Brian could have done it by themselves, but what if there were other people there, helping?"

Cammie runs her hand through her ponytail. "Someone who was there would know all the details. They would know what really happened to Laura."

"And if she was someone who helped with the cleanup operations," Mike says, rubbing his chin, "she would've had access to those manuscripts. She could have kept them for herself instead of burning them."

I stop short of smacking myself on the head. "And she might have access to the security code for our house. Felton said he told his father. Fuck! Why didn't I see this before?"

Cammie hands me my phone again. "It's okay. Just call Lazarus, ask him about his female employees. See if any of them match your description."

"Just call Lazarus, yeah," I say, my breathing picking up. "Yeah…because he's likely to believe me after I insulted him all evening." I don't feel like doing Lazarus's job for him and if these books weren't torturing Felton, I might just let them go. But if this woman is behind everything, I don't want her to reach the final end of her plan, whatever that might be. Because I'm sure it won't be good for anyone, especially Felton.

"What if you called Abagail instead? She might be more receptive," Cammie suggests.

I shake my head. "I just don't know. Lazarus might be right there over her shoulder."

"What's your alternative?"

She's right. If we want to find out who this woman is, we don't have a choice. Hopefully Abagail knows all of her husband's employees.

I scroll through my contacts and dial.

After three rings she picks up. "Hello?" She answers in a cool, soothing voice. It's almost easy to forget the daggers that could hide behind that voice.

"Good morning, Mrs. Byrnes."

"Winter. How are you feeling this morning? You left in quite a hurry last night."

"I'm fine, thank you. How is Brian? Is he going to be okay?"

"Don't concern yourself with Brian." She lets the words hang in the air until I'm uncomfortable. But I have no choice but to continue.

"The reason I'm calling is I hoped you might be able to identify someone on your husband's payroll. A woman."

"Why don't you talk to my husband? I'll go fetch him since I have nothing better to do this morning."

"No!" I say a little too loudly. I can almost *feel* the smile growing on Abagail's lips. Sweat droplets form on my forehead. I wipe them away with my sleeve.

"Oh, I see. A *private* matter, then. May I ask, what will you offer in return for any information I might provide?"

"What do you want?"

"What can you give me, Winter? What can only you give me?"

My heartbeat picks up. What was this woman asking? And why was everyone in this family so damn transactional? "I don't have much. A couple hundred dollars in the bank. Maybe some pull with the city as far as engineering goes."

"Let me tell you what I find most important in life," Abagail says. I glance at both Cammie and Mike, shaking my head. This is going to be bad. "The most important thing to me is family. Family is the bedrock of everything. Do you agree?"

I'm at least smart enough not to argue with the woman. "Yes."

"Excellent. So then perhaps you can imagine what you might be able to provide me that I do not already possess."

My heart sinks. "A grandchild."

"Grand*children*," Abagail corrects. "Now I know your age may be a factor, so this must be engaged immediately."

Children. After my relationship with Thomas fell apart, I stopped considering kids as an option. Early on, Thomas and I had decided we'd wait until we were ready, and as things only deteriorated between us, that time never came. By the time I realized it, I was pushing thirty-five. Felton and I had decided we didn't really need kids in our lives; we like them well enough, but the opportune time would have been five or ten years earlier. And we had careers we wanted to focus on, maybe do some traveling. I've never really had that biological urge other women talk about. Daisy had a little boy, and I'm more than happy to dote on him whenever we get together for holidays. But actually having kids of my own had long since passed from my mind. And Abagail knows it because Felton had told them outright. I thought it was no big deal. Right up until this moment.

"Winter? Are you still there?"

"You want me to give you grandchildren in exchange for one piece of information?"

"One very important piece of information. And my silence."

How bad do I want this information? What if this woman is dangerous? Could Felton be in danger? I did give him her number, after all. The problem is I just don't know. But is it important enough to make a sacrifice this large?

Screw it. I can always claim complications later, find a doctor to help me come up with a medical reason why I can't do it. Right now, this is more important.

"Okay, Abagail. You have a deal."

Chapter Forty

"FOR WHOM ARE YOU SEARCHING?" Abagail asks in that uppity way that rich people try to demonstrate how much smarter they are than the rest of us.

"Black hair, about five-foot-six. Wears glasses, maybe. Hazel eyes, soft voice. Mid-thirties." It's the best I can do. What if "Laura" used a disguise with me? The glasses very well might not have been real. She might even have contacts.

"Anything else?" Abagail asks.

"Smoker. She smokes," I say, recalling my indiscretion.

"I want at least two grandchildren, you understand."

Wait, she's confirming the deal. "So you know who she is." Cammie leans forward with wide eyes.

"The woman you are looking for is named Rene Lawson. And she does not wear glasses, if you're interested."

"Who is she? She works for you?"

"She has worked for us for over ten years. Lazarus recruited her out of college. She's cunning and ruthless. She's one of my husband's most...efficient...employees."

"You mean she's killed people." Mike stiffens, baring his teeth.

"I mean she does what she's told to do."

"Did you tell her to torture your son? To beat him down psychologically?"

Silence on the other end.

I shoot up out of my chair, suddenly angry. "Did you?"

"No. She was never given a job like that. Not to my knowledge." Abagail's voice is reduced somehow. It's the first time I've ever heard weakness from the woman.

"Where is Rene now?"

"She's not working today. I believe it is her day off."

"Do you know where she lives? I need to find her. I need her to explain herself."

"Winter," Abagail says, her voice returning to normal and now tainted with impatience. "This is not someone you wish to find. If you could even find her. She is one of my husband's best, reserved for only what he considers troublesome cases. As you are now significantly more important to me than you were five minutes ago, I implore you not to seek her out. In fact, why don't I have someone come collect you? If Rene is behind all of this, both you and my son may be safer here. Until my husband can sort this out with her."

No way. I'm not going back into that house with that man. In fact, part of me just wants to go back to my life with Felton. I have a very bad feeling that my leaving him might have put him in more danger.

"Can't he just...call her off or something?" I ask.

"If you'd like me to inform him...perhaps. But if Rene is running her own agenda, he may not be able to stop her. My husband is not as spry as he was in his youth."

I shake my head but keep my eyes on Cammie and Mike, mouthing: *these people are fucking crazy.*

"Okay," I say, relenting. If Rene is as dangerous as Abagail is making her sound, I doubt I can convince her to stop whatever it is she's doing. Maybe it's better if Lazarus takes care of it internally. He might even have other people who can…stop her.

"Does Felton know?" I ask.

"About Rene? I don't believe so. I'm not even sure they've ever met."

I nod, even though she can't see me. I can let them take care of this. And now I've roped myself back into their lives. But if it gets this woman under control before she does whatever she's trying to do, I think that's a better outcome. There's no telling what she has planned, and honestly, I don't want to find out.

"Send the car. I'm at my friend's house. I'll give you the address."

"See? You're not as stupid as my husband says you are." I roll my eyes and give Abagail the address.

"Don't worry," Abagail adds. "You're part of the family now. We take care of each other."

But at what price? I don't respond, only hang up.

"Jeez, Win. Children? And who is Rene? Is that Laura?" Cammie asks. "What the hell did you just agree to?"

"They're coming to collect me. And Felton. To keep us safe," I say. "I guess I won't be able to get out of this one." I give her a sheepish smile.

"Is she that dangerous?"

"Apparently so."

"What if Abagail was playing her up? Making her sound more dangerous than she actually is? What if all this is just a setup to get what she wants? She might not even know who Laura really is."

I shake my head. "Maybe. I don't know. I just don't know anymore. So many secrets and lies. I hate all of this." I struggle to keep the tears from falling.

"Oh, honey." Cammie gathers me in a hug and lets me release. We stand there a moment, just holding each other while the tears fall on her new work shirt.

But I can't stay here forever. "I guess..." I pull back and wipe my eyes. "I guess I should call Felton. Let him know what I've just agreed to. He deserves to know the truth. And I should probably try to smooth things over from last night. I kind of implied he'd never see me again."

"Maybe you guys can make it work," Cammie says.

"Maybe." I don't know. So much has happened, how can I ever look at him the same way again? I open his quick contact on my phone and put it to my ear, letting it ring. "He's not picking up." My chest grows tight. He never lets my calls go to voicemail, even when he's in the john.

"Maybe he had a rough night," Mike says. "You know."

"He doesn't drink," I say.

"Even when the love of his life leaves him forever?" Cammie says.

She could be right. And honestly, how much do I even know about the man? He's lied to me, concealed his past, a prior marriage, made up excuses, and possibly worst of all, defended his family to me. Something I never thought I'd hear from his mouth. If someone could erase the woman they loved so completely from their life, what else were they capable of?

Or am I just looking for excuses again, like I always do? Looking for another reason to turn away from him? And with Rene out there, that might be the worst thing I can do right now. We need to be united, at least for now. I've made the commitment, I need to follow through.

"Maybe I should just go over there. In case he *has* drunk himself into a stupor. I want to make sure he's okay."

"Is Abagail sending a car for him too?" Mike asks.

"I honestly don't know, but it's probably not a good look if the car shows up and he's fall-down drunk. I should probably try to sober him up before the car arrives."

"Here, we can take you," Mike says, grabbing his keys from the counter. "Get in the truck."

"I have my own car," I say.

Cammie smiles. "Just in case. It never hurts to have a couple of friends around, right?"

"Don't you have dogs to wash?"

She puts a hand on my shoulder. "Some things are more important than stinky dogs."

Chapter Forty-One

FELTON

"GOOD MOOOORNING!" THE SING-SONG VOICE PERMEATED the air, rousing Felton from sleep. He was groggy, heavy. His entire body felt like it was full of lead. He tried lifting his head, finding it more difficult than normal. What happened last night? He didn't even remember. He'd followed Winter back to the house, he'd tried to explain about Laura, and then she'd left him.

His head snapped up.

She'd left him. For good. The one person he loved more than anyone else had rejected him, just as he knew she would once she learned the truth. It had been doomed from the beginning. There was no chance of her being okay with what happened with Laura. He'd tried so hard to forget, to just move past it all. And for some reason his past had come back with a vengeance.

"Felton? Honey, are you there?" He turned his head towards the voice. He wasn't alone after all. He'd thought the voice had been part of a dream. The room was still dark and he didn't feel quite right. His joints were stiff, like he'd been at the gym all night. Had he been at the gym? Why couldn't he remember? The last thing he did after Winter left was sit on the couch and watch his cell phone, in case she called or changed her mind. Had he fallen asleep on the couch? Why did his body feel so strange?

Light flooded his eyes and he shut his eyelids reflexively, crying out at the sudden change as the curtains revealed it was much later than he'd thought.

"Oh, sorry. Guess I should have warned you." Who's voice was that?

"Who…" he asked, trying to squint at her, but his eyes hadn't adjusted yet. All he could see was a dark outline against a bright, white room.

"Don't you recognize me, love? It's Laura. I came back. I couldn't bear being away too long. The divorce just isn't working for me." She tapped his cheek with a cool hand and more of her came into view. The hair was dark, similar length, and she wore the same glasses as Laura, but it couldn't be her. Laura was dead.

"I don't understand," Felton said, trying to move. He realized he was bound to something, in a sitting position. Was he tied to a chair? He tried kicking his legs, only to find they were tied down as well.

"Now don't move too much. I don't want you getting away from me," the woman who was not Laura said.

Felton's vision finally cleared. The woman was familiar, he'd seen her face before, but she wasn't Laura. Not by a long shot. Maybe if he'd been a hundred yards away and only seen her from the back. She had a similar build, but everything else was wrong. Her hands, her nose, her eyes. And yet she looked familiar.

"Who are you?" he said with more conviction. "And what are you doing in my house?" He'd been positioned in the living room, which itself had been rearranged. The couch was moved back and the rug had been rolled up again. The trap door was exposed but remained closed beside him.

"Not doing it for you, huh?" the woman said, facing him. "It was worth a shot." She removed her glasses and stuck them in a small bag. She extracted the book he and Winter had received last week. *Simple Desires.* "Funny title. Maybe funny is the wrong word. Ironic title? What do you think?"

"Who the hell are you?" Felton asked.

"Oh," the woman said, placing her hand on her chest and feigning a shocked expression. "You don't recognize me? You don't remember me at all? That really hurts."

"Should I?"

"I work for your father, you moron," she said, deadpan.

"I barely have any contact with my father's employees. Or him for that matter."

"I know," the woman said. "I just thought you might remember the person who helped you clean up your mess the *first* time around." She raised the book up and brought it down hard on his thighs, creating a slapping sound that echoed throughout the house.

"Ow! Dammit, what was that for?"

"Just testing it out." She smiled. "The funny thing about you, Felton, is you don't see the obvious. Now I can't figure out if it's because you're just dumb, or if it's because you're just naïve. Either way, it's probably not good for you." She tossed the book onto one of the couches. "Being an observant person is a skill everyone needs, and I'm afraid you just don't have it. Which is probably why you're in that chair, and why I'm standing here explaining this to you."

Felton shook his head. "I still don't get it. What do you want? Why are you here? Are you looking to impress my father? Bring me in like I'm a bounty?"

The woman threw her head back and cackled. "You wish! No, no, my dear, blind Felton Byrnes. My employment with your father officially terminated at one-fifteen a.m. this morning, when I broke into your house and drugged you, allowing me to strap you to that chair you've found yourself in."

"You quit?"

"I quit. Yes." After a beat, she added, "I don't care about your father's business or his shortsighted attempts to rein control over this small corner of the northeast. I don't care about the work he hired me for, nor do I have any loyalty to him. What I care about…is you. It's always been about you." She leaned down and stared him directly in the eyes.

"Me? Why?"

She shot back up. "See, this is why I have to keep coming back to your observance. You just don't have it, honey." The woman tapped her lips with one finger. "Which is kind of distressing, knowing what you do for a living. If you don't take into account all the variables, how on earth can you design a structure that will withstand the test of time?" She glanced all over the room.

"Just tell me what you want from me," Felton said, dropping his head. Most of this barely registered for him. He'd lost something precious. Who cared if some crazy woman broke into his house and threatened him? Did any of it really matter anymore?

"You are so frustrating!" the woman said, storming from the room. "Don't go anywhere! I'm coming right back!" she called from the office. Felton managed to turn his head so he could see the clock mounted in the kitchen. The time read 8:55.

She stormed back in with another book in her hands. But this one was thinner, with a glossy cover.

"What is…is that *my* yearbook? How did you know where that was?"

"Oh, baby, I know where everything is. I spend a lot of time in this house."

"What?"

The woman clicked her tongue against her teeth a few

times. "I mean, I tried to put everything back as I'd found it, but sometimes you just forget." She slapped herself upside the head. "Silly Rene."

"Rene? Now I remember you. You were here the night Laura died. You helped destroy her belongings."

"That's what I was supposed to do, yes."

"But you looked so much different then. What happened to you?"

"Really? You're going to give me grief over a little plastic surgery? I have literally cut a man's toes off while he watched, his mouth sewn shut so he couldn't scream, and I'm not allowed to get a little work done? Men." She opened the year-book and flipped a few of the pages. "I don't look *that* different."

She dropped the yearbook in his lap, pointing to one photograph. "Rene Lawson," he read. "We went to school together?"

"Sure did, dummy. But you wouldn't remember. We never crossed paths. In fact, I loathed you for most of my school career. You and your easy money, your easy life. But I watched you. I thought, Rene, what makes him deserving of so much and me of so little? What has he done that makes him better than me? And you know what I discovered?"

Felton shook his head.

"Absolutely nothing. You were no better or worse than me. Maybe a little stuck up, but overall you did what most kids did. It wasn't until I found out about your family before I became really interested." She leaned in close to him. "And then I thought, maybe if I get close enough to his world, maybe then I'll figure it out. There had to be something that made the universe choose you to have this privileged life, and not me." She paused. "Now," she said, her voice like a middle school teacher's, "I already know the answer to this, so don't bother lying. But I want to hear it from you. What is the most important thing in your life?"

"Winter," he said, not even hesitating.

Her hand moved faster than he thought possible, striking his cheek and sending spittle flying from his mouth.

"Try again."

"It's true. She is. More than anything."

SMACK!

"One more time. Think now."

He furrowed his brow. His cheek ached and was probably swelling. He'd never been hit by a woman before, but Rene packed one hell of a punch. "Escape." he finally said, hanging his head.

"Ding! Winner!" Rene smiled wide. "The only thing you've ever wanted was to get away from your upbringing, your life. And I couldn't quite understand it. I started working for your father right out of college. I'm sure he thinks he recruited me, but I made sure all the pertinent information fell right into his lap at the right time. I'm good at organizing. But as I continued to work my way deeper and deeper into your home life, all I saw from the shadows was you shunning it, pushing it all away. And maybe I'm just a fool, but I needed to understand it. Your family was what I'd been looking for my entire life. And you wanted to throw it away!"

"Because they're toxic!" Felton yelled. "Can't you see that?"

Rene grew quiet for a moment. "Maybe." She flipped through the yearbook again. Coming to another page, she held it up for him. "Look familiar?"

Felton squinted. It was a picture of the band practicing, the black-and-white grain of the photo blurring some of the details in the distance. He'd probably seen the photo before, but never thought anything of it. He hadn't been in band as a student and neither had anyone he'd known.

"Right here, hot shot," she said, tapping the page. Off to the side were two girls, laughing at something, but only one of them was turned towards the camera enough to capture her face.

"Is that…Laura?"

"That," Rene said slowly, "was my best friend." She sighed. "That's where you first met. In high school. Of course, you didn't date then because Laura wasn't interested in you. The boy with the weird family and all the secrets. But I watched. I saw the way you looked at her." Rene turned around and sat on the couch opposite Felton, her forearms on her knees and her hands hanging down.

"So it's a jealousy thing, then. I never paid any attention to you, and you're getting back at me for it."

Rene reared back, laughter erupting from her lungs. "You think I'm attracted to *you*?" she asked as soon as she caught her breath.

"It makes sense."

"No, it doesn't. Because I'm not interested in your kind."

"Guys?"

"*Toxicity*," she spits.

"What the hell are you talking about?" Felton could feel the heat rising in his chest. This woman was crazy and this had gone on long enough. He wasn't about to be tortured by some high school crush gone awry.

Rene picked up the discarded book on the couch, flipping through its pages. "Do you know why she wrote these?" she asked. Felton didn't feel like giving her the dignity of a response. "She wrote them as an outlet. As a way to vent all of the pressure you put on her."

"How could you know that?" Felton shifted uncomfortably in his chair. The ropes had cut into his skin and were rubbing it raw.

"Working for your father allowed me certain access. We kept in touch. I told her not to pursue you, way back then. She saw you as an up-and-comer and I told her, I said, 'Laura, you don't know everything about him. Don't get involved.

He's got too much baggage.' But did she listen?" Rene's voice had dropped a few octaves.

Felton just shook his head.

"No. She decided to pursue the relationship. And I kept tabs on both of you. As time went on, it became very clear to me she was unhappy. No one writes five books in a year unless they're going through something. It was her only outlet, you callous peon."

"It was you. You killed her that night," Felton said, his eyes going wide.

"No. I *saved* her."

Chapter Forty-Two

WINTER

MIKE BRINGS THE TRUCK TO A HALT IN THE DRIVEWAY. Felton's car is the only other one there. Good, we aren't too late. He must be sleeping off the hangover or something, that's why he's not answering my calls. I open the door and slide out.

"You guys stay here. I don't want him to feel like he's been ambushed. If I don't text you in two or three minutes, come on in."

"Which is it? Two or three?" Cammie asks.

"Three. Just give me a minute to wake him up. All of this will be a shock to his system."

"That's a bit of an understatement," Mike says. "What do we do if someone else comes along?"

I glance down the long drive. "Get the hell out of here. It isn't worth risking your lives over. If this woman really is dangerous, she might not be very discerning."

"Win, maybe this isn't a good idea." Cammie's face is awash in worry.

I shut the door and place a hand on Cammie's arm through the open window. "It'll be okay. We'll be out in a few minutes and then you guys can drive us over to the Byrnes house. And...and we'll..." I exhale. "We'll just go from there."

Cammie doesn't say anything else, only holds my gaze until I turn and walk up the steps to the door. I take another deep breath, trying to figure out how I'm going to talk to him after everything that happened last night. First I have to make sure he's lucid. Then we can deal with everything else.

I slip my key into the lock and the deadbolt turns. It might be the fact that the door doesn't beep three times like it always does or that a strange smell catches my nose as soon as I pass over the threshold, but I'm immediately on edge.

"Hey there."

It takes me a second to take stock of the scene in front of me. Felton, tied to chair in the middle of the living room. Laura, or Rene, rather, standing behind him with a gun to his head, smiling.

"Close the door behind you, and walk forward," Rene says. She's not wearing her glasses, but otherwise looks the same as the last time I saw her at the café. My feet feel like lead bricks as I take in the scene before me. But I manage to follow her instructions.

Three minutes. Stall for three minutes and you'll have help.

Rene leans to the side, looking past me. "That's not your car."

I turn, realizing she can see Mike's red truck through the sheen covering the window. She can't make out any occupants of the truck but she knows what car I drive from when we met.

"Had a chauffeur, did we?" she asks, cocking her head. "That's...Cammie? Yes? I've never met the woman, but she's probably your only friend. Besides me, that is." She lets out a little chuckle that sends shivers down my back.

"What…what is going on here?"

"Winter, run!" Felton says. "Just get out of here. She killed Laura. She's crazy!"

Rene lets the butt of the gun fall on Felton's crown. Hard enough to make him wince.

"Let's see. You're not supposed to be here…hmm." Rene looks past me again. "Toss me your cell phone."

I hesitate until she presses the barrel of the gun to Felton's ear. I pull it from my pocket and toss it over.

Rene caught it, the gun still on Felton. "Password?"

"One-zero-two-one-eight-five."

"Thanks. Here we go, Cammie." Rene talks as she types. "Everything…is…cool…hang…tight. There, sounds pretty hip, right? Or do you spell it k-e-w-l?"

"That's fine," I reply, dropping my shoulders.

"Sure?" Rene asks, digging the gun deeper into Felton's ear.

I nod.

"Aaaaaand, send. Perfect." She turns off the phone and opens the exposed trap door, tossing it down into the hole. "Now. Why in the hell did you come back?" She sounds genuinely curious.

"I…was worried. I couldn't just—"

"Walk away? Why not? I gave you the perfect excuse! I was trying to spare you all the pain this man can't seem to help but cause. You've walked away from every other relationship in your life, why not this one? He's so much worse than Thomas!"

I tense. Who *is* this woman? "You know about Thomas?"

"Sweetie, I know about everyone. I know about your father, about your high school boyfriend and that whole mess. I know it all."

"How?"

"She works for my dad. He does his research," Felton says,

his eyes pleading with me. He wants me to run, to leave him here. He's strapped to a chair with a gun to his head and all he cares about is my safety. I have been a terrible judge of character.

"Correction. Worked. Past tense," Rene says, motioning with the gun. I enter the living room and take a seat on the couch opposite Felton. Beside me sits the book that first arrived last Tuesday, the title *Simple Desires* scrawled across the front.

"Gaudy, isn't it?" Rene asks, following my gaze. "It was the best I could do on short notice. I didn't have time to hire a cover designer. Can you believe they average six weeks just for one cover? What the hell is that about?"

"So it was you. You did all of this." I look directly into her eyes. "Why?"

"Because you were about to make the same mistake as Laura." Rene glances down to my ring finger where Felton's engagement ring had recently lived. There's a light band where the ring had been.

"What mistake?" I ask.

"Marrying this one. Things started out okay for Laura, but they only got worse and worse. It would have been the same for you."

"Okay, yes, we had problems, every couple does," Felton yells, his face turning red. "But we were working through them. Neither of us was completely happy, but who is? The perfect relationship doesn't exist. It's a myth!" Rene lowers the gun and looks at him with an expression of pity.

"No," Rene whispers in his ear. "It does exist. It's the kind where you watch from afar, where you control every part of it. The kind where you can't be hurt because the other person doesn't know who you are. No fights. No baggage. Everything is smooth. You can't get hurt. Winter knows what I'm talking about."

"What? No, I don't."

"She's playing dumb," Rene says to Felton. "She's like me. She doesn't like for there to be a lot of…drama. Everything is out in the open and there can be no secrets. And I'm telling you, Winter," she turns to me, "the best way to make sure you know everything about a person is to do some reconnaissance. The more, the better. Then you can't be blindsided."

"That's how you know so much. About me. About Laura," Felton says quietly. "Did we ever have a private moment?"

Rene scoffs. "A few. But I was looking out for *her*. I tried to tell her to get out when she still could. But she refused, said you were worth fighting for. And then you had to go and do something stupid."

"The bruise," Winter said. "You were telling the truth about that part, weren't you?"

"See? She gets it!"

"And so you kill her?" Felton yells.

Rene's face grows red. "I tried to reason with her! After you left that night, I came over. I tried telling her this was only going to escalate. If not physically, then emotionally. I even offered to help her pack. But no, she was adamant about staying! She was so sure you could work things out. She said she could change you, that you weren't a bad person. And there was no other way. And the more she talked, the more I could see this was only going to get worse. She'd come back and maybe next time you smack her around. Or accidentally push her on the couch. And then it becomes slaps across the face, black eyes. It only gets worse from there. To spare her a lifetime of your special brand of torture, I had to save her."

"Oh my God," Felton says, hanging his head.

A tremor has welled up from somewhere deep inside me and I can't control it. My hands, legs, my very core all trembles in unison.

"I tried to do the same thing for you," Rene says,

addressing me. "This little fucker can't be trusted with a solid relationship. Way too many skeletons, if you know what I mean. I tried to be coy, maybe a little too coy with the book. I know how skittish you are and I figured one book would do it. But it wasn't enough. You needed me to play the part. And then I thought maybe I could scare you off with the second one." Rene shook her head. "But you just couldn't leave it alone. Even after I told you where I'd hidden a couple of backup copies." She glances down to the trap door.

"The mobile home…that was you," Felton says.

Rene bends down and looks Felton in the eye. "I know how your brother works. He's an amateur, at best. A strange car near the neighborhood is like catnip to him." She smiles at me. "The man thinks he's a detective." She scoffs again. "Give me a break. I just didn't figure he'd bring you with him. And I couldn't let you die in that mobile home. Your punishment is you get to keep living. Alone and estranged from everyone. Forever. Death is too good for you."

"You're not going to kill me?" Felton asks, his voice small.

"Not unless you make me. You're going in the hole. I'll keep you fed periodically. Just enough to keep you alive. You can finally be with your precious Laura."

"Wha…what?" Felton asks, looking up.

I don't want to believe it, but I already know. "She's down there," I say, looking into the blackness. "You put her down there. She's been here the whole time."

"Jesus!" Felton yells, scooting his chair away from the trap door. He pushes too hard and the chair falls, taking him down with it.

"Whoops!" Rene says, tucking the gun behind her and righting him. "Baby go boom. Your fiancée is pretty slick, F, I'll give her that. But just a bit too curious."

Everything coalesces for me. It all makes sense. "I'm going down there too," I say.

Rene shakes her head in disappointment. "I tried to warn you. You were free to go, and all you had to do was stay away. I never wanted to harm you, Winter. I genuinely like you. If you'd never walked back through that door you probably could have had a nice, long, happy life. And I hate that you've lost that now."

"I almost did." The words escaped my mouth before I can stop them. "I was almost done."

"What brought you back?"

I drop my eyes, not really looking at anything, just thinking. Why *had* I come back? I've left other relationships for a lot less. "I guess I realized leaving never fixed anything. I keep running into the same problems. No matter what I do."

"You want too much," Rene says. "You want intimacy, but you also want perfection."

"No. Not perfection."

"What, you think I don't know about your little tests? The hoops you make men jump through just to qualify them?"

"Tests? What tests?" Felton asks.

"She pre-screened you. She keeps a list…it's in one of your apps, right? A list of undesirable behaviors or actions or past instances. Anyone she dates has to make sure not to earn a check on the list before she proceeds with the next phase of the relationship."

"Winter?" Felton asks, his eyes watering.

I can't bring myself to admit it. The list was for my eyes only. No one is supposed to know about it. Plus, it didn't work. Felton had passed and look what happened.

Maybe that was the whole problem. What if I never had a list? What if I'd just let things develop naturally, instead of trying to control every little thing? Maybe there were no relationships that didn't hurt…at least sometimes. My eyes meet Rene's. This woman has done what I never could. She'd built the "perfect" relationship for herself, but she was still isolated.

Still alone. She was fooling herself into thinking she had someone in her life.

Rene makes a comical grin. "Guess you both have a few secrets." She takes a breath. "Okay, Winter. Would you mind getting in the hole? It will be much easier if I don't have to drag your lifeless body down there. Do a friend a solid, huh?"

One thing eludes me. "How did you do it? Get Laura's body in here? This house wasn't even on Felton's radar when she died." Laura had been gone almost ten years and Felton only finished the house a few months ago.

"She stayed with me, most of the time." Rene shrugs, pulling the gun back out. "Gave me someone to talk to. And it helped develop my embalming skills. She had been my best friend, after all, and I needed to make sure she was properly taken care of. Unlike some people." She turns and kicks Felton in the ribs, the move swift and hard. He cries out in pain as the momentum knocks him over again and he hits the ground with a thud.

"He's just not a fighter," Rene says, bending over to pick him up.

Before I can think about what I'm doing, I'm on my feet, rushing the woman. Rene has one hand on Felton's chair before turning her head in time. She tries raising the gun, but I get to her first, grabbing her and knocking her over. We both hit the ground behind Felton.

"Winter, no! Run! Get out of here!" Felton cries.

I punch and kick as hard as I can, not knowing if I'm doing any damage. Rene still has the gun in her hand, but she's flailing back and forth with it. I'm praying it doesn't go off, I just need to get it away from her. But Rene manages to get a knee up between us and pushes me off her like I'm nothing.

"Not very strong, are you?" she says, pushing herself up as I fall back against the couch. "Gotta make everything difficult." Rene points the gun at Felton and fires twice, not even looking at him, instead she keeps her eyes locked on me.

"No!" I cry out.

Rene turns the gun on me. "You've just killed everyone you love," she says, her eyes burning with hatred. "Some people just refuse to listen."

I turn away from her and bear down. I don't want to die right here, but at least I didn't run again. I stood my ground for once in my life, and I was willing to put in the hard work, to stop running away. I just turned out to be harder than I ever expected. Just as I'm about to close my eyes, I realize I'm looking at the book, that stupid cover staring back at me. I lurch to the side at the same time Rene fires the gun. Pain shoots through me, but I don't register where. It doesn't matter. If I'm going to die, I'm taking this psycho with me. I grab the book and swing it around, hitting Rene's hand which sends the gun scattering away.

Behind me the front door swings open, something of which I'm only barely aware. But it's enough to provide a diversion. Rene looks at the door as I bring the book back around and hit her again, this time across the face. She falls back, blood spurting from her nose. I straddle her, bringing the book down again and again, its weight smashing into her face over and over until someone grabs me from behind.

"No! Let me go!" I yell, but someone snatches the book from my grasp. I turn to see Cammie, holding the bloody book as Mike drags me away from Rene. "Call 911! She shot him!" Winter yelled, pointing at Felton.

"Already did, as soon as we heard the gun," Mike says. Cammie leans over Felton as Mike picks me up and sets me on the couch. "Hold here," he says, moving my right hand to cover my left shoulder. There's a weight against my foot. I look down to see the gun laying on its side. I don't know why, but I lean down and take it in my free hand.

At the same time Rene sits up, her face disfigured from the

beating. She looks nothing like herself anymore. But I catch the glint of metal in her hand.

Before I know what I'm doing, I empty all the chambers of the gun into her chest. She stills for a moment before looking at me, a smirk on her face, then she falls back, a knife clattering from her hand.

Chapter Forty-Three

"MA'AM. PUT THE GUN DOWN."

I'm frozen in place, staring at Rene's limp body. Four of my shots hit their mark, and two missed, hitting the back wall, where there are now two small black holes.

"Ma'am!"

I turn. Four officers stand behind me, their guns trained on my back. Mike and Cammie are both bent over Felton, who isn't moving, a crimson pooling beneath him. Is he dead?

I drop the gun and put my hand up. The other one still covers the bullet wound in my shoulder.

"She's been shot," Mike says. "By her." He points to Rene's limp body.

Two of the officers come around the couch and help me up, leading me out of the room and into the kitchen. As I'm leaving, paramedics come running through the front door.

"You stay here with her," one officer tells the other. "Keep pressure on that." He points to my wound. The officer who remains removes my hand and applies pressure with a towel he's found somewhere. It's all happening in slow motion around me. I try to get up but he gently presses me back down.

"I need..."

"Ma'am, please," the officer says. "They're taking care of it."

"Will he be okay?" I ask. "She shot him. Twice." I feel like none of this is real, like I should be screaming my head off, but I'm stuck in this fog. I don't quite know how to process what's happening.

"They will do everything they can for him," he says. "But for now can you tell me—"

"What the hell?" a booming voice yells from the living room. The officer stiffens at the new voice. It's one I recognize.

Warren bursts into the kitchen, his face flushed like he's just run a marathon. His presence here is ethereal in a way, almost like none of this is real. I just saw him last night, when I was with Felton.

"Miss Southerland, what...?" He runs over and checks my wound. "Dean, I've got this," he says to the other officer. "Get a paramedic in here when they're done."

"Right," the officer named Dean says.

Dean disappears from my view and I look up at Warren, who is now holding my shoulder. The towel is soaked through with blood. "Is he going to live?"

"Don't worry about that right now," he replies. "I need you to tell me what happened. I picked up the 911 call when I was on the way to your friend's house to pick you up. What are you doing here?"

I try looking around him to the living room. Part of me feels like this isn't over, like Rene might jump back up again. "Is she...?"

"Who, Rene? She's dead all right. I assume that was your handiwork out there," he gives me a warm smile. "You're not a bad shot."

"Did you know her?"

He sighs. "Unfortunately, she's on the payroll. Mr. Byrnes

saves her for some of the more...messy deals. Was she... impersonating Laura?"

I nod. "She sent the books. And blew up the mobile home. I think she was trying to kill Brian."

"She's usually not sloppy like that. I mean, she doesn't normally miss."

"She didn't expect Felton to be with him at the mobile home," I say.

"Ah. That explains things. She must have panicked when she realized they were both inside." He glances back to the living room. "Where is that goddamn medic?" he yells.

A paramedic comes in, bag in hand. "Let me inspect that wound," he says.

Warren takes the towel away and goes to wash his hands in the sink while the paramedic inspects my arm.

I look up to realize Cammie and Mike have come into the kitchen. Neither of them looks very good. "I'm so sorry...for everything," I say.

Cammie just shakes her head, then gives me an awkward hug around the paramedic.

"I need to move her to the ambulance," the paramedic says. "This went straight through, but there's a lot of blood loss. We need to get her a transfusion, immediately."

"Is Felton..." I begin.

"They just took him out to the other ambulance," Cammie says.

"Ma'am, if you'll come with me?" the paramedic says. I look at Warren. He nods. For some reason I trust him now, maybe because he was the one who finally convinced me Felton and Lazarus were telling the truth about Laura.

"I'm coming with you. I need to know exactly what happened." He looks at Cammie and Mike. "Can you two stay here for me? A man named Jackson will be by in a few minutes. You're to tell him everything, understand?"

Cammie nods, tears falling from her eyes. She reaches out

and takes my good hand, holding it until the paramedic leads me outside where they have a stretcher waiting for me. Part of me struggles, I don't want to get on that thing, but with Warren's help they finally manage to help me up on it. Moments later I'm loaded into the back of the ambulance. Warren climbs in, and I notice the sleeve of his suit is stained with my blood.

"How's Brian?" I ask as they close the doors.

"Better this morning. Fortunately the third degree burns are minor. But he did suffer a collapsed lung from the explosion." I look at the paramedics working on me, are they supposed to know about what happened? "He should recover fine in a few days. The burns will heal in about a month." He leans forward. "Now, tell me everything that happened, start to finish."

I relate the story as best I can. From the moment we arrived in the driveway, through Rene's ramblings up until the point when I shot her dead. I still can't believe I did that. But she had that knife she'd pulled from somewhere. If I hadn't fired, she could have hurt Cammie, or Mike, or me.

They manage to clean and dress my wound in the back of the ambulance. Apparently it looks worse than it is. They've started an IV and are keeping an eye on my vitals, but I'm starting to feel a little better now that I'm not bleeding all over the place.

"Mrs. Byrnes wants me to bring you back to the house as soon as possible," Warren says. He looks at the paramedics. "Is there any need for her to visit the hospital?"

"We'd prefer to take her in, just to make sure," one of them says. "The wound isn't too serious, but in cases like this we like to be safe rather than sorry."

"Did she tell you?" I ask, trying to hold back tears. "About our *deal*?"

"I'm afraid so," he replies.

I shake my head. "It might be a moot point anyway. But I

don't want to go back to that house." I turn to the paramedics. "Take me to the hospital. I want to be with Felton."

Warren looks like he's having an internal battle with himself. Finally he nods. "Very well. To the hospital."

THEY WHEEL ME INTO THE HOSPITAL WHILE WARREN STAYS AT my side, checking over his shoulder constantly like he's afraid someone might see us. But the hospital is already a flurry of activity. I'm taken into an urgent care facility where the paramedics hand me off to the hospital staff. They perform many of the same tests the paramedics did, as well as checking my wound and the rest of me for any other trauma.

"How are you doing?" one of the nurses asks me absently and I can tell this is going to be a long process. I don't want to be here on this bed, I want to see what's happening with Felton.

"Where did they take him?" I ask.

"I'm sorry?" she's checking charts and not really paying attention. I look to Warren for help, pleading with him inside my mind.

"The man they brought in before her," he says. "Where did they take him?"

The nurse looks up. "Oh." She knows who we're talking about. It isn't often they see multiple gunshot wounds in this town. "I'm sure he's in surgery already."

"Okay," I say, pulling the IV out of my arm.

"Ma'am!" the nurse says, rushing to my side, but I wave her off.

"I'm fine. I need to see him."

She tries to help me back on the bed. "You've just been shot and you may be in shock. We need to make sure you're—"

"It's okay," Warren says, coming around to the same side of the bed. "I'll make sure to keep an eye on her."

The nurse looks from him to me. "I can't just let her walk around. She's a patient. The hospital has a liability—"

"The man they brought in is my fiancée," I say.

She gives me a pitiful look. "Stay here one second." She rushes off and I sit on the edge of the bed, my arm sore from where I pulled the IV out.

"You might want to consider staying here," Warren says. "There's nothing you can do for him right now."

I shake my head. "I have to know. If he's not going to make it, I want to be there."

The nurse returns a moment later pushing a wheelchair. "Here," she says. "Get in." Warren helps me into the chair and the nurse wheels me out of the urgent care area. "I shouldn't be doing this, but sometimes our policies aren't very…"

"…practical?" I say. Now that she's taking me to him, I can't stop my hands from shaking.

"I was going to say compassionate." She wheels me along with Warren following behind down past the ER and into the surgical unit. "He's down in there," she says, pointing to the large doors. "I can't take you any farther, but I will let the on-call know you're out here. They'll come let you know his condition as soon as they can. Okay?"

For the first time I feel tears slip down my cheeks. It's all I can do to nod. She looks up at Warren. "You'll stay here with her? Make sure she doesn't leave?"

"I will," he says.

"Okay." She gives me a sad kind of smile. "I hope everything works out." Then she disappears through the large double doors, headed for a station on the other side. As soon as the doors open for her a code alarm sounds from somewhere inside the department.

Before I know it I'm on my feet as three more people rush

in through the double doors. When I see the nurse's face who helped me here fall, I lunge forward, only for Warren to grab me, holding me back.

"I have to get in there!" I've lost all semblance of the outside world. It's just me and those two doors that are rapidly closing to the most terrible sound I've ever heard.

"You can't," Warren says, "Let them help him."

"You don't understand!" I yell. "I need to see him. I have to tell him I'm sorry! Before it's too late!"

Warren holds me back, no matter how hard I struggle. At some point someone comes up to try and help me back in my wheelchair.

"I have to tell him," I whimper. It can't end like this. It just can't. Felton will be okay. I'll get to talk to him again. He's young and strong, he'll make it. He has his whole life ahead of him. I try again to wrench from Warren's grasp, but he's too strong.

Eventually I collapse back into the chair.

There's nothing more I can do but wait.

Chapter Forty-Four

I STAND before the huge oak double doors, doubting if I can go in. I've come to hate this house with a passion, and the last thing I want to do is come back here. But this is the last time I will ever see this place, that much I'm sure of. I wince as I reach out with my right arm, pressing the doorbell and listening to the ancient chimes echo within the cavernous home.

Warren appears at the door, a new, clean suit on from the last time I saw him in the hospital. "Miss Southerland. Please come in."

"Thank you," I say, removing my small black hat. Has it really been a week since I was last here, arguing with Lazarus, then watching Brian be shuffled off to the "surgical wing" of this house, burned and barely conscious? And then running away from *him*, afraid of what my life might look like if I attached myself to this place?

"You can follow me," Warren says. There's something sympathetic in his gaze. Something I'm not sure he's supposed to show. I haven't spoken to him since the hospital, but he was there for me when I needed someone, so I'm grateful for that, at least.

We twist through a bevy of rooms until coming to a giant atrium, the twelve-foot windows looking out on the back of the property. The room teems with people huddled in small groups, chatting, making small talk. And in the middle of the back wall sits a metal casket, one which has haunted my dreams for the past week.

"Visitation is until seven," Warren says. "The funeral will commence in the morning."

"Thank you," I reply, barely keeping my shit together. I won't be staying. The only reason I'm here at all is to say goodbye one last time and then I'm gone. Warren managed to get me back into the surgical unit at the last minute. *He* was unconscious by then and he'd already crashed, so they were working on him frantically. But there was nothing they could do. After they called it, they let me see him. I didn't think I'd have the strength, but somehow I did. I know he was already gone at that point, but I swear I felt some part of him linger in the room for only a few minutes. I told him how sorry I was and that I loved him and would miss him. Warren never left my side the entire time.

"Hey."

I turn to see Brian beside me. His black suit is loose on him and he has a couple of bandages on his face, but I can tell he's already healing.

"How...um...how are you?" he asks.

"Fine," I reply, no emotion in my voice whatsoever. I'm glad to see he's okay, but its small consolation to the reality of the moment. I indicate the casket. "Closed?"

Brian drops his voice. "Mom made the call. She didn't want people seeing him like that. Said it would be better if they remembered him like he was, not...whatever he is now."

Imagine that, something Abagail and I agree on. Still, I can't stop tears from escaping my eyes. Not that I wanted to see him again, there's just something about a closed casket that's so...final. Is this what it means to love unconditionally?

To hurt so badly? I've been doing a lot of soul searching the past week. And I realize that even if he'd made it, I don't think I could have stayed. Not because I don't believe he was a good person, I just finally realized my own personal well-being is more important than finding a partner. And the emotional baggage of this family is too much.

But that doesn't mean I'm not angry.

"Where are they?" I ask, my voice almost a growl.

Brian resigns himself and scans the room. "Far side, by the south windows. Talking to the mayor."

I turn towards them, my face turned into a sneer. I promised myself I wasn't going to do this here, but seeing that closed casket has just changed my mind. It's strange, these people are the architects of so much destruction and yet here they stand, talking with the mayor, still alive and free from consequence. Maybe some of my statements to the police will change that. But for right now, I can't help but be infuriated.

As I approach them, Abagail spots me first and removes herself from the conversation, meeting me in the middle of the room.

"Winter, so glad you could make it." She reaches in for one of her light hugs and I step back, putting distance between us. I'm not about to participate in this dog and pony show.

"Don't touch me."

Several people turn their attention to us.

Abagail gives me a placating smile. "Perhaps we should go—"

"Somewhere else to talk?" I say, loudly. "I don't think so. Your son is dead because of you, I hope you realize that. If you'd just told me who I was looking for, none of this would have happened."

She tilts her head. "Maybe. Maybe not."

I address the entire room. "She only agreed to help me find who was torturing her son if I agreed to give her grandchildren." The room has gone completely quiet, no one is making small talk anymore. "Maybe if you'd been less concerned about what you wanted, and thought about the needs of other people, your son might still be alive right now!"

I point to Lazarus, who is watching us along with everyone else in the room. "And you! You and your little deals, your back-room negotiations and under-the-table transactions. Don't think everyone doesn't already know what you do."

A dark form appears in my peripheral. Warren.

Abagail takes a step back, her eyes burning with anger. Lazarus appears behind her, taking her by the shoulders. "I think it is time for you to go," he growls.

"Happy to." I turn and storm past Brian, who tries to reach out for me, but I push his hand away. As I reach the exit, I stop and turn. "All of this," I indicate the house, "this isn't your legacy. That is." I point to the casket. "Forever."

Without another word, I leave the room in silence.

"WHAT WILL YOU DO?" CAMMIE ASKS, SITTING ON THE EDGE of the bed as I pack.

"Get out of here, first of all. I need a new start. Those people, the hold they have on this town, it's toxic."

Cammie nods, looking back through the spare bedroom door behind her. "I know what you mean. If you find somewhere, let me know. This whole experience has soured me on the northeast."

"Thank you for letting me stay here," I say, packing the last of my clothes.

"We couldn't let you stay in that house, not after everything that happened there."

I smile. "Yeah, plus the fact I was sleeping with a corpse less than twenty feet away kinda gave me PTSD. My next house isn't going to have a crawlspace or a basement or anything under the floor. It's going to be on a concrete slab, nothing else." The house has been designated an ongoing crime scene anyway; it isn't like I could have stayed there if I wanted to. From what little information I've been able to glean, the police managed to exhume Laura's body from the crawlspace where it had been buried. And both Lazarus and Brian are under investigation in connection with her disappearance. Though I'm sure in the end, the police will eventually determine Rene worked alone. Dead people often make convenient scapegoats, especially for the rich. As for me, I've seen more than my fair share of the inside of police interview rooms.

"How did she even manage to do that? Get in the house?" Cammie asks.

"She had the code from Lazarus, and she'd copied the key at some point. Warren told me they found some embalming liquid and salt at the mobile home Brian and F—" I stop myself from saying his name. "At the mobile home. I guess that's where she'd prepared Laura's body so she wouldn't stink up the house. I don't know how long ago she buried her there, but I'm betting it was before the house was finished. It would have been easy to sneak on to the property while it was still being renovated."

"And she was going to keep him down there with her? Like a prisoner? Why?"

I pull the zipper tight. "She was convinced F—*he* was the cause of all her problems. I guess because he was rich it seemed to her like he had it easy. Like he didn't have any complaints, while her life growing up was hard. And she couldn't take her best friend being with her worst enemy. I think when she found out he'd hurt Laura, something in Rene snapped. And when she couldn't convince Laura to leave him, she figured the only way to keep her 'safe' was to make sure he couldn't hurt her anymore."

"That's so twisted," Cammie says.

"Tell me about it." I've relayed this story to the police again and again, and they told me Rene had some mental problems in the past, things she was able to cover up in order to work for Lazarus. It's probably what made her so efficient at her job. But I don't see how he doesn't face some sort of consequences for employing someone like that. "I just hope they find Lazarus liable somehow. Either by hiring her, or in whatever jobs she did for him."

"Have you heard from them?"

I shake my head. "No, and I don't expect I will. Now that the secret about Laura is out, I'm no longer a threat. Plus, I was nothing more than a means to an end for Abagail, and a nuisance or maybe even an obstruction as far as Lazarus was concerned."

Cammie helps me heave my suitcase off the bed. There's another, smaller one right beside it. "Did you talk to your partners yet?"

"Yeah, I turned in my notice shortly after the funeral. Sidhara wanted me to stay, but I don't think Henry cared one way or the other. Despite the fact they ended up getting *both* bridge contracts."

"You always were good at your job."

I glance out the window at Cammie's dog-grooming van. "And you're great at yours. Plus, you get to play with puppers all day."

Cammie smiles. "Yeah, whenever I get the chance to actually get started. This last week has been a little chaotic." She reaches over and hugs me. "You'll let me know where you end up?"

"Of course."

"And you'll be safe?"

"Always."

"I just can't believe you're leaving. You've lived here all your life."

"I know, and I think that's part of the problem."

Cammie wipes away a tear. "Then get out there and fix it. Start something new."

I grab the large suitcase and wheel it out of the guest room, down the hall to the front door. Mike is splayed out on the couch, watching T.V. As soon as he sees me, he's up, wrapping me in a bear hug.

"You out?" he asks.

"I'm out," I manage. It feels like he's crushing me.

"You're a good person, Win. Take care of yourself out there." Ever since *he* died, I knew there was no way I was staying in Connecticut. It's only now in the presence of my friends am I reconsidering my future.

Cammie comes up beside him as he releases me and she grabs me again too. They're not making this easy. "You take care of yourself," she whispers. I nod, barely keeping it together. If I don't get out of here right now I'll never leave.

I pull away from them and they stay together, arms wrapped around each other's waists. Part of me has always been jealous of Cammie for finding Mike so easily. For getting *lucky*. But I realize now I don't feel that anymore. I'm glad they have each other, but I don't necessarily need that for *my* life. I deleted *the test* off my phone last week. I'm never using anything like that ever again. If I find someone, great. If not, that's okay too.

"Do you need any help with the bags?" Cammie asks.

"No," I say, looking towards the door. "I think I got it on my own."

THE END

Thank you for reading *FORGOTTEN*. I hope you enjoyed the story and found the characters engaging.

If you haven't already, check out my newest series, starting with *HIS PERFECT CRIME*. It follows FBI Agent Emily Slate as she works to track down a killer who seems to have left no trace behind. You can order it on Amazon right now.

Thanks again for taking a chance on a new author. I hope to continue to entertain you for years to come!

-Alex

Scan the code below for *HIS PERFECT CRIME!*

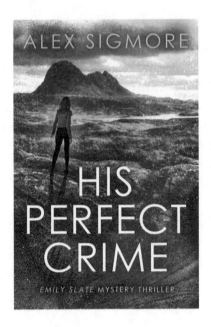

Emily Slate Series

The Emily Slate FBI Mystery Series

Free Prequel - Her Last Shot (Emily Slate Bonus Story)

His Perfect Crime - (Emily Slate Series Book One)

The Collection Girls - (Emily Slate Series Book Two)

Smoke and Ashes - (Emily Slate Series Book Three)

Her Final Words - (Emily Slate Series Book Four)

Can't Miss Her - (Emily Slate Series Book Five)

The Lost Daughter - (Emily Slate Series Book Six)

The Secret Seven - (Emily Slate Series Book Seven)

Coming Soon!

A Liar's Grave - (Emily Slate Series Book Eight)

The Girl in the Wall - (Emily Slate Series Book Nine)

His Final Act - (Emily Slate Series Book Ten)

Standalone Psychological Thrillers

Forgotten

About the Author

A lifelong reader from the start, Alex has always been fascinated by what drives people. What events in our lives shape us to become the people we are today? After a few other careers, it became clear that writing was the only way for Alex to explore this eternal question.

When not writing, Alex enjoys long walks in the woods, where it's easier to dream up stories about serial killers and the heroes who catch them.

Made in United States
Troutdale, OR
01/06/2024

16737494R00170